# THE NUCLEAR FRONTIER

## EVERGREEN BOOK 5

## MATTHEW S. COX

DIVISION ZERO PRESS

The Nuclear Frontier
Evergreen Book 5

© 2020 Matthew S. Cox
All Rights Reserved

ISBN (ebook): 978-1-950738-30-4

ISBN (paperback): 978-1-950738-31-1

# CONTENTS

1. Some Regrets Last Forever     1
2. The Natural Way     11
3. Waiting to Die     20
4. No Normal but What We Make     28
5. The Thing About Stuff     34
6. The Seventh     41
7. A Bit Too Wild     46
8. Quiet Time     52
9. A Place of Safety     60
10. A Curse Broken     72
11. Down From the Clouds     77
12. Perimeter Watch     89
13. The Express     101
14. Just Camping     108
15. Search Party     120
16. Helping Dad     131
17. Marksman     141
18. No Signal     148
19. Dinosaur Pasta     154
20. All the Way     168
21. The Notebook     177
22. The Smarter Option     192
23. Sixty-Two Miles     196
24. Foraging     206
25. Fairplay     219
26. The Mushroom Cloud     228
27. Civilization Take Two     236
28. Haunted     245
29. Every Moment     256

*Acknowledgments*     265
*About the Author*     266
*Other books by Matthew S. Cox*     267

# SOME REGRETS LAST FOREVER

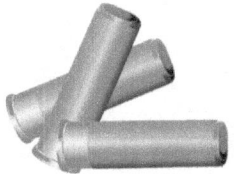

S urvival in a broken world made demands of Harper she'd never be proud of.

Things she'd done as well as things she'd been afraid to do ever lurked in the quiet places between other thoughts. It still didn't seem wholly real to be walking the streets of Evergreen, Colorado, carrying Dad's Mossberg 930. It felt *less* real to think about having killed people. Self-defense or not, she'd ended human life more than once. None of the millions of random thoughts, fears, dreams, or hopes she had swirling around her head a year ago included how to process civilization grinding to a halt or how it felt to shoot a man in the head.

*Late July already… almost a year since the world lit on fire.*

Harper stopped a few paces past where Canyon Circle met South Hiwan Drive, looking around at the houses and trees. North Evergreen, just southwest of the golf course, appeared pretty much the same as she imagined it did before the war—except for no functioning cars driving by, no radio or television sound, and not a single aircraft anywhere overhead. She could almost pretend the world hadn't gone insane.

Only, it had.

She'd shot a man in the face not far from here when he tried to kidnap Mila Cline, who'd had her tenth birthday only a few days ago on July 19. The poor kid still had an edge of creepiness to her, a bit like a real-life version of Wednesday Addams, but she no longer deliberately tried to freak people out. Mila behaved fairly normal considering the craziness she'd suffered before arriving in Evergreen.

Harper sighed to herself. *Everyone is a little messed up.*

The trees scattered around the homes didn't hold any sense of natural peace or serenity. She saw only hiding places and cover, or memories of gunfire. Prior to the man grabbing Mila, she'd been shot at by a bunch of nut-jobs, one of whom she'd recognized as Scott, a barista from the Starbucks she used to visit with her mother and sister all the time. He and some other guys invaded a home here, shot at the militia, and died for it.

What bothered her more than anything is it didn't bother her much anymore.

A dingy grey sky and a bit of drizzling rain fit her mood to a T. Everyone's panic over radioactivity in raindrops had lessened considerably. Perhaps a downpour would get people to stay inside, but a day like this where the mist seemed to simply hang in the air didn't faze anyone. She resumed walking, trying to conjure up less morbid thoughts.

The farm defied the odds, turning into a viable source of food. They didn't have much variety, but 'not starving' mattered more than not eating the same thing three times a week. It would still be a few years before the farming reached a point where the town wouldn't be quite so susceptible to any minor bad event turning catastrophic, but she'd gotten over her constant worry about it. Even the best-managed farms could be wiped out by a severe enough weather event like an unseasonal cold snap, plant disease, locusts, or whatever. Fortunately, the town had like twenty people who'd come from ranches or farms in the surrounding areas and legit knew how to run a farm or take care of livestock. Evergreen had the advantage of not relying on a bunch of suburbanite couch potatoes trying to figure out how to stick seeds in the ground.

Rather than spend the last weeks of summer hanging out with friends, going to the mall, going to dance class, or whatever... her little sister Madison and the other kids spent five or six hours every morning at the farm, learning and working. Harper couldn't believe none of them complained once about it.

*Could be worse... they could be asked to work from sunrise to sunset. At least they let the kids play in the afternoon... and it's not like they're being made to do hard labor.*

Cliff, who had for all intents and purposes become their father, sometimes told them about his childhood. He'd grown up in the Eighties—as he put it, back when kids played outside. To him, the sight of kids running around the yard felt like a time machine. No video games or television keeping them inside, no long periods of inactivity making kids gain weight. Of course, for *anyone* to gain weight at the moment would be a task, and also likely earn them scorn for taking more than their fair share of food.

*We're not standing at the edge of starvation anymore but we can still see it from here.*

She resumed walking. Gone were her thoughts of it being boring to hike in circles for hours along the streets in this neighborhood. Boredom had become lovely because it meant no one had any problems. At first, when she'd joined the militia, she'd done so purely out of a need to keep Dad's shotgun, both for sentimental value and to protect Madison. It didn't even occur to her until weeks later people here might view her in a different light because of it. Some of the kids she'd gone to high school with feared or hated cops. Harper never had a bad encounter with the police, but her personal experiences didn't define reality. The internet and news told a different story.

However, the Evergreen Militia existed primarily as a means to defend the town from outside threats. Citizens didn't look at them like 'cops' per se, rather as the only thing standing between them and gangs like the Lawless. For the most part, the citizens 'policed' themselves since almost everyone carried a handgun or knife. But... the militia often stepped in if a situation escalated to violence.

Mayor Ned hadn't made anything official about law enforcement.

Any citizen of Evergreen could 'detain' a troublemaker and bring them before the town management. The militia didn't 'legally' have any special powers or protections, even though most everyone here treated them as if they did. She figured it came from at least half the militia, like Roy Ellis, having been cops before the war. Some of the guys had the 'cop attitude.' Hearing them talk with authority tended to make people see them as having authority even though the entire legal power structure of the United States had evaporated. She still couldn't quite pull off the 'do what I say or else' tone. Whenever she tried to bark commands, she felt like a bratty kid having a tantrum, embarrassed at herself for raising her voice. Despite knowing it came from her fear of public speaking and she didn't *really* sound like a petulant child, she still tried to rely on logic and speaking calmly whenever possible... which didn't always work.

Be it due to the shell shock of nuclear war or knowing the militia's role primarily involved town defense rather than worrying about what the people living there did, the citizens—at least the ones in her patrol area—smiled and waved at her, a few curmudgeons aside.

At some point over the last several months, Harper stopped dwelling on the 'how did I end up here' aspect of her present life. As Cliff told her, the only way to handle an event as major as the complete destruction of civilization is to keep moving forward. Deal with the here and now. Society collapsed. All her hopes and dreams burned. She and Madison lost both parents to the Lawless. Any one of those things could break a person, but somehow, Harper still hadn't crumbled.

Her need to protect Madison overpowered her fear and aversion to violence.

She fussed at the Mossberg. Despite not having fired it in a while, Dad's ghost pestered her about taking proper care of it. *Her* shotgun, a simple Remington pump, may or may not still be in the gun safe in their house in Lakewood. Dad handed her the 930 when the world fell apart, due to it being semi-automatic. He'd called it a 'combat shotgun.' The day he'd bought her the Remington, neither one of them imagined she'd fire buckshot at a person... only targets.

Up until the skies burned, she'd never thought of her shotgun as a 'weapon,' only a piece of sporting equipment.

*I should probably clean it. At least once a month, even if it hasn't been fired. Can't let it stop working before I run out of ammo.*

Some people called Dad a 'gun nut,' but he didn't own a huge collection of weapons, only five: AR-15, the Mossberg, a 7mm magnum rifle (for hunting), Beretta 92, and a Springfield 1911. Technically, the Remington pump shotgun belonged to Harper. He also didn't feel like he needed to carry a gun to Starbucks or to go grocery shopping. To her, a 'gun nut' loved waving their weapons around in everyone's faces, showing them off, worshipping them. Dad—and even Mom—appreciated firearms and enjoyed using them at the range. Neither felt the need to have one in hand at all times, so she didn't consider her parents 'gun *nuts*.' He had, however, been almost obsessively meticulous in regard to maintaining them. Every Saturday, he'd spend at least an hour cleaning one weapon.

The AR-15 and Beretta ended up in the hands of the Lawless after they invaded the house. Harper neither wanted them back nor had any inclination to go hunt down gang members for revenge, but it hurt to think about all the care he'd put into those weapons only to have them end up being used by criminals.

*I need to let go of the past. Easier said than done, but I'm working on it.*

While being bored on patrol reassured her, it also made time drag. She recognized the need to patrol—no one had phones anymore. The people responsible for reacting to danger or crisis had to be nearby to arrive in time to matter. Citizens of Evergreen couldn't simply call 911 if something happened. Her mother had once said smart people become bored more easily. Harper never considered herself exceptionally smart, certainly not one of those kids who finished college at fourteen. Still, she managed to get mostly As and Bs while barely putting in effort. Both parents wanted her to go to college, often telling her she had the smarts to do anything. Despite their encouragement, she hadn't been able to decide what to study. She'd hated feeling so confused about her future, but all those problems seemed so petty now by comparison.

*No point wondering what I would've majored in.*

Harper sighed at the Mossberg.

*I've got 222 shells left, then this thing becomes a club.*

Hammond Rutledge, one of a handful of people who'd lived in Evergreen before the war, had been talking about the possibility of manufacturing gunpowder like they used to back in the mid-1800s. Most people considered him a 'maker,' the sort of person who could fabricate just about anything given enough time and the correct materials. Rumor had it he'd worked for a movie studio before the war as a day job, and also ran a YouTube channel to show off side projects he did for fun.

*Everyone had a YouTube channel... even me.*

Admittedly, her father did most of the work. She hadn't been at all interested in becoming a celebrity, insofar as a few thousand total strangers knowing her name made someone a celebrity. Some people thought it really cool a thirteen-year-old set records on a shooting competition course. Others accused her parents of 'child abuse' for allowing her to touch a weapon. Dad needed to screen all the comments posted on the videos before he let her look, weeding out the nasty ones.

*People can be real assholes. What kind of moron makes death threats at a child or her father for participating in sport shooting because guns are dangerous? Oh, you shouldn't let that little girl play with guns because she could hurt herself, so we're going to kill her and you to teach you a lesson. Ridiculous.*

If Hammond could manufacture gunpowder, shotgun shells would be the most likely result since they didn't require precision machining and it would be a whole lot easier to melt plastic into new shells than make brass casings for rifle or pistol bullets. Sure, they could refill old ones, but it wouldn't do any good without unfired bullets to put in them. Shotgun shells could be packed with any sort of metal shrapnel and still be somewhat effective.

He detailed a means to make saltpeter using urine, cow poop, and rotting vegetation at the last public town meeting. The process took months and didn't produce much, but he felt for sure it would work. However, they ran into a problem—gunpowder required sulfur, which no one seemed to know how to obtain in a world without

Amazon or eBay. A few people thought it had to be mined out of the earth near volcanic regions. Walter, the head of the militia, mentioned oil refineries produced it as well, but… global nuclear war resulted in a 'mild' downturn in oil processing. As in, no one believed a single refinery remained operating… at least not within the USA, Russia, or most of Europe. Alas, they couldn't come up with a good place to get any sulfur from, which killed the idea of making new gunpowder.

No one really knew the extent of worldwide damage, though Cliff had serious doubts any of the major countries fired nukes at Latin America, Central America, or the Third World. Other than the potential damage from migrating fallout or climate effects due to all the dust in the air, those countries might have escaped the worst of it. Whether or not they'd rush to help any former superpower rebuild any semblance of civilization remained unclear. Most in the militia believed the US, Russia, North Korea, and China had been pummeled into debris-strewn wastelands wherever major metropolitan areas used to exist. The UK as well as most of Europe had also likely been reduced to rubble. As with the mountains of Colorado, it stood to reason remote areas far from big cities probably avoided direct strikes and may hold pockets of survivors clinging to a pre-industrialization level of society.

Cliff figured India and Pakistan wiped each other out in some 'well, everyone else is firing nukes, now's our chance to get the bastards' mentality. He also felt pretty certain North Korea turned South Korea into a parking lot and then ended up glowing due to a retaliatory strike from the US… which prompted Russia to cut loose. For all anyone truly knew, computer glitches killed everyone without any human being making the decision to attack. The whole 'war' came out of nowhere. Harper couldn't remember hearing anything on the news or from her parents about rising global tensions… at least nothing significantly worse than the general worry and unrest all over the globe for most of 2018.

"Either a computer messed up or someone snapped and went insane overnight. Doesn't really matter what caused it…" She sighed. "It won't change anything to know who did it."

A lack of sulfur meant no new gunpowder—at least not in Evergreen. No one knew if nuclear strikes in Europe had thrown up much more dust than what happened here. A giant cloud of sunlight-killing dirt could be making its way across the planet even now, though she figured it would have already blotted out the sky if it existed by now. The noticeable haze in the sky remained, thick enough to blot out the stars at night... but it let through enough sunlight for crops to grow. Any countries not politically significant enough to nuke may well have been crippled by the aftereffects— either direct damage from fallout, starvation to crop failure, economic collapse from global trade halting, riots, civil unrest.

*It's possible the entire world collapsed.*

Some people, including a few on the militia, feared Mexico or some Central American country might attempt a military invasion to take land from the US while the nation had no ability to defend itself. Considering it had been almost a full year since the nuclear strike and no sign of any organized federal government showed up, everyone naturally assumed it gone. Washington DC most certainly had been hammered by nukes. Whether or not the president escaped death didn't sound terribly important when the infrastructure no longer existed. One man plus a handful of staffers couldn't do much. Maybe they'd set up shop in another city like Evergreen, trying to restore society.

But, ten years from now, would anyone give a damn who'd been president or have any respect for the 'authority' of the old government?

*Will we even still be here in ten years? The Lawless could find us. Other gangs might attack.* Harper frowned, not thinking the Mexican military presented a threat. *If* they did anything, they'd invade and take control... not massacre civilians.

*I'd learn Spanish if it would keep Maddie alive and let the world go back to normal. Does that make me a traitor? Can anyone be a traitor if their country is gone?*

Still, 222 shells sounded like a lot, but she'd burn them quick if a hostile force attacked Evergreen. Hell, she used to go through 400 or so merely from one day practicing for an upcoming competition.

Given their relatively short range, shotgun shells would last longer than rifle ammo for the simple reason she wouldn't have any targets until a hostile person made it close enough. Still, in the chaos of an actual fight, people could easily close distance. She could tear through fifty or a hundred shells in a serious engagement—assuming she didn't die. Harper also feared the ammo would eventually rot to unreliable—or dangerous—junk, so she didn't have an obsessive need to hold onto them at all costs beyond her distaste for killing people. She'd try everything she could to avoid having to fire on someone, but 'conserving ammo' would not be a point of hesitation.

*If it can save my life or protect someone, better to use them than let them rot.*

A random, bizarre thought of Mom checking 'best by' dates on plastic-wrapped packages of shotgun ammo at the grocery store—as if buying them there like any other necessary item seemed normal—made her glance down at the Mossberg and sigh. "Someday, you're going to become a decorative wall-hanging that reminds me of Dad."

A flicker of memory haunted her. Thinking of her father brought a wave of guilt for his death. A member of the Lawless gang had kicked in their front door, locked stares with Harper, and had one disgusting thing on his mind—until he saw the shotgun. Her hesitation forced Dad to protect her, leading to him being shot from behind when he took his attention off the patio door in the kitchen.

For the longest time, Harper blamed herself for his death. She'd finally decided to talk with Dr. Tegan Hale about it after the woman witnessed her rage-kill the Lawless who shot Dad. The gang attacked them months ago when they'd run into the city for medicine, before gasoline ran out. By random chance, *that* guy jumped on the back of their van and tried to get inside. As soon as Harper recognized him, she lost control.

Though a medical doctor, the woman had experience with mental health counseling. The day Harper grabbed Madison and fled the house after her parents' deaths, a large pack of Lawless chased them for blocks. She still didn't quite know how they managed to get away. Even if she *had* been able to shoot the guy who came in the front door, they might have still been overrun.

It had taken her eleven months, but Harper finally put ninety percent of the blame for her father's death on the Lawless instead of herself.

Overcome with grief, she stopped walking, bowed her head, and shivered from the weight of emotion. Most of the time, she held it together, but every so often, a moment of desperately trying to wish it had all been a dream brought her to the edge of tears. She sometimes hoped if she closed her eyes hard enough and wanted it bad enough, she'd wake up to find herself back home.

*No one's stupid enough to actually launch a full-scale nuclear war on purpose, right?*

Harper bowed her head.

*Nope. I'm still here.* She opened her eyes. *Guess people really are that stupid.*

She wiped a few stray tears from her face, then resumed walking, almost laughing at herself for being maudlin out of the blue. Had to be the drizzly weather affecting her mood.

"I'm probably never going to be able to think about Mom and Dad without feeling sad and guilty... but I guess that's normal. It would be way scarier if I had no feelings at all. Dad knew I'd have trouble shooting someone or he wouldn't have been watching me. Okay. I'm fine, really."

One deep breath led to another—and the odor of acrid smoke.

"Crap!"

Something burned, and not a fireplace. This stank too much to be a simple wood fire. All thoughts of the past disappeared. She faced into the breeze, looking around for the source. A trail of dark grey-black smoke leaked from a house on Brookline Road.

Harper sounded one long blart from her air horn can, a 911 tone, then ran toward the house.

# 2

# THE NATURAL WAY

S moke poured from a ground-floor window of an otherwise nice two-story home.

The house sat below the level of Brookline Road, its roof only a little higher than the street surface. Harper disregarded the long driveway off to her right, scrambling down the steep tree-studded embankment to the asphalt-paved area in front of the house. A double-ended driveway connected to Brookline on her right and out to South Hiwan Drive on her left.

"Mr. Vitelli?" yelled Harper, still feeling a bit too young to call an almost-forty-year-old by his first name, Joe.

No response came from inside, so she barged in, slinging the Mossberg over her shoulder on its strap. A thin layer of dark smoke clung to the ceiling in the hall, seeping out from an archway on the left up ahead. The place looked otherwise normal, the fire seemingly confined—at the moment—to one room. She pulled her T-shirt up over her face as a mask, then hurried through the arch into the living room. Joe Vitelli lay face-down on the rug next to a glass-top coffee table. A fairly small patch of flames chewed on the rug not far from a fireplace. Harper hauled ass to the kitchen, grabbed a stock pot from a shelf, and ran to the bathroom to fill it in the tub.

An air horn pip went off not too far away, which meant other militia people responding to her request couldn't tell where to go. *They must be too far to see smoke past the trees.*

While the pot filled, Harper stuck her air horn out the bathroom window and sounded another long tone.

"Where you at?" yelled Darnell in the distance.

"Here!" shouted Harper. "Fire! Joe Vitelli's house. Brookline Road."

She cut the water and lugged the pot to the living room, dumping the water on the burning spot, already larger than it had been a minute ago. In the midst of her pouring, people tromped in the front door out in the hall. Water splashed over the rug, smothering the patch of fire into a few tiny areas of burn.

"Harper?" called Leigh.

"In here." She stomped on the squishy, ashed carpet, tamping out the last of the flames.

Darnell and Leigh appeared in the archway. Joe Vitelli abruptly pushed himself up onto his knees and began speaking as if having a conversation with someone about selling a house.

"Mr. Vitelli?" asked Harper.

He ignored her, continuing to reassure a non-existent person the house passed all inspections.

"Oh, damn." Darnell coughed, walking over to the burn mark. "Looks like you got here just in time."

Leigh waved her hand in front of the man's face. "Joe? Are you feeling all right?"

He looked up at her, seemingly bewildered. "I told them purple was off the table. Why did they insist on painting it purple?"

"Uhh…" Harper blinked. "Is he on something?"

Darnell kicked at the burned spot. "Looks like an ember went flying out of the fireplace. This could'a been way bad."

"Joe?" asked Leigh, louder. "Earth to Joe."

He glanced down at a big plastic cup on the floor, which he'd likely dropped earlier when he blacked out. Still seeming confused, he picked the cup up, examined it for a second as if he'd never seen such an object before—and crushed it.

"Something is really wrong with him," said Harper.

Darnell closed the screen in front of the fireplace. "We should get him to the medical center. This fire's pretty much died down, but we can't leave it going in an empty house. Harper, you mind getting another bucket?"

"Yeah, sure..." She hurried to the bathroom.

Darnell and Leigh continued trying to get Joe to respond to conversation while Harper filled the stock pot. The man replied babbling, or spouting mixed-up sentences unrelated to their questions, such as exclaiming 'frogs can't fly' when they asked him if he knew where he was.

Harper lugged the pot of water to the living room.

Joe picked up a TV remote from the coffee table and put it on the floor in front of him. He picked it back up and put it on the table... then repeated the back and forth three times.

"What the actual eff is he doing?" asked Harper while dumping the water into the fireplace.

Darnell shrugged. "Don't look at me. Leigh's the one who used to be an EMT."

"I'm thinking either he's got a brain tumor or he's having a sugar crash." Leigh took Joe's arm. "We need to get him to the medical center."

Harper's stomach knotted up at the words 'sugar crash.' It meant diabetes, which meant he would likely die fairly soon in a world where insulin no longer existed.

"Joe, man, can you walk?" Darnell took his other arm and helped Leigh lift the man to his feet.

"The house is listed fair," said Joe—six times in a row. He gave a wild laugh while rocking back and forth.

"C'mon, Joe." Leigh tugged on his arm.

They walked him out to the driveway.

Harper accompanied them, mostly out of worry and curiosity than any true need to provide an escort. Joe ambled along, babbling random phrases, growling, chuckling, or whistling. Twice, he started singing Eighties hair band music. They followed Brookline to Route 76, the straightest path to the medical center they'd established in a former office building. She still didn't understand why they hadn't used the dental place next to the Wendy's, since it already had a bunch of medical equipment. Maybe the doctors didn't want to put the medical center in a building so close to the edge of town out of fear of potential attack?

For that matter, Evergreen had an actual medical center farther south on 74 behind the Big R. There'd been talk of relocating services there, but so far, no action. Between the lack of ability to transmit electricity from the solar panel farm there to—she assumed—no one thinking it worth the bother, the converted office building remained their 'hospital.' The citizens of Evergreen had more or less accepted society would end up in some strange version of the early 1900s as far as medical technology went for the foreseeable future.

Also, the fancy technology in the *real* medical center wouldn't do anyone any good without more power than the solar panels had the ability to create. Jeanette and her electrical team managed to energize the former power grid in a limited area, and it still crapped out if too many people turned on too many lights at the same time. Trying to switch on an MRI machine would cause the solar panels to melt.

Most of the houses around the old golf course (where Anne-Marie assigned people with children to live due to proximity to the school) had power, as well as the improvised medical center, city hall, and numerous houses as far south as Hilltop Drive, where Harper lived. They'd been working to salvage or replace pole wiring as much as they could, but the fairly small solar array could only generate so much juice. If they innervated too much of the former town's power grid, the wires alone would be so much of a drain there wouldn't be enough power left to turn on three light bulbs. Harper still didn't quite understand why long wires caused power loss, but trusted the electricians to be correct.

Chasing bears off, walking around a quiet suburb, and helping sick people to the medical center didn't come close to what the movies made nuclear war survival sound like... but she had no complaints. She far preferred the mundanity of it to having gangs of crazed leather-clad freaks who flipped a coin to decide between cooking their meat or eating it raw chasing her all over a desert wasteland. The constant Hollywood threat of suffering cannibalism, sexual assault, or some weird gladiatorial fiasco if captured had fortunately not proved out to be truth. Then again, those movies usually portrayed a time set many generations after the war when no one alive remembered what society had been like.

She wanted to believe what Anne-Marie, the town manager, said. The woman believed deep down every person had good in them, and society, no matter what form it took, would generally cling to civilization. Roving bands of psychos existed only in movies, or so she wanted to believe. Harper had seen at least two—possibly three—groups she'd classify as a 'roving band of psychos,' perhaps not so much on the 'roving' part. Obviously, the Lawless, then the group of gang punks camped out beside a highway where she found her former physics teacher, Ms. Tiller, and finally, the small army of convicts who'd attacked Evergreen in revenge for liberating the people they'd enslaved to work on farms at Kittredge.

*Yeah, nuts exist. Most people might be good, but the world's got plenty of idiots.*

Joe slipped in and out of consciousness, forcing Darnell and Leigh to carry him for about half the trip. As soon as they went in the door of the medical center, Ruby Dorsey called for Dr. Khan. The woman managed the day-to-day stuff, and also helped deal with small problems like kids who'd scraped a knee. To Harper, she seemed like the 'front desk person' every doctor's office or dentist's office had, mostly because the woman sat at the front desk. None of the receptionist computers or phones worked anymore, but for whatever reason, no one had bothered removing them.

Darnell and Leigh carried Joe across the waiting room, meeting Dr. Khan at the start of the hallway leading deeper into the building. Ruby ran to grab a gurney. Between the four of them, they maneuvered Joe into a treatment room.

"What happened?" asked Dr. Khan, while giving Joe a cursory initial evaluation.

Harper hovered in the doorway. "I saw smoke coming out of the window. Found Mr. Vitelli unconscious on the floor. The fire was

pretty small, only about"—she held her hands about pizza-size apart
—"this big. I put it out. Don't think the smoke knocked him cold. He
woke up and started talking to someone who wasn't there and did a
bunch of weird stuff."

Leigh nodded. "Incoherent speech, repetitive activities... I'm
thinking he's probably in hypoglycemic shock... or he's got a brain
tumor."

Dr. Khan rummaged a tester from a drawer, seeming both
surprised and relieved when it turned on. He pricked Joe's finger.
His eyes went wide a few seconds later when the device beeped and
displayed results. "Excuse me a moment."

Harper sidestepped as the doctor rushed out of the treatment
room. He ran down the hall to a small break area, returning in a
moment carrying a cup, which he coaxed Joe to drink.

"What are you giving him?" asked Darnell.

"Sugar water. You're correct, Miss Preston." Dr. Khan smiled at
Leigh. "Blood glucose was forty-two."

Leigh cringed. "Holy cow."

"If he hadn't fainted, he could have put the fire out pretty easy,"
said Harper. "It's pure luck I happened to walk by in time to catch it
before it spread across the whole room."

"Dude's seriously lucky." Darnell whistled. "Kinda backward his
living room carpet catching fire *saved* his life."

"Mr. Vitelli probably shouldn't live alone." Harper bit her lip.
*Until he dies for not having insulin.*

"A legitimate concern." Dr. Khan set the empty cup on the
counter. "He should be all right in a few minutes once the sugar gets
into his bloodstream. With extreme dietary care, he can potentially
manage. The odds are better if he's type two. If he's type one, it's...
well... even with perfect dietary management, his prognosis for
survival in the absence of insulin is not rosy. Mr. Vitelli should not be
living alone."

"Yeah." Leigh bowed her head.

After so many months of patrolling the area around the old golf
course, Harper had a fairly good sense of who lived where. She
might not have known everyone on a 'first name' basis, but she knew

names and a little bit about each person. People like Joe Vitelli, single adults living alone, would likely be asked to relocate for a family with kids if the houses closest to the school ever filled up. However, they still had plenty of empties. Regardless, the guy needed to have someone with him pretty much all the time.

If he happened to be a type one diabetic, he wouldn't last much longer. Despite seeing him on and off while patrolling for months, she'd never realized he had a medical condition, which meant he either got astoundingly lucky or had a stash of insulin—or he'd only recently developed diabetes.

*The stuff goes bad pretty quick, doesn't it? And we haven't had working refrigerators for very long… and the power goes out all the time, sometimes for days.* Distribution of electrical power had become so iffy, Jeannette's team had installed a few solar panels and some kind of battery directly on the quartermaster building roof, dedicated to powering the 'community refrigerators.'

While the others discussed the possibility of talking Joe into moving, Harper decided she had no further need of being there, so made her way out. Head full of somber thoughts, she nearly walked straight into Arturo Rosales not far from the medical center door. He appeared to be on the way to go inside.

"Sorry," said Arturo, grabbing her arms for balance.

"My fault. I should have been looking ahead, not down."

He let go. "Everything okay? You look kinda glum. Usually, it's me who's the downer."

She managed a weak smile. Consumed by feelings of uselessness, the former lawyer had come close to shooting himself a while back. Talking about depressing things probably wouldn't help him much… or maybe hearing about someone in much worse shape than having skills the world no longer needed might help.

"Just found someone having diabetes problems. He's probably not going to last much longer since there's no way to get insulin anymore."

Arturo grimaced. "Ouch. Darwin's back to being king."

"Don't be a douche," muttered Harper.

"I didn't mean it like that."

She raised both eyebrows. "Not much other way to mean calling someone a Darwin Award winner."

Arturo chuckled, shaking his head. "No, not a Darwin Award. That's for people who die for extreme stupidity. I'm talking about how we've cheated nature, cheated death for a long time. Stuff like cancer, diabetes, even old age... nature had a design and we've been messing with it. Maybe we shouldn't have. Sick and weak animals die off in nature. Did we mess up humans as a species by not letting natural processes get rid of bad traits? I'm not saying it's a good thing people are going to start dying to stuff they'd never have died to before the war... just, you know, saying it's how nature would've worked if humans didn't have such big brains."

She fidgeted, wholly uncomfortable with his line of reasoning. *Sounds like some kinda evil pure genetics thing a bad guy government would do in a movie.*

"Eh, ignore me." He waved dismissively off to the side. "I'm having one of my nihilistic moods. Here to see Dr. Hale. You know, a therapy session."

The urge to call him an insensitive dick faded. "Cool. She's super nice. Hope she's helping."

"I'm still here, aren't I?"

"Don't talk like that. We still need *you.* Anyone who can successfully become a lawyer has got to be smart enough to help us out in some way. We're not the only settlement out there. Maybe if we keep growing, we'll eventually need like an ambassador to another town. You'd be perfect for that."

He chuckled. "I should be so lucky. We'll see. For the time being, I'm working at the farm. Eating is good. I'm kind of addicted to it."

"Yeah. Same here."

Arturo waved, then headed into the medical center, muttering under his breath about paying hundreds of thousands of dollars in tuition so he can plant turnips and shovel cow shit.

*Ugh.* She slung the Mossberg off her shoulder, then resumed walking back up Route 74 toward her patrol area. *If animals had the ability to save their offspring, parents, or siblings from 'natural selection,' they damn sure would.* It couldn't be true nature decided to kill off certain people. Arturo's comments implied some people had been determined 'genetic dead ends' and needed to be pruned from humanity's family tree. Though she'd call the Lawless 'genetic dead ends,' it infuriated her to hear someone so callously disregard inevitable death for no reason other than medical technology being thrown back a century or two.

*People in a modern country shouldn't die due to lack of insulin.* She stopped short, feeling like an idiot. *We're no longer in a modern country.*

Harper shivered at the idea humanity had lost the ability to defy nature's process. True, Evergreen had two *real* doctors plus some supplies. It put them far ahead of being literally in the 1800s, but the supplies wouldn't last forever and neither would Dr. Khan or Dr. Hale. The woman seemed quite young to be a medical doctor, barely into her thirties. Perhaps to be calming, she'd asked Harper to call her Tegan rather than Dr. Hale.

Despite her relative youth, even Dr. Hale would eventually die, leaving Evergreen without 'legitimate' doctors. They presently trained Grace as an apprentice, one of the cheerleaders who'd arrived on the bus with Logan and some other high school seniors. Their arrangement couldn't compare to actual medical school, but it beat having no doctors at all. When Grace and any other apprentices trained by the real doctors became too old to do the job, the town would have to rely on whoever *they* trained. Invariably, knowledge and expertise would be lost along the way. Eventually, they really would be back to 1800s medicine... unless some Third World country which had escaped total destruction assisted the rest of the planet in rebuilding.

*I'm not going to be around to worry about the second-generation apprentices... but if I have kids, they will be.*

She exhaled hard.

"Nothing I can do about it. Humanity survived the actual 1800s. We'll do it again."

# 3

# WAITING TO DIE

Madison balanced the big bowl of feed on her hip, opened the gate, and slipped into the chicken pen.

Sensing dinner, several dozen chickens swarmed her, scrambling around and crashing into each other in their haste. Happy coos and clucks came from all sides.

"Hello, guys," whispered Madison. "It's lunchtime."

She grabbed handfuls of feed, tossing it around evenly, smiling at the birds pecking it up as fast as they could. A few tosses at the back of the cluster helped spread them out so all the birds got something to eat. It took her a few minutes to empty the bowl by handfuls. Most of the other kids would dump it all in one spot to be done with the job as fast as possible. Invariably, leaving a single big pile set off a battle royal among the chickens. Madison didn't care how long it took her, she wanted to be nice to the birds.

Around twenty minutes later, Madison sprinkled the last handful of feed on the ground right in front of her, watching the kernels bounce off the dirt. One landed on her foot. A chicken ate it before she could twitch. She stared down and gave a sad sigh. Dirty, splitting apart at the seams, and uncomfortably tight, the pinkish-purple sneakers her Mom bought her looked about ready to disintegrate. She'd given them up for lost the day the bad guys forced her and Harper to run away from their home, but Cliff and some of the militia brought them back when they'd recovered usable clothes from the old house as a surprise for Harper's birthday.

The sneakers hadn't hit her in the feels at all until now.

Seeing them in such a sad state almost felt like being mean to Mom. Almost. Running shoes hadn't exactly been designed for farm work. Not that anyone made her or any of the kids under fourteen do anything seriously grueling, but farms had mud, animal poop, water, sharp things hiding in the plants... The sneakers, New Balance, hadn't cost all that much nor bestowed many style points. Up until this moment, she hadn't placed any great significance on them.

Seeing them in such worn out shape hit her as a shock. She'd expected to outgrow them after about a year, no big surprise they'd gotten tight, but their beat-up condition offered glaring proof of the world changing. Madison daydreamed about the day she got them. Mom had taken her to the mall last August for 'back to school' shopping. She'd grumbled and whined the entire time because the shopping trip got in the way of hanging out over Becca's house on one of the final days of summer break. Now, she'd have given anything to have even five minutes with her mom.

Silent tears rolled down her face.

*Nothing lasts. Not shoes... not parents...* Madison wiped her eyes. *Maybe that's why Lorelei doesn't care about clothes. She loves being with people and doesn't give a crap about things.*

She debated taking her shoes off to escape the annoying tightness, but decided against it due to not wanting to step in chicken poop. Going barefoot didn't bother her while running around with her friends at home... but on the farm, it seemed like a disgusting — and possibly dangerous — idea.

Her thoughts drifted from sneakers and Mom to chickens. It didn't feel like it had been long at all since she screamed when the chickens got too close. As much as she loved animals, she'd only ever seen dogs, cats, and hamsters up close. For some silly reason, having thirty some odd chickens gathering around her freaked her out the first week or two.

The crowd of—now about sixty—chickens didn't bother her anymore.

Madison crouched, patting random birds while they hunted the last few grains of feed. The idea many of them would eventually become food made her want to hug them all and hide them somewhere. Few people thought of chickens as anything more than stone dumb birds barely smart enough to comprehend their own existence. Of the kids tasked with feeding chickens, only Madison spent any time with them beyond the minimum necessary to drop off food or collect eggs. Everyone else merely dumped the feed and left. The chickens, some of them anyway, showed signs of affection toward her. One she'd named Rosie routinely followed her around and even demanded hugs sometimes.

She'd tearfully pleaded with Mr. Rollins, the man in charge of the farm, to spare Rosie. It killed her to think a creature capable of recognizing her and showing affection like a dog or cat might soon be slaughtered. Sure enough, soon after she crouched, Rosie leapt into her lap, resting her head on Madison's shoulder.

So soon after her dying sneakers reminded her of Mom, Rosie's show of affection broke the dam. Madison hugged the chicken, trying not to make too much noise while bawling over the creature's imminent death. Rosie emitted a contented coo.

*I gotta save her!*

A few minutes later, two voices whispering in the gap between the chicken house and the barn distracted her from a rapidly forming plan to smuggle Rosie home. She couldn't save all the chickens, but she could save the one who asked for hugs.

Madison stood, still holding Rosie, and crept across the pen to the building at the back end. Careful not to make a sound, she leaned left over the fence, peering around the corner of the chicken house.

Her 'brother,' Jonathan, and Mila Cline faced each other at the opposite end of the narrow alley between the two buildings. It still seemed weird to see Mila not wearing black everything. Her light purple dress made her seem almost normal, like any other kid in school. Jonathan had likely been born in a T-shirt and jeans. Madison backed off, hiding against the wall, watching them with only one eye.

Jon and Mila stood there looking at each other for almost a minute in silence.

"Are you going to do it or just stare at me?" asked Mila.

Jonathan fidgeted, clearly nervous. He waited a few seconds, then leaned forward, giving Mila a brief kiss on the cheek.

*Ooo!* Madison squeezed Rosie.

The chicken made a *bwawk* noise, but given all the other chickens around, neither Mila nor her brother noticed.

"Did I do it right?" asked Jonathan.

Mila shrugged. "How should I know? You're the first boy to kiss me."

"Did you like it?"

"Umm." Mila scrunched up her nose. "I think so."

Madison ducked out of sight before they noticed her, feeling a bit rude for spying. Of course, she already knew Jonathan was sweet on Mila, no big reveal there. She also had no intention to make fun of them or even tell anyone about it. Protecting her family included more than simply shooting guns at bad guys. She sighed. Her pre-war self probably would have made fun of him or at least teased him in private… but bad people drained most of the joy out of the world. Happiness snuck in here and there sometimes, and if doing something embarrassing with Mila made Jonathan happy, she couldn't dare ruin it for him. This post-war version of her couldn't, feeling only warmth at seeing him smile. Still, she sorta laughed a bit at their awkwardness. Harper and Logan kissed *way* different. She debated telling Jonathan to try kissing her on the lips next time like she'd seen Harper and Logan do, but couldn't without admitting to catching them.

She retreated back among the chickens, her whimsical mood falling flat again watching the birds peck at the dirt, stupidly trying to find feed where none existed.

*They're sitting here waiting to die and don't even realize it… just like us.*

Rosie appeared content to cuddle, so Madison kept holding her.

"Hey Maddie," called Eva.

Madison looked up.

Her friends, Eva Parsons and Becca Perry, rushed over to the fence around the pen. Madison had known them both since first grade. Every time she saw them, she had to remind herself she didn't imagine their presence. Eva *still* looked too skinny, her long mouse-brown hair as wild as a shell-shocked child survivor of nuclear war probably ought to look. She and her mother ended up at the Army survivor camp in El Dorado. Only by the sheer random chance Harper went on a delivery run there, she found them and brought them back to Evergreen. Madison still had no idea what happened to her other before-the-war friend, Melissa. Both of Becca's parents were alive and here with her, something Madison occasionally felt jealous about, but not too much. No bad feelings for Becca, she just wished she still had her parents, too. Eva lost her dad. Her mother survived, but suffered some mental problems as a result of stuff that happened in the camp no one had explained to her. Anything 'too bad' for Madison to hear at ten had to be *bad*. She decided not to push for answers, having enough things in her head to be sad about already.

"Why are you crying?" asked Becca, swiping her blonde hair off her face. Despite the state of the world, she still made time to style it as best she could—though no longer bothered trying to curl it.

Madison looked down, hugging Rosie a little tighter. "The chickens. I feel sad for them."

"Wow…" Eva blinked. "Seriously?"

Becca pursed her lips. "It's kinda stupid they made the vegan feed chickens."

"I don't mind taking care of them. It's what's going to eventually happen to them that makes me sad." Madison sighed. "Okay, I'm not really crying over chickens. They're part of it, but I'm really sad about lots of other stuff… you know… *everything*."

"Yeah." Becca folded her arms atop the fence and rested her chin on them. "I miss how it used to be, too."

Eva kicked at the ground. "Yeah." She glanced up for a second, seeming to swallow whatever she wanted to say next.

"What?" asked Madison.

"Sorry."

"Say it, it's fine." Madison relaxed her hug on Rosie, set the chicken back on its feet, then swiped her hands down the front of her T-shirt to knock away a few stray feathers.

Eva's lip quivered, but she didn't start crying. "I miss the way the world was, but I could deal with it better if Mom wasn't weird now. Sorry."

Madison walked over to her friends. "Why are you apologizing for being upset your mom has some issues? Everyone has issues."

"I shouldn't complain." Eva avoided eye contact. "My mother is still here. Yours… umm…"

"Not your fault. I know Becca's still got *both* of her parents and they're still normal." Madison half smiled.

Becca laughed. "Parents are never normal. They're parents… and they're not really the same now, anyway. They don't fight anymore, like ever. It's kinda weird. But nice."

Rosie wandered over and leaned against Madison's leg.

She crouched to pet the chicken. "How much trouble do you think I'll get in for bringing one chicken home?"

"Huh?" asked Becca.

Madison explained her plan to 'steal' Rosie because she didn't trust her request not to kill her for food would be honored. "… Mr. Rollins said they'd leave her alone, but she looks just like all the other white ones. The only way to recognize her is she runs over for hugs whenever I'm here. Someone's going to make a mistake."

"Everyone knows how you are about animals. You're not stealing extra food… and you're still a kid." Becca grinned. "Someone might yell at you, but I don't think you'll get in big trouble."

"Yeah, not unless you try to set *all* the chickens free." Eva crossed her eyes and twirled a finger around by her right ear.

Madison snickered. "I would, but then I'd get in real trouble. Animals deserve to live, but even they eat other animals. It's not like before when stores had all kinds of food and no one *needed* to eat meat. It's not right for me to risk other people's health because I cry about dead chickens… but I wanna save one."

"You're way too upset for one chicken." Becca poked her in the side. "What happened?"

"Nothing *happened*." Madison flapped her arms. "Just... thinking. My sneakers are falling apart and it made me think about how everything falls apart. Stuff doesn't last forever. My mother bought me these sneakers for school. It's really stupid, but I might keep them to remember her."

Becca giggled. "That's how people turn into hoarders."

"Hey, we're supposed to feed the cows," said Eva. "Are you done here? Wanna help?"

"Sure." Madison pulled herself up to sit on the fence. "I can come back for Rosie after."

Becca faced the farm, squinting into the sunlight. "Feels so weird to have to work. It's like illegal to make a ten-year-old have a job."

"It isn't *work*. We're surviving." Madison jumped down outside the pen. "More like having to do chores at home."

"Yeah." Eva wiped at a dirt smear on her left arm. "And they let us go home at lunchtime. Mom said a 'job' is working to help someone else get rich. So, this isn't a job."

A man's anguished scream came from the field off to the left.

Madison jumped back against the fence. Becca and Eva spun to stare in the direction of the cry. Several adults rushed into the tall greenery. Eva grabbed Madison, clinging and half hiding behind her. The girl hadn't spoken too much about the time she'd spent in the Army camp, but like her mother, she'd changed. Mrs. Parsons was sad all the time, barely cared about things other than her daughter. Eva had become easily frightened, afraid of the dark, afraid of being alone, jumpy at loud noises. For the most part, she acted mostly the same as before the war, but unexpected bangs or aggressive men made her run away and hide—or cling.

People shouted in the distance. One man yelled for something to make a bandage with. A woman called, "He's here" a few times. Madison put an arm around Eva. The three of them stood still, staring at the distant corn plants. Before long, five people emerged onto the dirt field between the small animal pens and the planting rows. Three men and one woman carried another man, who appeared to have passed out. A thin metal shard stuck out from both sides of his leg at the calf. Blood saturated his jeans.

Madison stared at the impaling blade—likely a broken scythe or piece of farm machinery—as they carried him right past the girls. Eva turned away, unable to bear the sight of blood. Becca took the scene in relative stride, eyebrows up in a 'whoa' expression. After seeing Harper shoot Lawless at close range with a shotgun, a piece of metal sticking out of a guy's leg didn't faze Madison much. She didn't *like* seeing it, but it didn't bother her.

She let a long sigh slip out of her nose. *Guess I'm a little nuts, too.*

They stood there in silence for a moment after the people rushed the wounded man out of sight.

"C'mon." Becca bumped Madison's arm. "Help us feed the cows."

"'Kay." Madison twisted to look Eva in the eye. "You okay?"

The scrawny girl took a deep breath. "Yeah. Thought someone was trying to kill us, but he had an accident."

*Stuff doesn't matter. We could die from anything any time.* Madison put her other arm around Becca and squeezed her friends together, beyond thrilled to have time with them.

"What are you getting emo about now?" asked Becca.

"A farm accident," said Madison. "The world isn't safe anymore."

"It wasn't safe before," whispered Eva.

"Yeah, but it's more dangerous now." Madison exhaled. "I'm trying to deal. Remember, I'm the crazy kid who kept talking to a dead phone."

Becca nudged her. "You're not crazy, just… trying to deal."

"I don't want you guys to die." Madison fought off the urge to cry. "I'm okay. Dr. Tegan said it's normal for me to get super emotional about small things after what happened. Part of the process."

"Yeah." Becca smiled. "Let's go feed the cows. They'll make you feel better."

"Okay." Madison smiled.

# 4

## NO NORMAL BUT WHAT WE MAKE

Harper sliced potatoes into chunks beside the kitchen sink. The repetitive soft *thunk* of the knife hitting the cutting board in the otherwise silent house proved relaxing. It wouldn't be long before the kids returned from the farm and their voices filled the air outside. Harper almost laughed at the idea of surviving a nuclear apocalypse and ending up cutting vegetables in a reasonably normal kitchen. She pictured herself in full 'apocalypse-chic' regalia, which for a girl her age probably meant a leather bikini with spikes all over the place, her hair dyed hot pink or something silly, and two big machetes on her back — at least according to Hollywood. The mental image of 'wasteland badass girl' slicing potatoes reached a point of ridiculous to where she laughed out loud.

"Probably why they don't show the normal stuff in movies, right? Hey, Bloodsaw, you wanna go cut some people's heads off? Yeah, sure. Gimme a sec to finish the potatoes first."

A streak of white dashing across the back yard made her look up, out the window.

*Why is there a chicken in the yard?* She chuckled. *Probably got out. Wonder how long it's been running around. Hope it's gone by the time Cliff gets home or it's going to end up in a pot.*

She kept cutting potatoes for the soup-stew-something she and Carrie intended to put together for dinner. Tonight, they'd use up the last of the boxed pasta, simple macaroni elbows... but it had to be the only remaining dry pasta anywhere in Evergreen. They probably would've used it months ago if it hadn't been stuffed out of sight in the cabinet. One box of elbows wouldn't work for her entire new family, but adding it to a stew helped stretch it over another portion or two.

Madison ran by in the backyard, the chicken following her.

*Oh...* Harper laughed in her head. *Guess she adopted one. Ack. Gotta tell Cliff not to kill it.*

Jonathan, Mila, Lorelei, Christopher Dominguez, Becca, and Eva ran around, playing some sort of 'laser sword tag' game they'd invented. One kid had a pool noodle—a.k.a laser sword—and tried to wallop someone else. As soon as they got a 'kill,' the person they hit took the 'sword.' Maybe they kept score, maybe they didn't. It looked far too chaotic and random to have any real rules.

Harper gathered the potato chunks into a bowl. "Wow. Time really is going backward."

"Huh?" Carrie looked up from the stew pot she'd been stirring. "What do you mean?"

"Womenfolk in the kitchen, kids playing outside instead of being in here on video games, Dad out doing 'manly things.'"

Carrie laughed. "We're making food because we're here. You know darn well Cliff cooks whenever he's got night patrol."

"Yeah, I know." Harper leaned on the counter. "Just making a joke. I should be used to the kids playing outside now. It's just like Cliff's stories about growing up. He says they didn't even have video games for the home until he was like eight or nine years old."

"Oh, the horror." Carrie fake gasped.

"Right?" Harper held her leg out. "And here we are literally barefoot in the kitchen."

"Hah. Be glad we still have a kitchen at all."

"No doubt." She grabbed the next potato and plonked it down on the cutting board. "Hey, can I ask you something serious?"

Carrie put the lid on the stew pot. "Of course."

"I'm kinda struggling with Lorelei."

"What now? Is she out there naked again?" Carrie approached to look out the window over the sink.

"No. I think she's starting to get the message clothes need to stay on except for bath time... or rain. I mean struggling in the sense it feels more like I'm her older sister than a mom. We're not far enough apart in age, I guess."

Carrie patted her shoulder. "There are plenty of older sisters and brothers who step up to take care of their little siblings when something happens to the parents. You shouldn't stress out about being 'mom' enough. Do the best you can."

"Yeah..." Harper cut another potato in half. "Tegan said something about being mom... I shouldn't like try to be her best friend. I'm just worried after everything she's been through. I don't want to put my foot down over something trivial and upset her. Am I being too soft on her? Mind letting me know if I mess up?"

"As much as I can." Carrie playfully elbowed her before returning to tend the pot. "Being older than you doesn't mean I know how to wrangle kids. I'll offer whatever advice I can. Not sure how much it applies anymore, considering the world ain't what it used to be. Just try to be 'mom' first, friend second. It's more important to do what's right for her than make sure she likes you."

Harper collected the potato chunks into the bowl. "This *is* Lore we're talking about. She likes everyone no matter what they do to her. The poor girl is broken."

"She ain't broken." Carrie reached for the spice rack, but sighed at all the nothing it held. "I sure do miss seasoning. How messed up is it that simple salt and pepper feel like exotic spices from a faraway land? Anyway, Lore ain't broke. She's just trying to come to terms with the cards life dealt her. Remember what Dr. Hale said. Keep on giving her a stable home and she'll be okay."

"Yeah." Harper sighed, moving on to carrots. "At least she's keeping her dress on more often than not lately."

Carrie laughed. "Small progress is still progress."

"She's doing really well. I've been trying to do what Tegan said and not make too big a deal about it to avoid traumatizing her into being ashamed of her body or neurotic about clothing. Hard to believe she had it so rough before."

"Abused?" asked Carrie.

"Not like that. I think her mother just neglected her to the point she didn't buy her clothes or didn't care if she wore them or not. Sorta took 'free range parenting' to a ridiculous extreme."

"Kids can be resilient. And a lot of them go through a weird phase with clothes. My sister's son loved streaking around the house. He outgrew it by six, though. And yes, I know Lorelei is six, but she's been coping with things kids shouldn't have to cope with." Carrie put the lid on the pot, turned to face Harper, and leaned against the counter. "I'm pretty sure her mother started off trying to do the best she could, then crashed hard. I'm no psychologist, but—"

"You Googled?"

"Hah. No. Saw a documentary a while back about a neglected kid. His mother didn't really feed him or even talk to him when he was a toddler. Police found him at like seven, nearly starved to death. In the documentary, they showed him at like sixteen. His adoptive parents had to lock the fridge, or he'd just eat everything until he threw up. Lore is pretty darn normal by comparison. Her mother had to have bonded with her in the critical early years, but fell flat on her face later on. Probably due to drugs."

Harper stared at the handful of carrots she held down to the board. "What is normal anymore?"

"Whatever we make it." Carrie waved randomly. "We're not quite back in the Old West, but we're also not really in the modern world anymore."

"Gotta pee!" yelled Madison.

Harper looked up at the window as her sister tossed the pool noodle to Jonathan, then ran inside, leaving a trail of bare dirt footprints across the kitchen floor before disappearing down the hall to the bathroom.

"See? *Now* I feel like Mom." Harper grabbed a towel and crouched to wipe the linoleum.

Carrie laughed.

A few minutes later, when Madison zoomed back into the

kitchen, Harper caught her. "Hey, you tracked dirt all over the floor."

"Sorry, Mom." Madison smiled.

Harper sighed, hugged her, then let go. "What happened to your shoes?"

"They're in my room. They're too small for me now and kinda hurt."

"Okay, yeah. It's been a while." Harper ruffled her sister's hair. "We'll go see if the quartermaster has anything after dinner. It's going to get too cold to go barefoot outside soon."

Madison looked down.

"What's wrong, Termite?"

"Heh. Just thinking about how much I whined at Mom when she took me shopping. I want to apologize."

Harper let out a long, slow breath. "Kids are kids. Mom knew you didn't intend to be annoying on purpose. If there's anything like ghosts or an afterlife, I'm sure she's forgiven you."

"I hope so," whispered Madison.

"There's a chicken in the yard."

"Rosie," said Madison.

"Explain." Harper folded her arms.

"I already told you about her."

"Yes, but not why she's here."

Madison pulled her hair out of her eyes. "I don't want her to be killed for food. She's a *pet* chicken, not a food chicken. She knows me and wants hugs and stuff. It would ruin me if they killed her."

"Okay..." Harper patted her shoulder. "I'm not going to get involved here, but if Mr. Rollins or someone from the farm management gets upset, you need to prepare yourself for the possibility they might want her back on the farm."

"I know." Madison tapped her big toe on the floor. "But we have so many chickens. They can let me save one."

*It's like the war to her. So many people where we used to live in Lakewood, but I only saved Madison.* "Okay."

Madison ran outside—and promptly ate a pool noodle to the face. Jonathan had been hiding against the wall by the door.

The 'hey, not fair' argument lasted five minutes, but ended with everyone outside laughing.

"Not bad," said Carrie. "Almost sounded like a mom there."

"Thanks." Harper gave a halfhearted chuckle... and resumed slicing carrots.

# 5

## THE THING ABOUT STUFF

The storeroom had shoes in Madison's size, if a little big.

Liz Trujillo, the quartermaster, joked about kids not needing shoes until their feet stopped getting bigger—to save time and materials—once the Walmart raid stash dried up. As far as Harper could remember, she stopped outgrowing shoes around fourteen. Madison promised to take good care of them so some other kid might inherit her new ones in a year when they no longer fit her.

Back home, Harper flopped on the couch and dared to crack open *The Secret Garden*. She'd made it up to chapter eighteen, but every time she tried to read it, *something* happened. Merely touching the book at all set her nerves on edge. However, she didn't believe in curses, jinxes, ghosts, shadow men, magic, or other forms of woo. Skepticism didn't stop her from worrying too much about becoming comfortable in Evergreen or taking risks like going out on expeditions. They'd found safety here. Leaving town felt like taunting a tiger.

Even accepting the town as a safe place seemed as if it would guarantee tragedy. The instant she let her guard down and tried to feel as if they might know happiness here, something bad would happen to Madison, or her... or the rest of her new family.

Plenty of bad already came their way, though. She'd lost both parents, several friends, the Tyler situation, had to shoot people. Her deepening love for Logan only served to increase her anxiety. As soon as she truly accepted she loved him, fate would take him away as it had done with Tyler.

Harper stared at the first page of chapter eighteen without reading it, thinking about Logan and whether or not she should suggest they go all the way in bed. They'd done just about everything possible short of that or 'butt stuff' as he awkwardly, jokingly referred to it. Granted, she didn't know a lot about sex, so 'just about everything' to her probably didn't encompass very much at all. Merely thinking about 'mouth stuff' made her blush. More than half the girls in her class claimed to have done that for their boyfriends, many talking about going down on them as no big deal. Whether or not they really had or simply bragged, she didn't know, nor wanted to.

Nearly losing Logan to a gunshot a few months ago erased her worry about going too fast to avoid being dumb and getting hurt. She really did love him, as much as she figured someone her age could believe themselves truly in love. Living in a reality where anyone could die tomorrow made the notion of 'saving herself' seem sad in a naïvely unrealistic way. She didn't want to throw away her virginity to be rid of it like Darci had. Her friend once believed doing so made her an adult. No, Harper wanted to share the joy of making love before anything happened to one or both of them. Afraid someone might catch her turning red in the face, she stopped thinking about Logan and turned her attention to the book.

"Ugh, not again," muttered Jonathan.

Harper peered over the top of the book.

Jonathan and Mila lay on the floor, attempting to use the PlayStation. It worked in stints between fluctuations in the electrical power that caused the system to shut off or restart. Naturally, it made playing games frustrating... but the kids kept trying.

*Might as well enjoy it while they can. I'm sure we'll see the end of electrical power as a thing in our lifetimes.*

Having developed and lost it could allow future generations to rebuild technology more easily, but it would still take decades. *If* she made it to old age, she might end up in a place like a 1930s or 1940s-era care home. Should she and Logan have kids, they'd probably keep 'grandma' as comfortable as possible until she died at home. Maybe society would reestablish a national power grid by the time she became elderly, but no guarantee. She thought it less likely she'd live past her seventies—if even *to* them—than civilization would get anywhere near back to what it had been before the war in her lifetime.

Madison and Lorelei played out in the yard, content to enjoy the last few hours of daylight.

Unlike her previous life, Harper couldn't spend all her free time hanging out with friends and goofing off, so she tried her best to enjoy idle moments whenever they happened. She read for a while, in between wondering what Renee and Darci were up to. Her new friend, Grace, put in long hours at the medical center, learning. Renee worked with a group learning how to make fabric from plants like flax, ultimately with the goal of manufacturing clothing by hand like in the old days. Darci still slacked, not having any official 'job.'

Cliff sat in his favorite recliner reading some sort of technical manual so he could help Jeanette out if the idea of making windmill generators ever got the go ahead. Solar panels wouldn't last forever. Replacing them required all sorts of chemicals and high-tech manufacturing processes humanity no longer possessed. Making wind turbines sounded like a much more sustainable idea. The Earth would never run out of wind, and it took much less of a technical infrastructure to produce mechanical parts—as opposed to advanced chemical composites, or whatever alchemy they made solar panels out of.

She read for an hour or so in peace.

"Harp?" called Madison from the hall.

"Yeah?" She looked up.

"C'mere."

*Figures. I dared trying to read this book again.* Harper stuffed the bookmark in place, got up, and headed down the hall to find Madison standing by the bathroom door, pointing. "What?"

"It's on the toilet seat."

She leaned in the doorway to look. A smallish beetle wandered around on the seat. *Why is Maddie afraid of a little bug?* With a shrug, Harper stepped into the bathroom and coaxed the insect to climb onto her hand. Madison followed her as she carried the bug outside, across the yard, and let it go on the wooden fence.

"Thanks," whispered Madison.

"It's only a bug. Nothing to be afraid of."

Madison smiled. "No, I meant thank you for still taking it outside. You didn't smash it."

"Huh? Why would I?" Harper blinked.

"Sorry. I was worried you having to shoot people might hurt you in the brain. I'm glad you're still yourself. I wasn't afraid of it… wanted to see what you'd do."

Stunned, Harper stood there in silence for a few seconds before pulling her little sister into a hug. "Yeah, I've changed a bit. We all have. But I'm still the same person inside." *Or trying to be.*

"Cool," mumbled Madison into Harper's shoulder.

"I'm glad to see you acting happy again."

Madison tossed her head to swing her hair off her eyes. "Yeah. I used to be sad about all the stuff we can't do anymore, all the stuff that's gone. But Mom and Dad always complained about being stuck in 'the rat race,' having to work all day. I dunno. Maybe this is better. I like taking care of the animals and being with them more than playing video games, and I don't have to study my butt off to get into college, then end up owing a ton of money only to get a job that makes me sad. Then I get married to have kids who'll do all the same things all over again. I think it's more important we live to be happy and to survive."

"Wow…" Harper whistled. "Where did that come from? Did Darci give you weed?"

"Yeah," said Madison, in a serious tone. "I got so high I tasted colors."

Harper started to laugh, but at her sister's continued blank stare, stopped. "Wait, are you serious?"

"Nah, just teasing." Madison giggled. "Your face."

*Whew*... Harper fussed at her sister's hair. "Getting kinda long."

"Guess it's time to go to the salon." Madison fake-gasped. "Oh, wait... we can't."

Harper sighed.

"Just kidding." Madison poked her. "I'm not upset about it. When I start sitting on it, I'll grab a knife and take off a few inches. No big deal."

"Are you really feeling better?"

Madison looked down. It struck Harper as weird to see her kid sister *without* nail polish on her toes. "I still get sad sometimes thinking about Mom and Dad, but it's not like I can change what happened, so I try to remember the good parts. No SATs, you're not gonna go away to college, I don't have to do homework ever again or worry about being fired from a job and ending up homeless."

"No such thing as being homeless anymore. Technically, everyone is homeless since there are no banks or police to enforce who owns what."

"Yeah. I mean..." Madison looked up at her. "If I could go back to the life we had before it all happened, I would totally do it. Computers, movies, video games, phones... we lost a lot of cool stuff. But... none of it matters. That's the thing about stuff. We can lose it and it sucks, but really, it's not that important. Losing *people* is way worse. Lore's got it figured out. She doesn't care about stuff at all, not even clothes. If she has stuff, cool. If not, cool."

*I can't lose her.* Harper squeezed Madison close, sniffling.

"Make you a deal. You don't die, and I won't become a basket case. Okay?"

"Deal." Harper chuckled. "Please tell me you're not going to turn into some weird hippie who casts aside all material possessions and runs off to live naked in the woods with feral chickens."

"No, dork." Madison smiled. "Just saying I don't miss the technology or the mall or cars as much as I thought I would. How messed up is it that I smuggled a chicken to freedom?"

"Not that messed up. You've always wanted an unusual pet. Mom wouldn't let you get a ferret."

Madison sighed, overacting drama. "I can't bring Rosie inside the house. She'll crap all over the place. Think Dad will help build a little coop in the yard?"

"Probably."

"Asking you to promise not to die is kinda weird." Madison bit her lip. "I know you can't control if someone goes crazy or whatever, just… please don't do anything stupid."

Harper bowed her head. "The hard part is realizing something is stupid before doing it. Some ideas sound utterly brilliant until they end in disaster."

"True, but you're not going to try flying with concrete wings like a *Bugs Bunny* cartoon. *Some* ideas really are dumb from the start."

Harper laughed.

They returned to the living room.

Cliff looked up from his technical manual. "If they're going to let you keep the bird, we'll make a little coop for it."

Harper and Madison both cringed.

"You heard us?" whispered Madison.

"Yep. It's one of the 'dad superpowers' men get soon as they're responsible for kids." He winked. "I can hear scheming anywhere in the house."

They laughed.

The PlayStation died.

Jonathan growled. "Dad, request permission to drop an F-bomb."

"Why?" asked Cliff.

"We've been playing this level for the past two hours. Finally got close to the save point after like fifty tries… and the stupid thing shuts off before we can save."

Cliff shifted his gaze back to his book. "Request denied. I'll let a dammit or a 'shit' go for it, but not the big F."

Jonathan sighed, then screamed, "Auugh!"

"Howls of generalized anguish are perfectly acceptable as well." Cliff smiled.

"You okay, Mila?" asked Harper. "You don't seem upset at all."

Mila rolled on her side to look up at her. "I'm not. It's just a video game. When we finish it, it will be boring. It's annoying to have to keep repeating stuff, but it makes the game last longer."

"Good way to look at it." Cliff chuckled.

"At least until the power's gone for good," whispered Madison.

*Click. Click. Click.*

"Chicken in the kitchen," said Cliff without looking up. "Deal with it, please. And someone please close the door."

"Rosie!" Madison ran over to collect the bird.

Harper flopped on the couch again and resumed reading. *Hmm. Maybe I'll finally finish this cursed book.*

# 6

# THE SEVENTH

S aturday, August third arrived with little fanfare.

The preceding week hadn't brought much excitement beyond Mr. Rollins giving Madison the okay to keep Rosie the chicken as a pet. Dr. Hale said the bird amounted to therapy, and killing it would certainly inflict mental harm. Also, even Mayor Ned pointed out they should consider it a miracle she only tried to 'pardon' one chicken. In the midst of the conversation, Harper learned a handful of other people, especially in the south part of Evergreen, already had small populations of chickens apart from those on the main farm.

Cliff went with the kids to scavenge up some scrap wood, and they'd built a little coop in the back corner of the yard. Madison often let Rosie out to run around and play, but the bird had a safe place to sleep at night. They'd need to build something a bit warmer eventually so Rosie didn't freeze to death over the winter.

For the past two days, Harper undertook a clandestine operation on par with anything the CIA did during the Cold War. She, Carrie, and Renee conspired to prepare a birthday party for Lorelei without the girl finding out. Tragically, it didn't take much effort to keep her unaware. Though the child knew her birthday fell on August third, she also said her mother never paid much attention to it, so likely wouldn't expect a party or even people saying 'happy birthday.' However, they'd had celebrations for Harper's eighteenth and Jonathan's eleventh since Lorelei became part of the family... so she might be secretly hoping for one, too.

Harper wanted to give her a party to make up for the previous six non-birthdays.

She'd spent a few hours next door at Carrie Rangel's house helping bake. The boxes of cake mix they'd found expired six months ago, but smelled okay and didn't have anything crawling around in them, so they trusted it. Few supplies remaining at the quartermaster had expiration dates, only things like cake mix, brownie mix, and so on, nonessential 'treats' someone grabbed when raiding various stores. At this point, they'd exhausted all the pre-war food. Someone even ate the nasty stuff like sardines and deviled ham.

It seemed so stupid to be emotional over the idea of never again having canned food, microwave meals, Hot Pockets, or even the 'lame but somehow awesome' grocery store chicken nuggets. Most of the time she spent at Carrie's, she'd been in a weird frame of mind thinking about the food situation. Everything people in Evergreen ate came from the farm, from hunting, or from fishing. Without even noticing the moment they'd done so, they'd become self-sustaining.

She found it unnerving not to have the security of being able to go to any of a hundred different stores carrying a seemingly unlimited selection of food. The 'plenty' of civilization had evaporated in the searing glow of a nuclear fireball. No one cared about high fructose corn syrup or excess fat or 'organic' anything now. Hell, even Madison ate meat whenever it got put in front of her. Most of the time, she didn't even cry while chewing anymore.

A vegan eating venison without complaining surely proved the end of the world had come and gone.

Last night, they'd taken a bath before bed, Harper, Madison and Lorelei still sharing a tub. Harper decided to let her sister make the call when she'd outgrown it, and worried a little about how needy-slash-clingy her sister had become. Sitting together in the tub like something out of the pioneer days always reminded her of their initial escape from Lakewood when they'd stopped in some random abandoned house near the mall to wash fallout ash off themselves. The promise Harper made while sitting behind Madison in ice cold water had perhaps been the only thing to happen over those few weeks Madison truly remembered during her shell-shocked haze. In that moment, she'd become not only big sis, but Mom.

On August first, Harper sent Jonathan, Madison, Becca, Eva, and Mila off to hunt through unused houses in search of toys they could give Lorelei for her birthday. She used a visit to the medical center for a checkup as an excuse to separate the six-year-old from the other kids for a couple hours.

The morning of the third, Harper pretended like any other day, waking the girls, nudging them to get dressed, and heading out to prepare breakfast—only Cliff beat her to it. Some days, breakfast consisted of nothing more than toast or some fruit. Today, he'd made eggs, pan-fried potatoes, and something they called 'deer bacon.' The only resemblance it had to actual bacon came from being cut into thin strips.

Lorelei, as usual, ran around powered by limitless cheerful energy. She practically climbed all over Cliff as he tried to move plates to the table. He ended up holding her upside down by one ankle in the manner of a fisherman proud of his catch. She squealed and giggled until he maneuvered her upright and set her seated in a chair.

After breakfast, Harper announced she had the day off from patrolling. She suggested they do something fun in the yard for a bit. As soon as she took Lorelei's hand, the girl looked up at her with a 'wow, really' expression. Harper couldn't keep a straight face, and grinned.

"Yay!" cheered Lorelei.

A small crowd of kids and some parents ambush cheered when they stepped outside. It seemed as if every child between six and twelve showed up to wish Lorelei a happy birthday as well as Darius, Jimmy, and T-Bone (who no longer used his street name and went by Terrence). Being thirteen and fourteen, the oldest kids at the party, they mostly hung with the parents rather than run around playing 'little kid' games.

A little before noon, Carrie gave her 'the look.' Harper scurried over to help retrieve the two cakes. As soon as he noticed them sneaking off, Cliff went inside as planned to collect the gifts from Jonathan's room.

All the kids—even the older ones—cheered when Harper and Carrie brought the cakes into view. Carrie made vanilla-ish icing from scratch, using sugar she still had on hand. Mrs. Parsons, Eva's mother, set up a makeshift table. Due to limited supplies, a single candle decorated one of the two cakes. Cliff lit it with his 'forever match.' Everyone chimed in to sing happy birthday.

Harper guided Lorelei over to the cake. "Okay, Lore. Since it's your birthday, you should make a wish, then blow out the candle."

"Okay." Lorelei fixated on the burning candle. Her permanent, contagious smile gradually melted away to a grim expression.

*Whoa. I don't think I've ever seen her look serious before... like* ever. Harper squeezed the girl's shoulders. Lorelei looked up, staring at Harper for a long minute before hastily puffing out the candle and cling-hugging her. Harper crouched, wrapping her arms around the child.

Lorelei leaned in close and whispered, "I wished you aren't gonna want me to go away like my first mom. Tyler, too. He said he's gonna take care of me, but didn't really want me."

"Oh, Lore..." Harper held her tight. "I will never want you to go away. Can't promise I'll be a perfect mom or big sis, but this is your home forever and I'm not gonna abandon you."

"'Kay," whispered Lorelei before breaking down in tears.

Not once had she ever before seen this girl cry. The child barely even stopped smiling in her sleep. Holding onto the tiny girl as she sobbed stole Harper's voice. Unable to speak, she patted Lorelei's back and rocked her side to side. Most of the kids watched in stunned silence. Madison's jaw hung open. Mila gave her a 'who do I need to stab?' glare.

A minute or so passed before Lorelei quieted. "I'm sorry for being sad on my birthday."

"It's all right." Harper kissed her atop the head. "You need to cry. You've been holding it all in for so long."

Lorelei leaned back, looking her in the eye. "I'm not sad. I'm really happy. My cryer must be broken, 'cause it's not s'posed ta make tears when I'm happy."

"Well, sometimes when people are *really* happy, they cry." Harper booped her on the nose. "It's normal."

"I'm happy to have a real mom and family. And friends." She spun to grin at everyone. "I don't wanna be sad now. Can we have cake?"

The kids all cheered.

# 7

# A BIT TOO WILD

L ate in the afternoon, Harper relaxed in the backyard watching the kids kick a soccer ball around.

Renee and Darci reclined in the grass on either side of her, talking randomly about stuff the way they used to—only the particular 'stuff' changed. No one mentioned school, teachers, jobs, dating gossip, boys, or movies. Renee mostly spoke of progress making fabric and turning it into clothing. Her 'team' had grown to ten people. Turning flax and wool into usable fabric took them a while to learn. After significant amounts of trial and error, they'd gotten to the point of producing basic cloth. Renee joked everyone would end up looking like medieval peasants in a few years, but it beat having nothing but leaves and loincloths to wear.

Darci didn't say as much, mostly discussing Elijah, the boy she'd essentially adopted after his father accidentally killed himself by bringing irradiated junk back from scavenging trips. Something didn't seem quite right about her, too wired, too alert. The girl had always been unusually thin, so Harper couldn't tell if she'd gotten hooked on something brutal like meth or whatever. Granted, it didn't make sense anyone could even *make* meth now, what with every pharmacy in hundreds of miles having been scavenged to bare shelves months ago. Darci didn't have any weight to lose, especially after her time in the Army survivors' camp.

*Gee, I hope she's not on some other drug than pot. I haven't seen her this 'unmellow' since grade school.*

"... he gets kinda moody sometimes," said Darci. "But I don't blame him for it after losing his dad like that. I mean, how is a five-year-old supposed to handle grief?"

"Good question." Renee sighed.

Darci fidgeted at the grass. "Lucas is helping out a ton, though. Not sure I could do it without him. He and Elijah have hit it off pretty well."

"So, Lucas has kinda adopted both of you?" asked Renee.

"Not exactly." Darci chuckled. "He's more boyfriend than father."

Renee gasped. "Dude... he's like thirty."

Darci examined her fingernails. "Thirty-two."

*Eek.* Harper winced internally.

"Wow." Renee whistled.

"Yeah, yeah. I know." Darci shrugged. "It's icky or whatever. I'm eighteen, he's thirty-two. But if I was thirty and he was fifty, no one would care. Besides, *I* made the first move. He's a great guy. Feels weird though."

Harper glanced over at her. "What does?"

Darci squinted up at the sky. "Having sex for fun instead of in trade for food. For a while there, I didn't think I'd ever want to again. Guess it's true what they say. Turning something fun into a job makes you want to avoid doing it."

"Darce, are you okay? You seem... somewhat brittle today?" Harper rested a hand on her friend's shoulder.

"Yeah, I'm fine. Just coping with losing my dad and the whole world changing so much. Guess it took a while for the truth to seep into my weed-saturated brain."

Renee chuckled.

"Okay." Harper patted Darci on the back. "If that's the story you're going with."

"What's up with Maddie and the chicken?" asked Renee.

Harper glanced over. Her little sister carried Rosie around like a child with a teddy bear.

"She's a little young to be so obsessed with cock, isn't she?" asked Darci.

"Darce!" Harper swatted her on the arm. "That's my sister!"

"And she's holding a hen, not a rooster," said Renee past embarrassed laughter.

*She always says something shocking to change the subject when she's feeling cornered.* "Now I know something's wrong." Harper nudged Darci. "I get you don't wanna talk about it, but I'm here if you change your mind. 'Kay?"

Darci again dodged eye contact. "I know. You're always the listener, Harp."

"Yeah, so they tell me. I—"

Gunfire went off in the distance.

"Shit!" rasped Harper while scrambling to her feet. "Watch the kids!"

She ran into the house, mentally yelling at herself for not having the .45 handgun on her hip. Wearing a weapon to a newly-seven-year-old's birthday party didn't feel right, even now. By the time Harper got to her bedroom, the shots stopped. Still, she grabbed the Mossberg and rushed out the front door, following the sound of yelling down Hilltop Drive. Thanks to Cliff and his idea of 'keeping fit,' she knew going from their house west to 74 Frontage Road covered 1,200 feet. Running it once didn't wind her too much, though she'd never done it barefoot—or in a dress—before.

Another rapid two-shot rang out from the right.

Harper ran north up the 74 Frontage road. Two men came running out of the Evergreen Brewery, ducking their heads as if afraid of being shot in the back. Darnell appeared in the distance, sprinting south toward the Brewery. He beat her to the parking lot by six seconds, raised his AR-15, and approached the building.

"It's over," yelled Earl from inside. "Damn fools."

Harper followed Darnell through the door. The scent of gunpowder hung in the air along with a fair amount of smoke. She nearly tripped over Summer Vasquez, the young woman she and

Cliff found running away from the Lawless gang, unconscious near the entrance, covered in gore. One man lay in more or less the center of the room, dead to multiple gunshots, including one in the forehead that blew out the back of his skull. A vast amount of blood pooled out on the floor beneath him. A second man sat slumped against the wall behind the table, seriously wounded, but alive. Three others crawled out from under a table covered in playing cards and coins. One bled from the leg, though didn't appear to realize he'd been hit.

A few people had guns out, but didn't aim at anyone specifically.

Leigh Preston ran in behind them, hand on her sidearm. "Heard shooting. What's going on?"

"Everyone chill," said Darnell. "What happened?"

Harper looked around the room. No one appeared particularly threatening at the moment, mostly freaked out, so she crouched to check on Summer, who didn't appear to have any injuries. Bits of bloody matter resembling beige scrambled eggs covered in ketchup all over her had to have come from someone else. Based on the massive hole in the back of the dead man's head, she figured the 'scrambled eggs' to be brain. Harper's stomach did a backflip. She'd cored out a man's head with the Mossberg once, but didn't stoop to study the mess afterward.

*She must've fainted.*

"Jesse there"—Earl pointed at the badly wounded man —"accused the idiot, Larry, of cheating. Said idiot pulled a gun. The results are pretty damn obvious. Everyone else lit him up."

"Damn." Darnell whistled. "Over a freakin' card game? Seriously?"

Earl pointed at the man who'd been grazed. "Randy, ya fool, yer hit in the leg."

"Aww crap. Didn't even feel it." Randy poked at his leg. "Hell."

Four guys grabbed Jesse and carried him out, likely heading for the medical center.

Harper patted Summer on the cheek until she came to. The woman sat up, lurched to one side, and vomited bile. Hearing—and smelling—puke on top of looking at brain bits everywhere caused Harper to retch.

"She was standin' right behind Larry when his brains blew out the back of his head," muttered a guy close by on the left. "Caught most of it straight in the face."

Summer puked harder.

Harper bit her forearm, trying to stop herself from erupting as well.

"A shootout in a bar over a card game," muttered Leigh. "Wow. We really are in the Wild West."

"A little *too* wild," said Darnell.

Harper stood, cringing as a slimy nugget squished under her bare foot. It took her a second to swallow rising nausea so she could speak. "Hey, everyone... can we please save bullets for actual threats? If someone cheats at cards, just punch them, okay?"

Most of the people around her chuckled.

"You can go on back to the little one's party." Darnell nudged her. "Don't want to be walking around in this mess without any shoes on."

"Already stepped in brain. I can stay if you need," said Harper.

Summer gagged.

"Nah. Nothing really to do here except mop the floor." Darnell clapped her on the shoulder. "Appreciate the backup."

"Thought we were being attacked again." Harper slung the Mossberg over her shoulder. "Money doesn't mean anything anymore. What kind of moron pulls a gun over a card game when there's no real stakes?"

Earl gestured at the body. "Like I said. An idiot."

"All right. Guess I'll head back to the party." Harper helped Summer up. "Are you okay?"

"Physically? Yeah. Never had a dude's head explode all over me before." She shuddered. "At least it happened so fast I didn't have time to scream."

"Huh?" asked Harper.

"My mouth was closed. Nothing got in." Summer heaved again but didn't throw up.

"Eww." She wiped her foot off on the mat by the door. "C'mon, I'll walk you home so you can clean up."

Summer followed her outside, trying not to touch anything. "This is so nasty. Hey, what did you mean by party?"

"Lorelei's seventh birthday. I'd say we have cake left, but I don't think you're too hungry."

"Ugh." Summer closed her eyes. "If there's anything that'll make me consider eating ever again, it's cake. Let me wash up and see how I feel."

Fortunately, Summer still lived close by, in the giant house she shared with Anne-Marie. Harper went inside with her, collected the brain-soaked dress after Summer peeled it off to take a shower, and carried the garment outside pinched between two fingers.

"In the real world, I'd have thrown this right in the damn trash." She dropped it on the street. "But we're not in the real world anymore. Clothing is too valuable... gotta try to wash it. And what the heck is wrong with me? Why aren't I throwing up all over the place? This is brain matter."

Harper sighed and headed back into the house to get a bucket of water for the dress.

"Life is weird."

# 8

## QUIET TIME

L ittle happened in response to the shooting at the Brewery.

Jesse died in the medical center less than an hour later. He'd suffered too much damage internally. Even in a fully operational modern hospital with all the technology and drugs available, he'd only have had about a twenty percent chance to pull through according to Tegan. These days, anyone taking five .45 bullets to the torso was pretty much doomed. Larry, the accused cheat, had the misfortune of catching a .44 magnum hollow point above the left eye, hence the mess everywhere.

Somehow, Harper managed to return home and continue with the party as though she hadn't seen a dead man or brain matter splattered all over Summer Vasquez. Honestly, she'd seen gorier deaths. Hell, she'd *caused* gorier deaths. Buckshot at close range didn't do pretty things to a human skull. Also, she hadn't watched the man die. He'd been dead already when she entered the Brewery.

Still, a shootout over cards at a bar, like something straight out of the Old West, felt surreal.

She couldn't say most people carrying guns was a bad thing considering the real danger of attack from gangs like the Lawless, random marauders, or even bears. Ammo needed to be saved for actual emergencies. If Larry and Jessy had merely had a fistfight, the militia wouldn't have even gotten involved.

Walter Holman had long ago sent word around town confirming the militia didn't have any intention of jailing anyone for more than a couple days while decisions happened. Sitting in a cell eating food other people worked to produce while doing nothing amounted to more of a vacation than a punishment. Anyone who shot or killed another resident of Evergreen over, as he put it, 'bullshit,' would end up in the ground or exiled unless they left town before justice found them. In the case of Jesse and Larry, the killer ended up dead before his victim. Five other people in the room at the time evidently agreed with Walter's opinion that shooting a man for calling him a cheat at a zero-risk card game amounted to 'bullshit.'

TWO WEEKS LATER ON A MONDAY NIGHT, HARPER SLIPPED AWAY with Logan for some private time.

In the woods west of North Evergreen, well out of sight from town, they sat together in the dark, naked and out of breath from a rather spirited session. She didn't quite want to call it 'lovemaking' since they hadn't done the deed fully. At first, she'd been nervous about 'hand stuff', due to something Darci said about her idiot boyfriends thinking they were down there to 'stuff a turkey' and had no idea how to do things right.

Harper had gone farther with Logan than with any other boyfriend—not difficult since she'd only ever kissed before. He'd been the first to see her fully naked, the first to touch her all over, the first to use his tongue... Logan was also the first boy she ever went down on, a few weeks earlier. He didn't complain, but she couldn't help but feel she didn't do it all that well. At least he didn't laugh at first when she—clueless what to do—treated it like a popsicle and started licking. Not like she could hit the internet and do 'research' now. Her alter ego, Introvert Prime, hadn't exactly been interested in steamy movies or porn. She also couldn't quite bring herself to ask Darci for advice due to embarrassment. She believed Logan telling her he hadn't done more than kiss any other girl, so what did it matter how good she was at any sex-type stuff? Neither one of them had any other experiences to compare to.

The more she thought about being there with him, the more her fear faded away. Just sitting beside him like a pair of hippies naked in the woods made her feel like they did something simultaneously wonderful and against the rules.

"Next time," said Harper before she changed her mind, "if you wanna do it like all the way, I think I'm ready."

Logan put an arm around her. "I'd love that, if it's what you want."

"Yeah. It is. But... I'm not ready to get pregnant."

"I'll do everything I can to avoid it, but without a... umm, condom... it's a coin toss. Can't promise it won't happen." Logan leaned his head against hers. "It's fine if you want to wait until you're open to the idea of maybe ending up pregnant."

Harper leaned against him, adoring the warmth of his chest, smiling.

"Gee... all the stuff we've scavenged." Logan chuckled. "No one thought of those things."

"They're not essential to survival." She laughed. "Actually, they're kinda an impediment to survival if you think in terms of humanity as a species."

Logan kissed her for a wonderful few minutes, then stared lovingly into her eyes. "If some genie showed up and gave me the choice between putting the world back the way it was or staying here with you, I'm not sure I could save all those people."

"I know you would. You care too much. Then, since you went back in time and would remember me, you could go to Lakewood, find me, and I'd fall in love all over again." She brushed her fingers down his chest. "I was pretty much broken up with my last boyfriend when the war happened."

"Maybe... though we'd also have to find Lorelei and kick her birth mother's ass. Not literally. I mean get CPS on her, not physically kick her."

"Yeah. It would be difficult to find her. Lore doesn't know what her last name was, and I'm still not exactly sure where she lived." Harper snuggled closer to him. "Doesn't matter. Genies and wishes aren't real."

"Alas," said Logan. "Sorry if I sound like an idiot right now. Still trying to process you saying you want to go all the way. You're really sure?"

"I am. Virginity is such a stupid concept. I guess like everyone else, I had this whole big faerie-tale idea of what it would be like to lose it. You know, there I am in this super special Hallmark romantic moment. Now, I'm scared I'll keep waiting and waiting for everything to be so perfect it'll never happen."

He gently lifted her head by a finger under the chin, kissed her, and smiled. "Perfect moments don't just happen. We have to make them. Even in this messed up half-burnt world, being with you makes me feel like it's still possible to be happy."

"I feel the same way about you." She threaded her arms around him. "After my parents, then the whole Tyler thing, I was ready to give up on feeling any emotions other than fear and sadness ever again."

Logan tossed a hunk of wood off into the trees. "I'm still not sure I've really accepted losing my parents and Luisa. Everyone says Colorado Springs got vaporized, so at least they didn't suffer... or even know what happened."

*There goes the mood.* "Whoever hit the button, I hope they died in a really painful way."

"They're probably still living in a luxurious bunker." Logan frowned. "The evil ones never seem to suffer consequences for what they do."

"Yeah." Harper let go of him. She stretched out on her back, pulling him down to lay beside her and gazing up past the branches at the indigo-blue haze overhead. "Thank you for showing me it's okay to be happy in this smashed-up world."

"I keep waiting to wake up. Being with you is like the nightmare went way off script. Bad dreams aren't supposed to have amazing parts."

She grinned to herself. "Look. The sky's starting to clear enough to let the stars out."

Logan stared skyward. "Your eyes are better than mine. I still only see fallout."

"It's not fallout. At least, it's not *fall*out until it comes back down. Just dirt thrown up into the sky by the explosions. The fallout's already gone." Harper scooted closer to him. "Are we really just hanging out naked in the forest like a pair of nymphs?"

"We are. No one's going to find us here. Even if they did, we won't get in trouble. Not like anyone's going to send a cop to bang on the window of the car and chase us away from lover's point."

She snickered.

"I want to spend all my time with you. It doesn't matter what we're doing, but this is nice."

"Who got the bright idea people needed to wear clothes, anyway?" Harper fake rolled her eyes. "This is really comfortable... except for that twig poking me in the butt."

He reached over and tickled her stomach.

Harper squealed, curling up and grabbing his arm. "Stop!"

He stole a kiss.

She collapsed half on top of him, trying not to laugh so loud someone heard and came to investigate. *Maybe it won't scare the crap out of me if I get pregnant. If it does happen, they'll definitely not send me out of town on a mission. Might not even let me patrol until the baby's a year old. Having so much time to spend with Madison while she's still young might actually be worth rolling the dice. Just have to live through giving birth first.* She huffed. *What the heck is wrong with me? Who seriously considers having a baby at eighteen on purpose? Does he even want kids? Having one might help him deal with the loss of his family. Everyone says Springs was vaporized but no one's gone there to look. Denver got hammered pretty bad, and we made it.* She bit her lip, thinking about his two older siblings, a brother in the Navy and a sister who'd gone out of state to college.

"What's on your mind? You look kinda sad or worried. Hope you're not regretting..."

"No." She swished her feet side to side. "Sitting out here like this and not being mortified about it is making me wonder if society's going to slip back to primitivism. Little by little, technology, all the little modern conveniences we've salvaged are going to stop working, break, or disappear. Renee and them are doing kinda okay making clothing, but it's not going to come out looking like anything we got at the mall."

"Yeah. We'll all be cosplaying peasants from *Lord of the Rings*." Logan chuckled. "Might as well since we'll be carrying swords again when the bullets run out."

"Okay, I'm lying." Harper rolled onto her side, head propped up on her hand, and stared into his eyes. "I just thought of that primitivism thing to not say what really made me feel sad because I didn't want to make you sad, too. I shouldn't play word games or lie to you. If we're going to do this for real, we've gotta be fully open with each other."

"Uh oh."

She smiled. "Relax, it's not too bad. But... I don't want to get in the habit of not being completely honest with you. I was really wondering how bad it really was in Springs, and what happened to your older siblings."

"Oh." He nodded once. "Never really let myself hope Springs might not be completely gone. It's kinda far to walk or even ride a bike. Too dangerous to just go there on a whim. The place could still be full of deadly radiation or who knows what kind of gangs. Not sure I could handle finding my old house gone. Or worse, finding it with bones inside."

"Sorry."

He laced his fingers behind his head, staring up at the sky again. "You don't have to apologize. As for Luis and Ana? I dunno. Last I heard, Luis was out at sea. Doesn't seem likely anyone could nuke a Navy ship, but there might have been more combat than nuclear missiles. Ana... there's no cars or planes anymore. She's so far away, Florida might as well be on another planet. It would take us months to walk there, and we'd have no idea where to even start looking if we survived the trip."

Harper rested her head on his shoulder, lying beside him in silence for a while. Someone far off to the east, back in town, shouting for 'Julio' to move his ass startled her into realizing she still hadn't gotten dressed. "What's going to happen to us?"

"Well, hopefully… we have a long, happy life together."

"I'd like that." She bit her lip. "But I meant us with a capital u, as in humanity. Like… there's no more insulin. Diabetes is a death sentence."

"True, but we're also not eating processed sugar in everything now."

"Diabetes happened a long time ago, too. Maybe not as often, but it happened. There are no more vaccines, no advanced medicine. In forty-five minutes, or however long it took the nukes to stop blowing up, we lost centuries of progress."

Logan sat up, legs crossed. "True. We don't have advanced medicine or vaccines anymore, but humans existed for centuries before them once already and didn't die off."

"Ugh." Harper also sat up, grabbing her head in both hands, elbows on her knees. "Yeah, but before vaccines, lots of people died."

"Yeah. Back then, people had to have twelve kids hoping three made it to adulthood."

She gave him side eye. "Please tell me you're making an observation about the past and not a suggestion. My uterus just quivered at the thought."

"Well…" Logan chuckled. "Totally up to you. If you even want to have kids, your body's going to be doing ninety-nine-point-nine percent of the work, so it's whatever you're willing to put up with."

"Not sure I'm ready for kids yet."

"Yeah, same. We're both a little young." He slid over to sit behind her, wrapping his arms around her middle. "I meant as a species, we're still here despite advanced medicine only being around not all that long in terms of history. Living like this might actually be a hidden blessing. You know, going all natural and stuff. No crazy stress from traffic, having to get a job, worrying about being laid off, losing your house… all that crap."

"Now you're starting to sound like Maddie."

"Huh?"

Harper leaned back against his chest. "Oh, she decided not to be depressed about living in the 1800s anymore."

"Glad to hear she's dealing."

"Yeah. I think she's going to be okay. At least, as okay as anyone can be now." She exhaled. "We should probably get dressed and head back before Cliff sends a search party after us."

He kissed her shoulder at the base of her neck.

A shudder ran down to her toes. "Dear Logan, are you trying to get us both in trouble? Do that again and we're going to be out here for another hour."

"I can't tell if you're asking me to do it again or sincerely asking me not to."

"What do you think?"

Smiling like a sly fox, he leaned in and kissed her on the same spot.

# A PLACE OF SAFETY

A few days later, the screams of multiple children came from the backyard.

Harper, barely two paragraphs into chapter 22 of *The Secret Garden*, put the book down and ran outside to find the usual crew: Madison, Jonathan, Lorelei, Becca, Eva, Mila, and Christopher standing there flailing at themselves in their underpants —except for Lorelei who'd gone full wood nymph. The little one mostly stooped over, raking her hands at her long blonde hair as if trying to clear it of leaf bits after jumping into a huge pile. The kids freaked out as if they'd been tear-gassed, flailing at the air, scratching themselves, shaking their hair around.

Mila, the most composed of the lot, walked over and informed her they'd discovered an abandoned house at the far end of Buchanan Drive full of bugs. The kids hadn't realized the extent of the flea infestation until everyone started itching. In an attempt to avoid bringing the fleas home with them, they'd abandoned their bug-riddled clothing on the front lawn and run back.

After telling the kids to stay there and not go inside the house, Harper ran a few backyards over to grab a small plastic kiddie pool to serve as an emergency de-bugging bath outside. After careful cleaning, it appeared only Jonathan, Christopher, and Mila had brought fleas back with them in their hair. All the kids had multiple bites, mostly on their arms and legs. Despite finding no signs of fleas in Madison's hair, she washed herself three times. Harper appreciated her sister's extreme caution since they shared a bed. Once satisfied the kids had become flee-free, Harper sent them inside the house to wait, then took the long walk to collect the discarded clothes in a plastic trash bag.

Merely thinking about fleas made her itch the entire way there.

Since the kids had only been in the place for about twenty minutes, she didn't think the fleas would have had time to lay eggs in any of the clothing, but she didn't want to take chances. If garments weren't a rare and precious commodity, she'd have burned the lot. Instead, she bagged it all bringing everything back home to boil in a giant soup pot on the cinder block grill, hoping the heat would kill any fleas or eggs in the fabric. The kids—except for the three who lived there—spent the day at the house wrapped in blankets or bed sheets until their clothes dried enough to put back on.

Bugmageddon had two major effects. It not only severely diminished the kids' interest in exploring abandoned houses, it served as an unpleasant and itchy reminder of civilization's demise—or at least ill health. Fleas and other pests existed in the 1800s. Any building left abandoned for over a year would probably have issues. The kids often found raccoons, possum, or other small animals inside houses where people hadn't been in a long time.

Harper brought the issue up to Walter the following day, which resulted in Anne-Marie recruiting a small group of volunteers whose job became tending to unoccupied houses in hopes of saving them from turning uninhabitable… and taking note of any houses with problems like a massive flea population.

Three days after the kids ended up covered in fleas, Harper took them to the pool after they finished working on the farm. It remained warm enough for it in late August, though she didn't expect they'd have many more opportunities to really enjoy the water before it became too cold outside for swimming. The somewhat embarrassingly skimpy bathing suit she'd gotten from the quartermaster months ago still fit, so she spent a little time in the water as well, amused at the idea someone thought a bikini a worthwhile scavenge. Then again, it hadn't taken up much room in the truck.

Being in a pool didn't have the same appeal it once did. Only a few years ago, she could've spent hours playing in the water and still be disappointed when she had to go home. Whether or not her change in enthusiasm came from simply growing up or as a result of the world falling apart, she couldn't tell. After little more than an hour, she climbed out of the pool and headed over to one of the lounge chairs, selecting one with an umbrella so she didn't turn into a lobster. As far as the sun went, her body had two color settings: white as chalk and bright red. From there, she could relax and keep an eye on the kids who would likely stay in the pool until she used a net pole to catch them.

Other than most people wearing normal shorts instead of bathing suits, the scene appeared fairly ordinary for a massive public pool. Adults tended to float and cool off. Kids swatted a volleyball around, tossed a Frisbee, or tried to see who could make the biggest cannonball splash.

*Wonder if the water's going to be usable next summer.* She glanced to the left at the big garage. *Yeah, most likely. They've got a ton of chemicals left and it's not exactly like hundreds of people are using the pool every day. I doubt it saw much use before... probably just a bunch of old rich people who played golf and brought their grandkids.*

She daydreamed about Logan, alternatively looking forward to and being terrified of going all the way. Considering how much they'd already done, it didn't feel like a big leap forward for one part of his body that hadn't touched one part of her body before to do so. She didn't trust any of her former boyfriends enough to go past kissing them. Surely, if she'd tried to have the same sort of 'almost but not quite having sex' arrangement with them, they would have lost control in the moment and taken more than she'd been prepared to give. Logan could easily have done so multiple times in the heat of the moment, but he hadn't.

At no point in her life before had she so completely trusted a boy. She'd allowed herself to become vulnerable in front of him, and he never once took advantage of her. Even if nuclear war hadn't happened, she'd probably never be able to find a boy like that again. She wanted to spend the rest of her life with him, even if it might only be five, ten, or twenty years. The area around her old home in Lakewood hadn't been *too* smashed, and her family made it to the basement before anything exploded nearby. Still, she couldn't put aside the nagging worry radiation exposure, however mild it had been, might shorten her life. Cliff reassured her that many survivors of Hiroshima and Nagasaki made it into their seventies and eighties. But irrational fears didn't listen to rational facts.

Watching the kids play in the pool sent her off down a depressing line of thought. With the exception of a handful of babies, everyone presently in Evergreen had most likely been vaccinated in the usual manner by modern society as far as she knew—barring morons who fell for anti-science internet conspiracy theories. Any children from here forward wouldn't have the luxury of modern preventative medicine. She, her friends, Madison, Lorelei, Jonathan… and so on had a decent chance of living to old age, notwithstanding violence or something like cancer. How many generations would it take for humanity to slide backward to the way things used to be, when reaching fifty was considered old age?

She couldn't remember history class enough to figure out if the average age of death moved forward due to advances in medicine or if it happened far longer ago due to people learning that taking baths and washing their hands fought disease.

Renee, in a pink half-tee and cargo shorts, jogged over. Her light-brown hair just about touched her shoulders. She slipped her shorts off to reveal bathing suit bottoms, then sat in the lounge chair beside Harper. "Hey."

"Still can't get used to seeing your hair so short," said Harper.

"I'm surprised you haven't chopped at least half of that bright red mane off." Renee crossed her eyes. "So much work. No, wait. I'm not surprised. I still remember that time you shrieked at your Mom for suggesting you cut it short."

Harper looked down. If it would bring her parents back, she'd give up her precious long hair. "Yeah... such a stupid thing to fixate on. Weird I never obsessed about styling it much, just having it long."

"Can't do a thing with mine. So thin and straight." Renee rolled her eyes.

"Pretty sure no one is going to care anymore if we run around like twelve-year-olds who don't realize hair styling products exist."

Renee laughed. "Tell that to Becca. She's more obsessed with her hair than Mandy Greer, and she's not even twelve yet."

"Oh, gawd." Harper laughed at the memory of their high school's former head cheerleader-slash-popular girl. "Hey, question. Serious talk."

"Hmm?" Renee raised one eyebrow.

Harper leaned close, lowering her voice. "I think the next time Logan and I are alone for some, uhh, fun times... I'm going to go all the way."

"Cool," said Renee.

"That's it?" Harper blinked. "Just 'cool'? No squeal, gasp, expression of shock? Not even a laugh of disbelief or some mild teasing?"

"Nope." Renee held up a bottle of sunblock, squinting at it. "Does this stuff go bad?"

"Don't think so."

"And yeah, just 'cool.' We're adults now. If you wanna do it, do it. People aren't going to talk about you like they used to whisper about Darci. It's awesome you're in love with him enough to do it. I'd probably wait a bit."

Harper fidgeted. Their entire high school somehow knew the day after Darci first had sex. Boys, as well as girls, tried to slut-shame her but she threw it in their faces, loudly admitting it and calling them cowards or 'little kids' for not having done it yet. She nearly got suspended for 'disruptive behavior,' but students stopped making fun of her, at least where anyone could hear them. Back then, Harper had been afraid of social shame, but she also never had a boyfriend she trusted. Besides, her parents would have completely freaked out if she'd done anything like that before eighteen... probably twenty-one.

"I'm not worried at all about what people will say. Hell, Darci's sleeping with Lucas and no one cares."

Renee squirmed. "That's a little... I dunno. Weird."

"This woman where Mom used to work had a husband twenty years older than her." Harper chuckled. "I remember going to the office on take your kid to work day, saw the dude's picture on her desk and said something like 'oh, your dad looks like a cool guy.'"

Renee gasped. "You didn't..."

"Not on purpose. I had no idea who the dude was. He *looked* like her father. So, yeah, Rita—I think that was her name—snaps at me 'that's my *husband*.' And she's all pissy with me and Mom the rest of the day."

"I remember. What were you like ten?"

"Nine."

They looked at each other and laughed.

Harper examined her fingernails. "Mom said she 'slipped' at the Christmas party four months later when she met him, asking if he was Rita's father."

"No..." Renee covered her mouth.

"Yeah. Totally not an accident. Mom's little revenge for Rita being so nasty to me making an innocent mistake."

"Epic," whispered Renee.

Harper laced her hands behind her head, gazing up at the giant green umbrella. "Why do you think I should wait?"

"Huh?"

"You said you'd wait a bit."

"No, I meant *me*. I'm going to wait. Still a bit freaked out at the whole 'about to be forcibly married' thing." Renee fought with the bottle of sunblock, which made farting sounds whenever she squeezed it. "Drat. Think I'm out."

Harper glanced over at her. "Are you okay?"

"Yeah. Pretty much. I mean, all the gang really did was lock me in a room and say mean stuff… make me carry a gun around and believe they'd shoot me in the head at any second, then tell me I was going to be some cretin's wife as soon as I got old enough to have sex with."

"Lower than roaches." Harper scowled. *Still can't believe they fell for her claiming to be fourteen.*

"Not really. Roaches you'd save and carry outside."

"Hah. I'm not quite *that* bad." Harper laughed. "Serious pests like roaches or bedbugs, I'd smash. My insect charity only applies to bugs who aren't a threat. Soon as something attacks me or carries disease, all bets are off."

"Oh."

Harper twirled a hand around in the air. "Never saw any kill on sight bugs back in Lakewood. My parents kept a clean house. First world problems."

Renee sighed. "Is it true some guy in the south part of Evergreen killed himself over Starbucks?"

"Umm." Harper cringed. "Not exactly. He didn't get upset at there no longer being Starbucks, more the total lack of coffee."

"Wow."

"Yeah. Dude had to have some other problems though. I love coffee more than most people, and Cliff adores it more than me. Neither one of us would end it all over not having java anymore."

"Right." Renee squeezed the bottle hard, making a wet, splattery fart noise. A few people close enough to hear it looked over, shocked. "Sunscreen!" She waved it at them.

Harper cracked up.

"Funny…" Renee shook her head and smeared the little bit of sunblock on her legs.

"So, you're waiting for marriage?"

"Nah. I'm waiting until we know for a fact we're not going to starve."

"Eek." Harper shivered. "I don't think that day will ever happen… unless the country isn't as smashed as everyone thinks it is."

"Maybe it is?"

"Doubtful. It's going to be September in like three weeks." She looked down at herself, her mind filling with flashing memories of Dad dragging her out of bed at ten to six in the morning, the mad panicked scramble into the basement, then thunder... "September 7th, 2018 at 5:58 a.m., Lakewood, Colorado burned."

Renee kept quiet for a moment before whispering, "Why are you making me cry?"

"Sorry. I meant it's almost a year now. If the country wasn't destroyed, we would've seen way more military people showing up with helicopters or supplies, letting us know the USA still exists. But there's been nothing. Not even one guy in a Humvee handing out pamphlets."

"Dammit. You made me think about my parents."

"I think about mine all the time," whispered Harper.

Renee laugh-sobbed, then wiped her eyes. "Of course. I meant the day it happened just jumped into my head like it was a minute ago."

"Same. I'm never going to forget it."

"Yeah, I—"

A loud *boom* went off in the distance to the south, along with a bright flash.

Renee, and a handful of kids in the pool, screamed.

Harper twitched.

Everyone faced south, trying to see what exploded—except for Emmy. The recently turned nine-year-old froze in mid-stride, on her way to the diving board. She trembled, staring into space, grabbing her stomach in both hands.

"Uh oh." Harper swung her legs off the lounge chair to stand.

"What?" asked Renee.

Emmy swooned to one side, falling to sit.

"Be right back." Harper ran over, crouching beside her. "Emmy? Are you okay?"

The girl didn't react, staring into space.

"Em?" Harper rested a hand on the child's shoulder.

"Sky fire's coming!" Emmy made a noise like she prepared to

vomit, then went wild-eyed. "We're gonna burn!" She started to bolt away—headed directly toward the pool.

Harper grabbed her. *This kid's gonna drown. She's not on Planet Earth right now.* Struggling to contain and carry the flailing child, she stood, whispering, 'you're safe. The sky fire is gone,' repeatedly. Roy Ellis, a former cop and current member of the militia, had been holding 'training workshops' every so often to pass on useful skills. She remembered him giving a talk about how to handle people having a panic or anxiety attack. He'd said something about getting the person to a place where they would feel safe. Emmy didn't have a particular fear of people, but wide-open spaces, specifically under open sky, made her nervous. The child saw people incinerated by a nuclear flash. By sheer luck, she'd been behind a large building blocking her from it, but someone in the distance hadn't been so lucky.

Harper rushed for the storage building—the closest structure with a roof—and darted inside. Surrounded by pool cleaning equipment and boxes of supplies, she hunkered down, holding Emmy still.

"Shh. We're inside. The sky fire can't get us in here."

Emmy continued screaming and flailing, trying to get away and run. After a few minutes, she gave up and hung limp in Harper's arms, breathing rapidly. Harper held her close, continually telling her she was safe in here and no 'sky fire' would hurt her.

Therese, the woman who'd taken the child in as a mother, ran in, skidding to a stop on her knees beside them. "What happened? Why is she in a panic?"

It took Harper a few seconds to process the woman's thick—possibly Nigerian—accent. "Something blew up. She thinks it's another nuclear attack. Brought her in here to take cover. Having a roof over her makes her feel safe from the sky fire."

Therese brushed a hand over the girl's head, moving her long, brown hair off her face. The child stared into nowhere, her expression terrified, pupils dilated wide. She continued to breathe rapidly, her heart racing.

"Something at the power system must have blown up," said Harper. "Maybe a transformer. It's not a nuke."

"Agreed. If it was another bomb, we would not be here to wonder what happened." Therese reached to take hold of Emmy.

Harper passed the girl over, patting the child's back reassuringly. "Breathe, Emmy. Slow it down, okay? You're safe."

Renee ran in, stopping short at the door to watch.

After another few minutes of Harper and Therese gently reassuring her, Emmy burst into sobbing tears.

"It's okay to be scared." Harper smiled. "There's no more sky fire. The bad people used it all up last year. They can't do it again."

Emmy made a face like she didn't fully believe it, but offered no protest. Harper smiled, patting the girl's cheek while sneakily checking her eyes—no longer dilated too wide.

"Are you ready to go outside?" asked Therese.

"Umm." Emmy glanced at the door. "Did they all die?"

"No, hon." Therese kissed her atop the head. "Everyone is just fine. No one died."

"I wanna see," whispered Emmy.

Harper stood.

Therese carried the child to the doorway. Emmy peered out at the pool—where everyone had more or less resumed having fun like nothing happened.

"Not sky fire." Harper smiled. "Someone probably just dropped a real heavy object."

"Nothing's heavy enough to sound like that if someone drops it," said Emmy.

"Big hollow trash dumpster? You're right, though. I don't think anything fell. But it wasn't sky fire."

"How do you know?" Emmy scrunched up her nose.

"Sky fire isn't a short, loud boom. It's more of a rumble that gets louder and louder until the whole world is shaking." Harper cringed at her memories of hiding in the basement with her parents, stuff falling from shelves all around them, the roaring outside so loud they couldn't even scream at each other and be heard. She swallowed the fear and sadness, somehow managing to keep a straight face for Emmy.

"Oh. Yeah." The child let out a big breath. "Okay. Do I have to go home now or can I swim more?"

"We can stay a bit longer if you want to." Therese smiled and set the girl on her feet.

Emmy hurried off toward the diving board.

"Thank you," said Therese.

"No problem."

Harper trudged back to where she'd been sitting.

Renee followed. "What happened there?"

"Em had a panic attack. Almost ran blindly into the pool. Water plus someone who isn't able to perceive the reality in front of them aren't a great combination."

"That poor kid." Renee sat. "How sad is it to think PTSD is the new normal. Anyone who *doesn't* have at least a mild case of it has gotta be a psycho."

Harper hugged herself. "Sign me up for a straitjacket then."

"You're not psycho. Just dealing with it."

"We all are." Harper hugged her, then sat on her chair. "Some more than others, but we're all fighting our demons. How are yours doing by the way?"

"Still quiet. Figure I've either mostly coped with everything or I'm going to fall to pieces someday at random."

Harper looked over at her. "'Nee…"

"Think I'm okay. You, Cliff, and idiot found me before anything seriously bad happened."

"Ugh." Harper angry-sighed straight up at the umbrella. "I still can't believe Zach shot you."

"I got super lucky. Just a little mark on the skin now. No like pain or anything. Easy to forget it happened. And if taking a .22 bullet was the price of freedom from those creeps, I'm happy to pay it."

Emmy cannonballed into the pool.

"My brain's about to explode." Harper massaged the bridge of her nose.

"Why?" Renee snickered.

"We're talking about you getting shot, having horrible memories about the day everything went to hell, and the kids are just playing in the pool like any other summer."

Renee poked her in the arm. "Little jealous?"

"Maybe a bit, but I don't envy them." Harper glanced to the south, wondering what exploded. "Let them be happy while they can."

# 10

# A CURSE BROKEN

Following a nice afternoon at the pool, Harper spent an hour trimming the grass in the backyard—with her teeth.

Unintentionally.

Cliff worked with her on self-defense techniques, which more often than not resulted in her flying face first to the ground. Madison and Jonathan—much to both of their surprise—wanted in on it, too. Lorelei sat on the porch watching, playing with her dolls.

Of course, by the time they'd returned home from the pool, she'd heard confirmation a transformer at the solar farm blew up. According to Cliff, Jeanette and her team believed they could get another transformer up and running via cannibalized parts. If they couldn't, they faced a choice between trying to find a way to salvage a comparable unit from the old Evergreen power station or hand-building a new one out of lower-tech parts. When they originally moved the now-dead one to the tennis court area, the town still had working trucks. Cliff intended to push the windmill idea. If they could make wind-powered generators, they could distribute them around closer to each house, thus removing the need for a transformer to push electricity over longer distances.

Fortunately, no one had been killed or seriously injured by flying shrapnel.

No electricity meant a return to candles and cooking by firewood for as long as it took to replace the bad transformer. Unfortunately, it also meant the hot water heater no longer worked. They would once again need to heat water in buckets and share baths only once a week to make the firewood last. Harper kept telling herself people survived not having electricity centuries ago, so she could deal.

When the self-defense practice came to an end, Cliff got started cooked venison outside on the cinder block grill. After eating, the kids played in the yard while Harper rushed to the couch and grabbed *The Secret Garden*, eager to get in as much reading as possible before the sun went down. No electricity also meant no working lights. As soon as it became dark, they couldn't really do much else but sleep or sit around in the void talking.

Renee and Carrie went home next door to do some cleaning. Harper pushed aside a little nagging guilt at knowing she ought to clean around the house a bit. Only a few chapters left to go. She could clean tomorrow afternoon. Cliff settled into his recliner and resumed studying the technical manual.

Not even twenty minutes later, it started raining.

Madison and Jonathan rushed inside via the back door.

"Lore! Come on. Rain's going to make you melt," yelled Madison.

"No it isn't," shouted Lorelei from the yard. "All the ray-dation's gone."

Madison leaned out the door. "Seriously, c'mon inside."

"Mom!" yelled Lorelei.

Harper kept reading for a few seconds before it hit her. *Oh, crap. She means me.* She twisted around to look over the back of the sofa at the kitchen and the door to the yard behind the house. "You're probably right about the radiation after this long, but it's starting to get chilly at night. Too cold to be wet outside."

"Aww, okay." Lorelei scampered into the house.

Madison shut the door, then huffed at the ceiling in a 'kids are *so* exhausting' sort of way.

Harper resumed reading while the kids dragged a board game out onto the living room floor. Jonathan grumbled occasionally about the electricity being dead, thus no PlayStation. Madison didn't seem to care much at all about losing power.

"Video games…" Cliff looked up from his book. "Light bulbs, hot water on demand, the stove, refrigerators, a handful of crap I don't understand at the medical center. All that stuff needs power, but the biggest loss is video games?"

"Uhh. No, it's not the biggest loss. Just the one that's annoying," said Jonathan.

"Losing hot water isn't annoying?" Cliff chuckled.

"No. It's worse than annoying. Not sure what to call it." The boy scratched his head. "Not having the PlayStation is annoying but doesn't mean anything."

"Really expensive junk," muttered Madison. "Without electricity."

"A lot of what we used to have is real expensive junk." Cliff chuckled. "I have warm fuzzy thoughts thinking about Lamborghinis and million-dollar yachts fried by EMP. All the money and resources society put into useless crap only a tiny percent of the people could use. Sometimes, I wonder if this whole thing is the Universe slapping us upside the head for being stupid."

Harper poked a finger into the page to mark her place. "Nukes… speaking of another stupidly expensive thing society made we shouldn't have."

"Yeah. They should have left war the way it was meant to be fought." Cliff raised a finger. "By people crawling through mud with guns that jam half the time."

"Huh?" asked Jonathan. "Why would anyone want a gun that always jams?"

"Ask the people who accepted the M-16," muttered Cliff.

Madison rolled dice for the board game. "We should get oil lamps. How did people get oil in old times?"

"Animal fats and seeds, I think." Cliff turned a page in the manual. "We can probably find something about it in the library."

Jonathan picked up the dice and rolled them. "Is the electricity going to work again?"

"The lights stopped working all the time where I used to live." Lorelei, sprawled on her front beside the game board, scissored her feet back and forth. "Just yell bad words at someone on the phone and the 'lectric will turn back on."

"No phones. I'd have to walk down the street and yell bad words at Jeanette. Pretty sure she won't appreciate it." Cliff winked.

Conversation petered out except for the kids talking about the game they played. Harper continued reading despite the weakening sun. She *finally* reached the end of the book with perhaps ten minutes of usable daylight remaining.

"Woooo!" shouted Harper.

She jumped off the couch, waving the book around over her head, screaming, cheering, and damn near crying tears of joy.

Cliff blinked at her. "You must be reading a different version of that than I did years ago."

The kids stared up at her in bewildered awe.

"The curse is broken!" Harper hugged the book to her chest. "I finished it!"

He chuckled. "I haven't seen a person *that* happy to successfully finish reading a book since I was stationed at an Army base in Alabama."

"Ouch," muttered Madison.

"No..." Harper held the book over her head in both hands like some ancient high priest making an offering to the gods. "This book has been my curse since we moved into this house. Now, it's broken."

"You are weird, Harp," said Madison. "But that's why I love you."

Harper fell over backward, landing on the sofa. "Every time I've tried to read this, some catastrophe would happen and interrupt me. I never thought I'd be able to finish it."

"Ahh." Cliff smiled. "Now your reaction makes a bit more sense."

"I don' wanna read books if it's gonna make me scream like that," said Lorelei.

"They won't. Harp's just being a dork." Madison handed Lorelei the dice. "Your turn."

"What do you need to roll to land on bed?" asked Harper.

"Aww," whined the kids at the same time.

She pointed at the window. "It's going to be dark in five minutes and the lights don't work. C'mon. Go brush your teeth and get changed while you can still see."

Lorelei stood, looked at the book in Harper's grip, then smiled. "Will you read me this story?"

"Augh!" wailed Harper in fake torment. "It took me months to read it once and you want me to read it again right away?"

"Uh huh." Lorelei grinned.

The kids laughed.

"Okay." Harper lightly bonked her over the head with it. "Can't start now since it's almost dark. Maybe when the lights come back, or tomorrow after dinner."

"Yaaaay!" Lorelei zoomed off down the hall, cheering.

"Sounds like you'll be at it for another whole year." Cliff winked.

Harper narrowed her eyes in challenge at *The Secret Garden*. "Nah. It's like a video game. I beat the final boss. Second playthrough is easier."

# 11

# DOWN FROM THE CLOUDS

E ach day closer to the anniversary of the world's end darkened Harper's mood a little more.

She expected to have *some* emotional issues to work out, but hadn't planned on them being primarily anger and disbelief. How could anyone have been so stupid and heartless as to set off a nuclear war, kill *so* many people all over the world, and push humanity's progress back by centuries? Most likely, the true sadness lurked two months from now in November, closer to the time her parents died.

Alas, by then, she'd lost track of time, so she didn't remember the day of the month when the Lawless invaded her former home. Second week of November came as close as her memory allowed. Perhaps she didn't want to remember the specific day.

Though the weight of loss sat heavy on her back, Harper didn't show it to the world. She figured everyone more or less had the same gloom to work out except for the youngest who hadn't really gotten used to the civilized world. One couldn't mourn something they'd never known. Walking patrol in the morning gave her both solitude and quiet to settle her mind. The kids would be at the farm until a little past noon. Once they came home, she'd be off duty. Dennis or Sadie alternated taking over the patrol of the area for the later shift.

Still August, though. Plenty of time to come up with a way to handle her emotions. She tried to cope with the oncoming gloom by ignoring the days as much as possible, hoping she'd realize at some point September was almost over without noticing it came and went. The idea started off as unworkable. She couldn't force herself to be oblivious to the start of September due to Renee's birthday being the midpoint of August, their former last great hurrah before the end of summer and school starting.

*Gotta be rough for her. Is she always going to associate her birthday with the end of the world?*

Memories of her best friend's seventeenth last year nearly brought Harper to tears, primarily because she hadn't seen Christina Menendez, Andrea Orton, and Veronica Jackson since the blast. She had no idea if they'd died to the strike itself, ended up somewhere safe like Evergreen, or anywhere in between. Her friends might be starving in some other Army survival camp, prisoners of a gang like the Lawless—if not the actual Lawless—or killed by random idiots.

Renee's seventeenth birthday had been the last time she'd been with all five of her friends at the same time. They'd spent the whole day at Renee's house goofing around, not so much a 'party' as it had been a day off from all the various clubs, sports, jobs, and other obligations intruding on life. On their last year of high school, they'd already gotten a taste of how little time the adult world would allow for getting together and doing 'friend stuff.' Not like when they'd been younger and could hang out for hours, without worrying about anything but how much time they had before their parents called, wanting them to go home. Even if the world hadn't blown itself to hell, she probably wouldn't have seen much of her friends by this point. Summer would be mostly over and they'd all have been going in different directions to various colleges or jobs. Andrea wanted to be an artist and talked of attending a place more like a trade school for graphic design than traditional college. Veronica always joked about becoming an action movie star or stunt double. The girl loved martial arts more than most people loved food.

*If any of them survived, it's her.*

Knowing her friends would be scattered around different states by now even if the war didn't happen offered little comfort. However, she also knew she couldn't do anything to change it, nor could she have stopped them from going to college.

*Ugh. Growing up sucks.* Harper kicked a rock off the road.

Living in a reality where she had no cell phone to tell the time bothered her far less than she could have imagined. She'd gotten fairly comfortable using the sun to determine the difference between before and after noon, enough to where when she couldn't say one way or the other, she figured it to *be* noon. Worked on nice days. When overcast, people tended to guess. The whole town still more or less stayed inside during heavy rain due to the old fear of droplets carrying radiation out of the upper atmosphere back to earth.

Considering they'd all been eating vegetables and meat from the farm for months, crops exposed to the rain, it didn't make a whole lot of sense to freak out over bad weather anymore. Whatever fallout might've hopped a ride on a raindrop back to earth had long since done so.

As Harper rounded the bend in South Hiwan Drive passing Pinehurst, Darci came running up the grassy hill off to the left. She appeared upset, eyes reddened from crying. An oversized olive drab T-shirt and black military-style pants with tons of pockets totally didn't fit the 'Darci aesthetic.' Her friend typically preferred goth clothes.

*Aww crap. I knew it. Lucas dumped her or they had a fight.*

Harper stopped short, waiting for her friend to run up to her. "Darce? You okay? What's wrong?"

"I'm... I... it's all gone. The whole world." Darci broke down in tears.

*Hello, Guinness? Is there a record for most delayed reaction to a massively significant event?* Harper couldn't think of anything to say in two seconds that didn't sound flippant, so she simply hugged her friend.

Darci cried unconsolably for a little while, muttering randomly about her father, their friends—except Renee who they knew to be safely here—teachers, other kids they knew from school, and random people like the waiter they both kinda crushed on at TGIF. She sounded as if she only woke up this morning and realized the world ended. Had Harper been playing a drinking game, taking a shot whenever her friend said 'I can't believe they're gone,' she'd have suffered alcohol poisoning.

Worry crept into Harper's brain. Darci almost always wore outfits designed to show off skin. She'd also been on the promiscuous side for the past few years, and ended up trading sex for food in the Army survivors' camp. Seeing her all of a sudden wearing oversized, baggy clothes like a female version of Shaggy from *Scooby-Doo* set off alarms.

*If she's only now realizing nuclear war happened, is she ashamed of what she did to eat?*

"Darce? Did something happen to you this morning or recently? I noticed you were kinda on edge the other day. It's totally not like you to freak out."

"Uhh." Darci sniffled.

"It's totally cool. I'm here for you. But I gotta know what's going on before I can help. Whatever you need, let me know."

"Umm."

"Except shooting children or dogs. Not gonna do that."

Darci sob-laughed. "Dork."

Harper smiled. "Yeah, that's me. Introvert Prime, full time geek, part time badass. Not really. I just play a badass on TV. I'm really screaming in my head the whole time."

"Don't sell yourself short. Renee told me about the guy who tried to get into the van. He totally deserved it." Darci wiped her eyes. "I'm not even freaked out knowing you killed a dude."

"Ugh." Harper scowled off to the side. "I don't really even remember it much except for seeing his face in the window before he opened the door. He's the one who killed Dad. One second, *he* looks at me, the next thing I know, we're driving away from a bloody smear on the road. Tegan thinks I disassociated from reality or something due to extreme emotion. But, enough about me. What's up with you right now?"

Darci folded her arms, looking down. Pale bare toes poked out from the floppy legs of her black BDU-style pants. "I'm, I dunno. Just freaking out."

"Wow. I don't think I ever remember seeing your toenails *not* painted black. Even when we were in fifth grade. Mrs. Connors tried to get you suspended for it."

"Bitch," muttered Darci. "She also tried to get Robin-what's-his-name kicked out of school for having long hair."

Harper fumed. "I hated that woman. Some people just shouldn't be teachers. You remember how when she couldn't get him expelled, she started referring to him as 'she' or 'missy'?"

"Yeah. I mean, 'Robin' is kind of an odd name to give a boy, but still. Not his fault. I don't understand why people who hate people become teachers." Darci wiped her face again, then stared up at the clouds. "Harp, I don't know if I can handle this."

"Sure you can. You're a badass. I only pretend to be one. Did something happen at the Army camp?"

Darci rolled her eyes. "Oh, yeah. A lot happened at the camp. Nothing I didn't ask for, though. No, it's got nothing to do with any of that."

"So…"

"It's been two weeks since I had any weed," whispered Darci.

Harper blinked in shock. "Most people don't say that in a tone like they're admitting to doing something wrong."

"Heh." Darci chuckled.

"Did you run out?"

"No… Lucas has plenty. We're growing enough for the whole town. It's just…" She looked down. "Oh, hell. I gotta tell someone."

Harper bit her lip, bracing for horrible news.

Darci lifted her shirt to expose a small, but noticeable, baby bump. "I stopped smoking as soon as I realized."

"Holy crap, Darce!" She stood there in shock, trying to process her eighteen-year-old friend having a baby with a dude in his thirties, though their age gap didn't surprise her as much as *Darci* laying off weed for the sake of a baby.

"Yeah…" Darci let her shirt fall back over her stomach. "Guess having Elijah has like showed me how to be responsible or some shit.

Don't wanna take a chance getting high will mess up the kid on the way, yanno?"

"You are awesome." Harper hugged her. "Can I say something you might want to hit me for?"

"Do I have to promise not to hit you?"

"No."

"Then go for it."

Harper grinned. "I'm honestly surprised to see you give up weed, no questions asked the instant you realized you got pregnant. That's like… really mature."

"Yeah… well… I'm a pothead, not an idiot. Babies can't handle it." Darci shivered. "But I haven't been sober this long since seventh grade. Or was it sixth?"

Harper gawked. "You started smoking weed at twelve? Didn't notice you were high until freshman year."

"Umm. Well, one joint a week at home is still more than a whole month without touching the stuff." Darci fidgeted at her thigh pockets. "I'm splitting the hairs of technicalities here. But, yeah. Being sober is making me deal with all the bullshit that's happened. It all kinda hit me at once and I'm losing it."

"The weed let you coast along like the world wasn't real. It's a crutch. And no, I'm not going to try talking you into staying off it after you have the baby, just saying." Harper exhaled. "Wow. I guess I should be more freaked out you're having a kid with an old man."

Darci raised both eyebrows. "The world's this messed up and you're freaking over his age?"

"Yeah, kinda." Harper flashed a cheesy smile.

"Umm, well." Darci laughed. "I kinda am, too. Dunno. Maybe I shouldn't have started being with him, but he really does care for me. He's not the oldest dude I've—"

Having no interest in her friend's next words, Harper clamp-hugged her. "I'm so sorry…"

"It's not your fault." Darci squeezed her back. "Couple days after I stopped getting high, all I could think of was the arguments I used to have with Dad"—she choked up—"how he used to get on me about going too far with the whole rebellious thing. We had an argument like two days before it happened."

Harper patted her friend on the back, listening as Darci tearfully rambled about various arguments she'd had with her father over the past year or two about drugs, cutting school, staying out late, having sex, and so on. Her friend had always been the serene, cool, laid back, aloof member of their little circle. Even if Darci's supernatural ability to stay calm in any situation came from being permanently baked, seeing her completely fall to pieces legitimately bothered Harper more than shooting a Lawless in the face at close range.

"… last time we talked, Dad was still kinda mad at me. We were just starting to get back to not being pissy and then he's dead. I'd be dead, too if my bedroom wasn't in the basement. I…" Darci shuddered from grief. "I don't think he even woke up."

"I'm sorry. None of it is your fault. Or his. Not like we knew civilization was going to end ass-early on a Friday morning."

"Bastards." Darci sniffled. "They could've at least waited until Monday. Had to ruin the weekend."

Harper didn't know if she should laugh, so merely sighed.

"Wasn't all bad. I had a test in Mr. Manning's class I wasn't prepared for," said Darci in a toneless voice.

"He gave the *worst* tests." Harper fake rolled her eyes. "The nerve of him actually expecting kids to study."

"Yeah, really." Darci glanced down the road. "Am I going to get you in trouble for just standing here?"

Harper scrunched her nose. "I don't think so. Not like I'm goofing off or sleeping. I'm helping a friend having a crisis."

"We can walk if you want. Sitting still is bothering me."

"Sure."

A minute or two after they began walking, Darci stopped.

"You okay?"

"Yeah." Darci squatted, pulled the legs of her BDU pants up, and tied the ankle closures. "Getting annoying stepping on my pants. Gonna wear them out."

Harper waited for her to stand, then continued walking.

"Guess I don't have to keep wearing baggy stuff." Darci flapped the front of her shirt. "Gonna be pretty obvious I'm preggers soon. Course, none of my clothes are going to fit when I blimp-ify."

"Oh shit," whispered Harper. *There are no maternity stores left.* "What are you going to wear?"

Darci held her arms out to either side. "Probably just sit around wearing a bikini top and no pants. It's going to be cold soon, so I'll just stay inside. Maybe I'll go Greek and wrap a bed sheet around myself when I'm huge."

"Uhh…" Harper blushed.

Her prior hesitation at having a child with Logan came mostly from fear giving birth might kill her. She hadn't even thought of maternity clothing. Bed sheets sounded like the most reasonable option unless Renee's team drastically upscaled their cloth production. She didn't think it would take them *too* much longer and had no problems waiting for handmade clothing before having a baby. Darci, however, didn't have the option to wait. However, the girl also had no shame. Unlike Lorelei who simply didn't care, Darci *would* streak specifically to shock people.

"Ugh." Darci scratched idly at her stomach. "How did women deal with it back in the day? Taking care of a house while barely able to walk. At least Lucas is amazing. He's going to take care of everything when I look like a telephone pole with a watermelon taped to it."

Harper cackled. "What? Watermelon?"

Darci struck a pose. "I'm like ninety pounds. In eight months, I'm going to look like a stick with a giant ball attached to it."

*Eek. For her sake, I hope Tegan is willing to do a C-section.* "Oh. Yeah."

"I miss my dad. More than I ever thought I would." Darci let out a long sigh. "I got what I wanted… and then realized I don't want it."

"Independence?"

"No. The total destruction of an oppressive, patriarchal capitalist society that exploited low-income people and treated women as objects." Darci half grinned. "It was edgy to talk about, not so edgy to live it as reality."

Harper looked over at her. "You miss society?"

"Hell yeah. I can deal with some societally programmed

unconscious sexism while walking from the car to the store. I am *so* fiending for some Doritos right now, it's not even funny. Or a Twinkie."

"I'm sure with enough searching, we could probably still find some edible Twinkies out there somewhere."

Darci laughed. "It's only been a year. The Twinkies survive nuclear war joke is a lot funnier when it's like two centuries later and everyone's carrying spears and worships an old car headlight as a god."

"I wasn't going for the apocalypse Twinkie joke… being serious." Harper feigned innocence. "So, wow… you're really holding off on weed until you spawn?"

"Yeah… at least until the pod person hatches. Maybe longer. Dunno." Darci waved her arms around randomly. "I'm so messed up right now, my thoughts are all over the place. They say weed's not supposed to be addictive or have withdrawal, but I feel so out of it."

At sudden motion coming toward them in the trees on the left, Harper stopped short and swung the Mossberg off her shoulder, not quite aiming it into the woods.

"What?" whispered Darci.

"Saw something move."

Seconds later, a deer bolted away from the area.

"Oh… just a deer." She slouched with relief and resumed walking. "So, yeah. Anyway. You went from like permanently supermellow to being normal. It's gotta feel like you're having a continuous anxiety attack, but you're not. This is how people are supposed to be. You spent the past four years a few degrees separated from the here and now. Just try to take stuff as it happens."

"Harp?" rasped Darci, her voice fried in grief.

"Yeah?"

Tears streamed down Darci's face. "I can't even remember the last thing I said to my dad."

"You guys seemed to get along great. Every time I came over, he was more like the cool uncle than dad."

Darci gave a sad sort of laugh. "Yeah. But we did have

arguments. Nothing real bad, though. But he's gone and I can't tell him I love him. I just wanna tell him one more time."

*Yeah. Me, too.* Harper hugged her, comforting Darci while she cried, alternating between talking to her dead father directly and telling Harper how much she missed him. She abruptly shifted from sobbing to freaking out, muttering, "Oh shit," "Crap," and "Dammit!" repeatedly.

"Whoa, whoa… what happened?" Harper grasped her by the shoulders. "Calm down. Talk to me."

"I might die. Having a kid could kill me."

"Giving birth could kill even before. The US had a pretty awful maternal death rate compared to other major developed countries."

Darci blinked. "Why do you have that piece of information at the tip of your brain?"

"Social studies project junior year. I did a report on it."

"Oh." Darci slouched.

"Hey, Beth gave birth to her daughter not long ago. She's doing fine."

Darci pulled up her shirt to show off her ribs. "Beth is normal. I'm a twig. *Gawd*, it's going to hurt so much, isn't it?"

"Ehh, probably about as painful as having Mrs. Carr's chemistry class first period after not sleeping the previous night."

"Ack! Just shoot me now if it's gonna be that bad," said Darci.

Harper cringed. "I'm honestly not sure what would be worse."

"Between Mrs. Carr's monotone or having a baby?" Darci laughed. "You're obviously kidding."

"No… I meant normal delivery or a C-section. They don't exactly have anesthesia anymore. We'd be wide awake for a C-section… and the stitches afterward."

Darci shuddered. "Okay, stop. Cheer me up with a happier subject. Like, let's talk about everyone we knew from school and guess if they survived or not."

"That's happier?" Harper kicked another rock off the road.

"Compared to how much this kid is going to hurt on the way out, it is. Yeah." Darci squirmed. "Damn. I feel like the girl in that one movie with the three-headed alien pilot."

"Don't remember…"

"The human girl had a bomb in her stomach and they had to get to some planet in time to remove it before it blew her in half."

Harper chuckled.

Darci looked at her stomach and made ticking noises.

"It's good to see you've still got your sense of humor."

"Can't have weed for at least another six months. Dr. Hale said most girls wouldn't even show yet. I'm too darn skinny. Guess I shouldn't have signed up for the apocalyptic survivor camp diet."

"Hope you're eating enough."

"Yeah. The big P is worth extra food allotment." Darci looked over at her. "Hey what happened to the bike? I thought you rode patrol now?"

Harper shrugged. "Usually, I do. Felt like walking today for some reason. Having a bad case of the glooms."

"How come?"

"September coming up. I keep thinking about *that* morning…"

Darci nudged her. "I've got plenty of weed if you want some to take the edge off."

"You know… if the war didn't happen, I might give it a shot. Have too many people depending on me right now for me to stick my head in a cloud. Only thing I can do is deal."

"Don't bottle everything up, either."

Harper glanced down at the Mossberg in her hands. "I'm not. It took me months to process everything and come to terms with what I didn't do, could've done, and what I've been forced to do. I'm not the same person I was a year ago."

"None of us are. Can I say something without you hitting me?" asked Darci, half smiling.

"Sure."

"You didn't ask if you had to promise not to." Darci cocked an eyebrow.

"Because you know I'd never hit you." Harper chuckled.

"Heh. Right." Darci gazed off at the sky. "You're the last person I ever expected to 'go hard' and kick ass. Figured you'd be hiding under a bed crying."

Harper laughed. "Pretty much what I did the first two months. After the Lawless… I had no choice."

"I'll make you a deal. If I lose my shit, I'll come talk to you. If you start falling apart, come talk to me. Okay?"

"Totally." Harper held up a fist.

Darci bumped it.

# 12

# PERIMETER WATCH

**M**adison trailed along at the rear of the pack, feeling a little bit like an outsider.

Nothing had particularly happened, but for whatever reason that afternoon, some weird invisible separation stood between her and the others. Mila had been 'the weird kid' everyone avoided and didn't want to be friends with back when she'd acted all sorts of creepy and morbid, but at the moment, Madison felt even more isolated. No one had done anything to her recently, nor had she purposefully alienated herself. For some reason today, she wanted to hang out with Harper—only Harper.

She recognized it as being selfish, so didn't act on it. Jonathan and Lorelei had become her siblings, too. Sometimes, she thought of them more as 'really good friends' while only Harper was her sister. But, Jonathan had been super upset the night Tyler almost killed Maddie. He'd probably even saved her from suffering frostbite or something by sharing a winter coat. As far as Lorelei went, Madison felt responsible for her and couldn't leave her to run off for something as dumb as wanting to pretend the war didn't happen or she had Harper all to herself.

*I'm jealous, aren't I?* Madison frowned at herself. This sudden resentment for Lorelei bothered her. The poor girl had an awful life before the nukes. Harper once said the war *improved* her situation.

Madison looked down at the road they walked on, accepting her moment of selfishness. Since she hadn't done anything more than feel inexplicably pissy without acting on it or saying anything mean, she didn't apologize to anyone. Cliff, who she now thought of as Dad, said thoughts didn't matter, actions did.

She let go of her moodiness and ran to catch up to the others.

Lorelei grinned at her as soon as she got close. The unbridled joy in the girl's smile made Madison cringe in guilt for her momentary wish 'family' still consisted only of her and Harper. She playfully palmed Lorelei's head and gave her a little shove, laughing.

*Love isn't pie. Harper can take care of us both.*

"Hey!" chirped Lorelei, before hugging her. "Don't push my head. I'll fall."

"Just playing around." Madison grabbed her in a gentle headlock.

Lorelei didn't fight, adoring being held.

*She's more like having one of those cats that goes totally limp when you pick them up than a sister.*

Jonathan, Christopher, and Mila at the front of the group discussed the plan to help 'defend Evergreen' by keeping a lookout for a while. It sounded fun, somewhere between playing soldiers and really helping to protect the town. Consequently, Jonathan had brought a pair of binoculars they'd found months ago. After the 'flea incident,' their old fun pastime of exploring unused houses around Evergreen no longer had as much appeal. Lorelei suggested an 'easy' fix would be to just leave their clothes outside so no fleas got into them. No one else liked the idea.

"We're not primitives," said Christopher. "People aren't going to be like that for a long time."

"Is not prim-tive." Lorelei pretended to scratch fleas. "Is smart. Fwees can't hide in clothes if we don't have any."

"Lore?" asked Madison.

"Yeah?"

"There's an L in fleas. Can you say *fleas*? Not fwees? You're too big for baby talk."

Lorelei grinned. "I'm not stupid."

Madison tickled her. "You're not. It's why I'm telling you how to say it because I know you're smart enough to say it."

"Fa-lees," said Lorelei, exaggerating the l.

Jonathan adjusted the machete he'd rigged in a back scabbard. "People might go primitive, but not until like our grandkids have grandkids."

"If we survive," muttered Christopher.

"We'll survive." Mila twirled one of her throwing knives around her finger. "Maybe not as long as we would have before, but we'll survive. It's not gonna be as bad as everyone thinks. People will be able to reinvent stuff because the hard part is getting the idea. We've already got all the ideas written down. Just gotta figure out how to *do* stuff all over again."

"Uh oh. Mila's saying happy stuff." Becca laughed.

Mila twirled the little knife around. "I am a happy person… who sometimes feels the need to cut a bitch."

Eva, Becca, and Christopher chuckled.

"She is." Jonathan turned to walk backward a few steps so he could look at everyone. "She only acted strange to protect us. The shadow men really had been after her. Since they're all dead now, she can be herself."

*He is totally in love.* Madison looked off to the left across Route 74 at the quartermaster's building and the old 'Bark Inn' dog place. To her, the idea of boys remained a solid 'eww.' She didn't understand how Mila liked Jonathan kissing her, the girl being basically a year younger than her. Harper thought neither of them truly understood kissing and simply did it out of curiosity. Madison didn't get how smushing lips against someone else was supposed to feel good. It kinda grossed her out. She hoped she didn't have something wrong with her making her not like a boy the way Mila appeared to like Jonathan. After all, she'd seriously thought her dead parents would call her on a fried iPhone. Then again, Mila had some 'head problems' too, as Dr. Tegan called them.

Up ahead, a stop sign stood on the edge of a grass 'island,' beside a rectangular green sign with white letters spelling out 'Evergreen Dental Group.' The boys veered right, following the turn past the former dentist's office toward the Wendy's restaurant.

As with most buildings in Evergreen, scavenging crews already removed the locks. The militia collected everything useful from most places in town before Madison and her new family of Harper plus Cliff and Jonathan arrived. The boys pulled the doors open and stepped into the place.

Somehow, it still smelled like a Wendy's.

"Wow," whispered Madison. "Does anyone else think this place smells like hamburgers?"

"Whoa, it *does*." Becca gawked. "Like they're still cooking in here."

"Yeah." Eva blinked. "So strange."

"I don't smell anything but old building," said Christopher.

"It kinda smells like burgers." Jonathan sniffed the air.

Mila looked around. "I don't smell anything. You're probably imagining it because you expect a fast food place to smell like a fast food place."

"Maybe." Madison shrugged. "I'm used to feeling sick from all the murdered cows. Mom used to say people smell and taste the stuff they hate more strongly than other things."

Christopher wandered behind the register counter. "My mom used to be a vegetarian. She doesn't really care anymore. She mostly hated the cruel factory farms."

"If Harper was here with us, she'd point at me and say 'don't get her started' or something." Madison exhaled, lips fluttering. "No point complaining about them anymore. They're gone. But they used to be really mean to the animals. Cutting off chicken's beaks. Forcing them to live in crammed cages, and—"

Becca grabbed her from behind, covering her mouth. "Shh. Let it go. Chill out. Nature won. Corporate farms lost."

Madison sighed out her nose and held a thumbs-up.

The boys explored the kitchen while Becca, Eva, and Madison reminisced about the time Madison drove the cafeteria lady nuts at their old school by debating her on the evils of meat and having a too well-reasoned argument for a frazzled cafeteria worker to process during a lunch rush.

"Aww. Someone's already taken all the money," said Christopher.

"Who cares?" Madison shrugged. "Money isn't good for anything anymore except starting fires."

"Or for wiping," said Jonathan from the kitchen. "They probably took it for TP."

"Eww," chimed Becca and Eva at the same time.

Lorelei played with one of the dead cashier terminals, pretending to talk to customers.

*Wow. She sounds just like a cashier at a fast food place. Did her mother work at McDonald's and bring her there?*

The kids explored the place for a while. Except for an assortment of knives, none of the equipment in the kitchen proved dangerous, useful, or terribly interesting. Someone had already cleared the place of food, though they'd left behind sauce packets no one dared open. After eleven months sitting around unrefrigerated, Mila declared them 'chemical weapons.'

Eventually, Jonathan located a ladder. Except for Lorelei, who continued playing cashier, the kids climbed up to the roof and used the Wendy's building as an elevated lookout point. Jonathan 'assigned' everyone to a spot, so they collectively had a wide field of vision to the north and east. Alas, their view mostly consisted of tree-covered hills surrounding the golf-course-turned-farm further north. However, if any bad guys came down Lewis Ridge Road, they'd definitely see them coming.

"This is stupid. We can't see anything from here." Mila pointed west, across Route 74 at the tall mountainous hills on the far side of the main farm. "We should go up there."

Jonathan scrunched his nose. "We'd be too far away to warn anyone if bad guys showed up."

"Up there, we'd be able to see bad guys for miles. Way more than from this roof." Mila rolled her eyes. "You're not thinking. If anyone attacked and we're up here, by the time we saw them, we'd be *chasing* them into town, not running ahead to warn anyone."

"We could ask for an air horn," said Madison. "Early warning."

Eva, flat on her stomach by the edge of the roof, looked over. "What happens if bad guys come over the hill? They'd get us first."

"We're not supposed to go that far away from town, anyway." Christopher took the binoculars from Jonathan and used them to look east along the road.

Jonathan scrunched up his face in thought. "Maybe we should go on the roof of the school. It's taller and it's basically the north end of town. There's lots of houses past it, but no one lives in those."

"That we know of," said Mila.

"View would be better from the school." Madison shrugged. "And if we're supposed to be scouts, we should be at or a little outside the edge of town. We're sitting right in the middle of it here, more or less."

"Yeah," said Jonathan. "But we might not be able to get out to the roof."

"There's like a shopping center on the other side of the school." Becca took the binoculars and looked through them. "It's not *too* far outside town. We shouldn't get in trouble."

Jonathan swished his feet back and forth, chin in hand. He looked far too serious for an eleven-year-old. "We haven't cleared those buildings yet. Don't know what's inside them. Probably not going to have bugs since no one keeps pets in a store. Tomorrow, we can check them out if you guys want."

"Okay." Christopher nodded. "We stay here now and practice?"

"Sounds good." Jonathan looked around at everyone.

Mila, Becca, and Eva appeared okay with it. Madison didn't care either way. Lorelei remained downstairs talking to 'customers.'

Becca handed the binoculars to Madison.

She took them, sighed, and held them up to her eyes, gazing up Route 74 as far as she could see. 'Playing soldier' had never interested her before, but they didn't really 'play.' Dangers that didn't exist in a civilized world could appear at any time from any direction, and the town only had so many militia people. Even kids their age could help out if only by keeping their eyes open.

The reality of laying on a rooftop seriously looking out for outsiders who might be dangerous put a sick feeling in the pit of Madison's stomach. She felt silly for ever being scared prior to a dance recital. The worst thing to result from her messing up or falling during a performance in front of an audience would be embarrassment, possibly some people laughing... maybe a sprained ankle. Screwing up here could get someone hurt... sort of. The town didn't officially rely on the kids for any early warning. If they all got bored and went off to do something else, no one would yell at them.

But, Madison wanted to help... or at least not be caught off guard.

She stared at the empty highway, thinking about how much the world changed. It had been months since she'd bothered practicing anything from dance class. Except for building flexibility and endurance, nothing she learned there would be of any practical use anymore.

*No more dance recitals. No shows, movies, theaters... School's all different now. We won't even have 'real' high school. College is definitely out.* She half smiled. *Won't have to get a bad job I hate.* She sighed away the sorrow from thinking about how her parents sometimes spent most of the night complaining about their jobs. Mom and Dad had been unhappy at work, but not so much so they'd wanted to quit and find new jobs. Dad seemed to believe it normal for everyone from middle management—whatever that meant—down to hate their jobs. It made no sense for *everyone* to work so hard to obtain and keep jobs they hated.

*Everyone has the same job now—staying alive. Dr. Tegan is right. I should probably stop hoping someone's going to fix the world and life will go back to normal in a couple months or years. We're really stuck like this. When I'm Harper's age, we'll be living in Skyrim.*

Eva, on her left, poked her. "Let me see."

Madison handed her the binoculars, then rested her head on her folded arms. "Knock yourself out. It's a road."

"I can't see anything. It's all super blurry."

Without looking up, Madison said, "You're holding them backwards. Look in the tiny lenses. Big ones point forward."

"Oh." Eva laughed. "Duh."

"Wow, she's not even blonde." Christopher laughed.

Becca threw a pebble at him, bouncing it off his head. "Take that back. I didn't mess it up."

"Wasn't talking about you being dumb. It's just a joke." Christopher rubbed the spot where the tiny rock hit him. "Ow."

"Do you have *any* idea how many times people think I'm stupid because my hair is blonde?" Becca rolled on her back and sighed at the clouds. "*So* annoying. Not so much anymore, but it used to happen every day. In school, I never asked questions because people would laugh at the 'stupid blonde' for not understanding. I had to pass Madison notes and ask her to ask."

"Truth," muttered Madison. "Girls with black hair are geniuses."

"And psychos." Mila smiled innocently.

Eva looked over. "What about brown hair?"

Everyone looked at each other, shrugging.

"Wow, you guys. I'm kidding." Madison lifted her forehead off her arms. "Black hair doesn't make anyone smart. Hair color doesn't mean anything."

Eva passed the binoculars to Mila, then wiped her eyes. "Those almost gave me a headache."

Mila observed the area for a few minutes, then passed the binocs back to Christopher.

He scooted to the roof edge, propped himself up on his elbows, and scanned the east. "What are we looking for again?"

"Anyone walking around you don't recognize," said Jonathan. "Bad guys might attack or someone could be out there needing help."

"It's after eleven!" yelled Lorelei from inside the Wendy's. "We don't have breakfast after eleven." Pause. "I *am* the manager."

Mila raised an eyebrow at Madison. "I'm not sure if that's cute or sad."

"Got something!" whispered Christopher. "Two people riding horses down the highway."

Jonathan crawled over to him. "Let me see?"

Christopher handed the binoculars over.

"Yeah. Wow." Jonathan looked for a moment, then handed the binoculars to Becca.

Madison squinted, straining to make out two indistinct figures approaching Evergreen at a walking pace. When Becca handed her the binoculars, she zoomed in on a suntanned man and black woman riding side by side on horses. Both looked 'old' to her, as in obvious grown-ups, though Cliff would call them young. They wore light brown long coats in the same style, like something out of the Old West. The coats appeared fairly new, obviously hand-made. He had a tired sort of expression while the woman flashed a big grin at the world. She also carried a rifle in a saddle sheath. The man didn't appear to be armed, but might have handguns or knives under the coat. Double saddlebags hung from both horses, all packed full.

They rode toward Evergreen in a casual manner, out in the open in the center of the highway.

"I don't think they're here to attack us," said Madison. "Maybe they're like merchants or something."

"Merchants?" asked Mila.

"Yeah, like from a video game. Wander from town to town selling stuff like healing potions or weapons." Madison shrugged. "I realize we're not in *Skyrim* and healing potions aren't real, but yeah. They could be selling other stuff. Clothing, ammo, guns... not 'healing potions.'"

"Mommy!" yelled Lorelei. "Please stop yelling at the lady."

"Ugh." Madison handed the binoculars to Eva and stood. "Be right back."

Jonathan followed her to the ladder opening. "Let's go see what they want."

The others ran over as Madison gingerly stepped onto the metal ladder and climbed down. She ran down the little hallway past the bathrooms and manager's office to find Lorelei pretending to have an argument with herself, playing the parts of angry mom and scared daughter. As soon as she saw Madison, she stopped making faces and grinned.

"You okay, Lore?"

"Uh huh."

"Did your mother yell at people like that?"

Lorelei shook her head. "No. My old mom was the stupid dumbass who wanted breakfast after eleven and started screaming over it and calling people bad words."

"Ack." Madison winced. "Someone called her that?"

The little blonde girl nodded.

"It's not nice to call someone that."

"I know. I wasn't calling anyone that." Lorelei grinned again. "Just telling you what they said."

The other kids ran across the room to the front door one by one.

"Well, don't say those words again until you're older. Harper will go ballistic."

Lorelei tilted her head. "What's go ba… liss…tick mean?"

"Get mad." Madison took her hand and led her to the door.

"She doesn't get mad." Lorelei ground her big toe into the floor. "If I do bad stuff, she gets sad."

Madison shoved the door open. "Yeah, that's Harp. Everyone used to call her 'too nice.'"

"How can someone be too nice?" Lorelei hurried to keep up with her as the kids ran up the road leading to Route 74.

"Like, you know how most people find a bug, they step on it? Harper carries them outside."

"Tha's not bein' too nice. Just bein' nice."

"She used to not get mad at people when she really needed to because she didn't want to make them feel bad. People took advantage."

"I don't know what that means," said Lorelei.

"I'll explain later."

"When?"

Madison ran a little faster to catch up to the other kids. "Three or four… years."

Lorelei laughed.

Jonathan reached the bus barrier the militia placed across the highway as a defensive sniper position first. He ran around to the 'inside' of the wall formed by a pair of city buses, announcing that his 'team' spotted two people riding horses down the road.

Cameron, standing on top of a bus behind a steel barrier, smiled down at him in a way that made Madison think he'd already seen the approaching people in his rifle scope. "Great work, Jonathan. Thanks for the heads up."

Madison pulled Lorelei around behind the buses, not caring they couldn't see the road due to metal plates covering all the windows facing away from Evergreen. She didn't expect violence from a group of two, but also felt safer having a wall and three adults between her and strangers. Eva, Becca, Christopher, and Mila gathered around her in a cluster.

Annapurna and Fred Mitchell walked out in front of the buses to meet the newcomers while Cameron remained up high to observe. A few minutes later, the clop of hooves on paving became audible.

Jonathan peered around the end of the bus.

"Afternoon," said Fred. "Welcome to Evergreen."

"Hello," replied a sweet female voice. "I'm Cerice. This is my associate, Wade. We got wind y'all had a settlement here."

"We do. Looking for a place to set down?" asked Annapurna.

"Got that already," said the man... probably Wade. "We're from the Express. You folks got anything like a mayor here? We'd like to talk to whoever's in charge about setting up an outpost."

"Express?" asked Fred.

"Sort of like the old Post Office," said Cerice. "We carry messages or small items between settlements."

Jonathan stopped peering around the bus end and jogged over to the group of kids. "Just people who carry mail. No threat."

"We can hear them from here." Mila folded her arms.

Madison snickered.

"Hey, wanna go to that house with the pool table and stuff in the basement?" Christopher held his arms out to either side. "Let's do something fun."

Lorelei looked up at Madison. "How did someone put a pool in a table?"

Mila giggled.

Becca narrowed her eyes at Christopher. "Don't say it."

He blinked, confused. "What?"

"Her hair." Becca folded her arms.

"Oh. Lorelei says stuff like that all the time. It's not a blonde issue. It's a being little issue." Christopher waved for the others to follow him and rushed off.

Chuckling, Madison tried to explain 'pool table' to Lorelei on the way to the sweet house with all the games in the basement.

# 13

## THE EXPRESS

**H**arper squinted up past wavering branches, gauging the position of the sun.

*Close enough to noon…*

Today had been quiet and kind of lonely. Having Darci with her yesterday made time go by quick, though admittedly cost her some awareness of her surroundings. Patrolling with a friend along probably equivocated to driving and talking on a cell phone. People having issues would remain obvious, but she might not have noticed a hostile party laying in ambush. Then again, idiots trying to raid Evergreen wouldn't exactly set a trap for a wandering sentry they had no way to know existed.

She still thought attacks would be most likely happen along roads or at the farm. The residential neighborhood surrounding the Hiwan Golf Club (now secondary farm) concealed the presence of edible crops from distant eyes, unless they climbed up onto the hills to the northeast. If an organized group of hostiles wanted to make trouble, they'd send in scouts first. Harper's job included noticing any potential spies.

However, she knew she couldn't shoot someone in the back for simply running away from her. Maybe she could shoot them if she knew for a fact they ran to alert a larger force of killers, but how could she tell what a person who bolted at first sight intended to do?

She kept going, eyeing the sun every few minutes or so until Sadie Walker emerged from a side street, apparently confused to see her. The woman still carried an AR-15, which meant the militia hadn't yet run critically low on 5.56mm ammunition. Fortunately, ever since the convicts who'd taken over Kittredge decided to attack Evergreen—not realizing a well-armed militia waited for them—things had been fairly quiet. No one had much reason to fire a shot. The hunting parties had taken to using compound bows as much as possible to save bullets for defense.

"Wow, did I lose track of time?" asked Harper once they met at the intersection.

"Either that or I'm a little early." Sadie shrugged. "Anything happen this morning?"

Harper shook her head. "Nope. All quiet. No trouble."

"Great." Sadie exhaled. "Well, I'm already here. You might as well head on out. Oh, I think I saw Maddie and the others walking south on 74, going past Chestnut."

"They're probably heading to that place on Tanoa Road... they found a house with all sorts of game tables in the basement. Ping pong, skee ball, a mini-basketball game, and one of those tables with the little football players on sticks. Whoever lived there must have worked in an arcade or something."

Sadie chuckled.

"Anyway, gotta grab food today. Gonna get going. Be careful and good luck." Harper slung the Mossberg over her shoulder on its strap.

"Thanks." Sadie waved.

Harper hurried southwest, cutting across woodland spaces between houses, taking as straight a line as possible, emerging a few minutes later from the trees at the intersection of Lewis Ridge Road and Route 74, not far from the bus barrier. She raised a hand to wave in greeting at whoever happened to be stationed there today, but froze in confusion at the sight of a pair of horses loaded up with saddlebags and other gear.

Curious, she walked over.

Annapurna, Cameron, and Fred wrapped up a conversation with two newcomers. The man looked to be in his late twenties, the woman a bit younger. Their long coats and hats almost made Harper laugh.

*Where are the cameras? Are they filming a cowboy movie?*

When Harper got a little closer, amusement shifted to being impressed. The coats didn't look like costume pieces. Someone hand-stitched them recently, exactly the sort of thing Renee and her team tried to figure out. Under the coats, both wore normal T-shirts and jeans. The guy had cowboy boots while the woman rocked a pair of hiking shoes.

Annapurna led them away from the barrier into town, probably heading to the medical center for a checkup—as they did with all newcomers—then to the southernmost building in the old La Plaza Office Park, which they'd repurposed into City Hall.

Harper jogged to catch up, falling in step beside Annapurna. "Hey, new arrivals?"

"Not exactly." Annapurna smiled. "Wade and Cerice are Express riders, asking to see Mayor Ned about setting up an office here."

"Whoa, seriously?" Harper blinked. "I keep thinking like we've gone back to the 1800s but never thought anyone would take it so literally. Pony Express?"

"Never heard of it." Wade shrugged. "But you probably remember it since you were still in school when the bombs fell. Been a while since I sat in a history class."

"Listen to this guy talking like he's some kinda old man." Cerice jabbed her thumb sideways at him.

"You guys ride horses to basically carry mail between towns?" asked Harper.

Wade nodded.

"Yeah. Pony Express. Basically." She offered a hand. "I'm Harper. So, are there really other survivor towns out there?"

"Sure are." Cerice grinned. "We know of about a dozen. They crop up here and there, mostly smaller places up in the hills far away from anywhere hit by nukes. Evergreen's the nearest one we've found to Denver. Didn't think anyone had the balls to settle this close to ground zero."

Harper's eyes widened. "Do you guys know how bad Colorado Springs got hit?"

"I've never been down that way." Wade scratched above his right ear. "Pretty much every major city took a beating."

"It's about the same as Denver, I hear," said Cerice. "Some parts are wide open nothingness where there used to be buildings. Other parts, not so bad. Ol' Lewis back at the main office thinks whoever hit us either didn't know about Cheyenne Mountain or knew enough to realize it was mostly decommissioned and not worth a bomb big enough to crack it—if anyone even had one."

"Umm, so wait..." Harper pressed a hand to her chest before her heart jumped out. "Are you saying Springs wasn't entirely vaporized?"

"Don't know for sure." Cerice offered an apologetic smile. "Sure, I've heard people say it's nothing but a radioactive parking lot or 'turned to glass.' One guy said it's a shimmering field of sparkling bits. 'Course, I also heard tell Denver looked like salt flats, and it ain't all the way gone. Some parts are pretty cleared out, but there are lots of ruins. Some places just a little messed up."

Harper exhaled. "Yeah... I used to live in Lakewood. My old neighborhood was all smashed up, but not *too* bad. Bigger problem is the Lawless. You guys should be extremely careful if you get close to Denver. Anyone with a blue sash around their neck is part of the gang. Better off shooting before they get close enough to realize you're a woman."

Cerice cringed. "That bad?"

"Yeah... they tried to grab me and my kid sister. They *did* kidnap my friend, Renee. Killed my parents, too."

"Sorry." Cerice bowed her head. "We haven't gone anywhere near Denver—or any big city for that matter. No plans to yet. Thanks for the tip, though."

Harper couldn't quite smile with thoughts of Lawless in her head, so she nodded once like some old Clint Eastwood movie cowboy. "No problem."

Wade looked around. "This here's gotta be the biggest, most organized settlement we've seen. Couple are close in terms of organization, but nowhere near the size, population wise anyway. Cameron back there says ya got about five hundred souls or so?"

"Yeah, something like that." Harper tried not to grimace. Evergreen being the biggest-slash-nicest town in the area didn't say good things about the other settlements. Perhaps it ended up being a good thing they presently lacked electricity. Rumors of them having an operational power grid (even if it only covered a small area) might make the town a target. "People keep trickling in. Farm's doing decent. We ran out of canned food and stuff months ago. Everything we're eating now, we're either growing or shooting."

"'Bout the same story as most places," said Cerice. "Like the severance package civilization gave us has run out. Sink or swim now is on us."

Harper hesitantly reached for the woman's sleeve. "Mind if I touch your coat? Curious where you got it."

"Go ahead, hon. Got some people at the main office make these coats for us. They're only for Express riders. Sort of our badge of authenticity."

She briefly examined the coarse, thick cloth. "What's it made out of?"

"Alpaca wool," said Wade. "Weird animals. Got a whole bunch of them up in Granby where the main office is."

*Hmm. Wonder if they'd be willing to trade for a mated pair?* "Cool. So, wow. We're really the most organized place you've found?"

"Pretty much." Wade grimaced. "Except for Goodland, over in Kansas. Except for not having electricity or working cars, place doesn't look like the war even happened."

"Not even nuclear bombs want to go to Kansas," muttered Cerice.

Wade chuckled. "It's an okay place if you can deal with the crazy. Fairly big, for a survivor town, surrounded by miles of farms. They ain't hurtin' for food but so damn creepy."

"Creepy?" Harper tilted her head. "How so?"

Cerice pursed her lips. "The people who live in that town think

God spared them, so they've made religion mandatory, fearing if they aren't devoted enough, the nuke that 'should have' hit them will come back and end it. They've publicly executed 'heretics' and 'godless free thinkers' in the town square. They went all sorts of old school. Women aren't allowed to talk to outsiders, especially men."

"Ugh." Harper frowned.

"They're real nice people," said Wade. "Give ya the shirt off their backs... as long as you tell 'em you believe in their god and don't get caught too close to a woman unless her husband or father is there to observe."

*No way am I ever ending up a man's property. Note to self: do not visit Goodland.* She bit her lip. *Sounds like something from a dystopian movie. Why are the crazy psycho cults always in places named things like 'Goodland?'*

Weird nuclear-god cults aside, the idea of numerous other settler towns existing intrigued her. Not in the sense she had the sudden desire to go traipsing around exploring towns like some manner of adventurer, but it gave her hope. If other settler towns had already established themselves, the recovery of civilization sounded more possible. Provided, of course, nutjobs didn't start another war. The people in Goodland would hopefully keep to themselves and not raise an army to forcibly convert nearby towns.

They walked down the road toward Mayor Ned's office.

"Umm, can I ask a dumb question about the Express thing?" Harper smiled at the riders.

"Of course, dear." Cerice returned the smile. "It's why we're here. To answer questions and get a feel for your town."

Harper gestured at the horses. "You guys take letters and stuff to other settlements... how do people know where to send things to? There isn't any way to communicate between places anymore. No phones, no internet..."

"Good question." Wade grinned. "We're collecting lists of names and keeping them in a big book at each Express station. It's not a list of everyone in a place. It's people who are looking for lost family or friends. They ask to be added to 'the book,' and copies are sent out to every office."

"Yeah." Cerice nodded. "The woman who started this whole

Express thing figured only people who had family or friends in other places would need to send mail at first, so she didn't see the point in trying to collect *every* name from a town. Only the ones who thought they might have people out there looking for them."

"It's all handwritten, so it gets a bit tedious." Cerice whistled. "Glad it ain't my job to make new copies. Eventually, a person will be able to go into any Express office and hunt through 'the book.'"

"Do you have a copy with you?" asked Harper, her voice rising on a wave of hope.

Both shook their heads.

"Not yet." Wade gave her a sympathetic look. "We don't copy the registry until we know for sure there'll be an office. Gotta ask your town if it's okay to set one up here first."

"Oh." Harper slouched in disappointment. "Well, I don't think Mr. O'Neill will mind. It sounds like an awesome idea. Civilization slowly coming back."

"Little bit at a time," said Cerice. "Some towns aren't much more than big campsites. Others feel like we've got a decent shot of finding some kind of new normal."

Harper walked with them to Mayor Ned's office, thanked them for talking to her, and headed across the street to the quartermaster's to pick up her weekly food allotment, her head spinning from anxiety and anticipation. Assuming the town management liked the idea of an Express office, she might learn if any of her other friends survived the war and ended up in settlements.

*Great. I'm not going to be able to sleep for weeks.*

# 14

# JUST CAMPING

A few days after the 'exciting' arrival of a pair of mail couriers, Cliff got the idea to go fishing.

The closest Harper and Madison had ever come to 'going fishing' involved standing behind Mom or Dad in the supermarket while they selected haddock, tilapia, or salmon from the seafood case. At least on a Saturday, Cliff had the whole day off. Spending it—or at least several hours—with the family on the shore of Evergreen Lake sounded nice, the sort of things families used to do before technology took over.

It took about an hour to walk there, a bit more than two miles from their house. Not like they could get lost, after all, as they had only to follow Route 74 south directly to the lake, and veer right a little.

Opposite a former restaurant named 'Lakepoint' according to a sign on the lawn, a narrow wooden bridge crossed the creek coming in from the west to a long, narrow strip of island near the northwestern shore. It appeared to be the start of a hiking trail circling the entire lake. Cliff decided to try fishing from the island, climbing over a wooden fence not far past the other end of the bridge, ignoring signs warning people to 'keep out' of the sensitive area.

Harper stopped at the fence. "Is it safe? What's it mean by sensitive area?"

"Where do you think the town's drinking water comes from?" asked Cliff without looking back. "That or some wildlife thing."

"Eww," said Madison.

"What do you think reservoirs are?" Harper poked her. "They have filtration."

"Which doesn't work too well without electricity." Jonathan put a hand on his stomach. "Maybe we should start boiling water before we drink it?"

"We could, but good chance the radiation already killed the germs," called Cliff.

Everyone stared aghast—until he started laughing.

Harper didn't know too much of what went on in the water treatment place. She'd ridden by it once while visiting south Evergreen. For all she knew, someone had already hooked up solar panels to power the plant… but it didn't seem too plausible. A place like that would take far more power than an improvised solar farm could generate.

*What did people do for drinking water before they had plumbing? Wells?*

Carrie, Harper, Madison, Jonathan, and Logan climbed the fence to follow Cliff. Lorelei ducked under the top rail. The little one started pulling her dress off and running for the water, but Carrie caught her.

"Not swimming today," said Carrie. "We're fishing. If you jump in the water, it will scare the fish away."

"Aww." Lorelei looked down.

"If she doesn't splash around too much, she could swim in the water on the other side of the island, near the bridge," said Cliff while handing out fishing poles to Harper, Logan, Jonathan, and Madison.

"Okay." Carrie gestured toward the creek behind the lake. "I'll keep an eye on her then."

"Yay!" Lorelei flung her dress off and waded into the water.

Carrie leaned on the bridge railing nearby, watching her play.

Except for Becca and Eva, the kids happily spent a few hours the previous day hunting for worms, which they'd brought in an old coffee can. Madison hadn't been happy about it, but she'd helped. She looked away as Cliff demonstrated how to put a worm on a hook. Despite having shot people at close range, Harper squirmed at the sight. Like Madison, she didn't really enjoy the idea of torturing an innocent creature. Impaling an earthworm on a fishhook didn't kill it. Even if the simple worm theoretically couldn't feel any pain, it *looked* to be suffering.

Harper clenched her jaw and put a worm on her hook. Logan had obviously never done it before, but didn't appear squeamish at the idea. Jonathan didn't hesitate either. Madison held the worm in one hand, barbed hook in the other. She tried a few times, but couldn't bring herself to puncture the worm.

"I'm sorry," said Madison after a few minutes, shaking from either grief or revulsion. "I can't do it."

Perhaps because she hadn't complained at all about going fishing, Cliff didn't insist she worm her own hook and did it for her. Madison looked about ready to cry as the worm writhed on the end of the line attached to her rod. Harper felt a little weird for wanting to carry bugs alive out of the house yet stabbing a worm.

*Sorry, little guy. Bugs aren't helping us eat.*

"All right. Push down on this lever here to free the reel." Cliff demonstrated. "Ease the rod back, then"—he swung his fishing pole forward—"cast it."

Logan, Jonathan, and Harper managed reasonable first-ever attempts. Madison swung her pole around, but the hook didn't go flying. Instead, it nearly hit Logan in the ear. He yelped and ducked.

"Sorry!" blurted Madison, trying to hand him the whole rod. "Here. Take it. I shouldn't be trusted with sharp things and dying worms."

Cliff rested a hand on her shoulder. "I know you're not thrilled about doing this. We've had this conversation over and over. Vegans are fine and all, but we're not in the first world anymore. A day might come where knowing how to catch a fish is the only reason you don't starve. Hopefully, it won't get to that point."

"She'd eat weeds and stuff," deadpanned Jonathan. "You've been showing us the ones we can eat."

"I know." Madison stopped trying to give her fishing pole to Logan. "Just... why does everything have to die?"

"We've been asking *that* question since people existed." Logan chuckled.

"Even veggies die when we eat them." Jonathan nudged her. "Only difference is a cucumber doesn't scream when you cut it."

She rolled her eyes.

"Push the release." Cliff pointed at the reel on Madison's rod.

She gingerly swung the rod back, fumbled at the reel, then managed a passable—if short—cast.

*And so the waiting starts.* Harper stared at the spot where her line entered the water. Cliff talked on and off about how to pull in a catch if they got a bite. Madison kept her head down the whole time, still mourning the worm death and torture.

"Birds eat tons of them," said Jonathan. "They're just worms. Gotta be millions of them in the dirt."

"I'm not a bird," grumbled Madison. "I don't need to kill worms just so I can kill a fish."

Jonathan shrugged. "Fish aren't even really animals. They're too stupid."

"Fish are not stupid." Madison scowled.

"Oh? Have you ever seen a fish play fetch? Or do tricks? Ever hug a fish?" Jonathan grinned.

"Ick," said Harper.

"Fish are pretty to watch swim. They're pets." Madison kicked her sneaker at the dirt.

"Stuff in your house that just sits there being looked at is furniture, not a pet." Cliff chuckled. "Fish are one step above plants. Like... plants that move around a little. And it's an awful lot of work to keep a tank clean."

Madison sighed.

*She's more like her old self.* Harper smiled. Having an overly sensitive animal-protecting little sister again gave her hope. The girl hadn't fully gone back to normal, as she hadn't spent the previous three days begging them to not go 'hurt fish.' *Maddie knows we have to eat. She'll probably eat the fish but doesn't enjoy the dirty work. Is it cruel to make her do this? I don't mind doing it for her.*

The random thought kids Madison's age back in the actual 1800s could probably kill chickens for dinner like no big deal made her cringe. No way would Madison *ever* be able to chop a bird's head off. Allowing her to keep Rosie as a pet made the idea she'd ever slaughter *any* chicken laughable. Admittedly, the chicken *did* show affection and appear to recognize Madison from the other kids. Most of the chickens Harper observed looked about as dumb and oblivious as could be.

*Rosie's gotta be some kind of Einstein chicken.*

Standing there on the lakeshore holding a fishing rod, idly talking to Logan about random stuff while Lorelei played in the water made it easy to pretend the war never happened. Except for not being flooded with hikers and tourists, her surroundings looked untouched by nuclear weapons... well, except for the hazy sky. She still hadn't gotten used to the *silence* of a world in which cell phones, cars, airplanes, helicopters, televisions, and radios didn't work. It never occurred to her how much background noise used to surround her everywhere—until it stopped.

However, the shores of Evergreen Lake embraced the quiet. Here, the stillness seemed natural.

*It's like we're just some family out camping... except for half of us carrying guns.*

She'd left the Mossberg home due to weight, deciding the .45 would be adequate for a trip across town. Cliff, too, only had a handgun. Carrie, who'd come along mostly as an assistant kid wrangler, not interested in doing any fishing, had Cliff's AR-15 over her shoulder on a strap. Madison kept twisting around to look at where Lorelei played.

*Maddie would totally rather be swimming than fishing. Bet she's got her fingers crossed no fish bite her worm. Or they get away with it and don't end up hooked.*

One hour bled into the next. Harper caught two fish, Jonathan four, Logan three. Madison had a nibble but reeled in an empty hook. Whether or not she intentionally lost the fish or merely didn't pull the line in properly, she seemed happy not to be responsible for 'fish murder.' Eventually, Lorelei became tired and a bit cold, so she climbed out of the water to wander around exploring the island, content to air-dry.

Cliff talked Madison into trying to cast once more, again impaling the worm for her while she looked away.

Jonathan progressively migrated farther and farther to the right each time he caught a fish. By the time he caught his fifth, he stood on a narrow strip of rocks leading from the western tip of the island to the bank on the other side of the creek.

On his way back with fish number five, something laying in the grass caught his eye; he paused to look at the ground, staring at a spot for a moment before pointing and yelling, "Dad? What's this? Is it going to explode?"

Cliff hurried over. Worried, Harper set her fishing pole down and followed, as did Logan. Madison, Carrie, and Lorelei remained behind. By the time Harper got there, Cliff crouched beside what appeared to be a mostly buried missile. A section of nose cone protruded from the dirt at a shallow angle, suggesting the rest of it lay almost flat under a few inches of dirt. Dark scorch marks covered it as well as a few dents.

"Hmm." Cliff brushed his fingers at the charred metal.

Harper tugged Jonathan back a few steps. Of course, based on the curvature of the visible piece, the missile had to be three or four feet in diameter and probably close to twenty feet tall. A couple steps away wouldn't make any difference to their survival if it exploded.

Cliff reached out to pat it a few times, then chuckled. He dug his fingers into the dirt, grabbed on, and lifted a piece of scrap metal shaped somewhat like a giant, warped slice of pizza. Both sides had burn marks, scratches, and dings.

As soon as Harper realized no actual missile lay buried, she let go of Jonathan—and started breathing again.

"What is it?" asked Logan. "Kinda looks like a piece from a rocket or something."

Cliff held it point-up. "I'm guessing here, but it's probably part of the outer nose housing of a MIRV warhead. Six or eight of these sections would've formed the nose cone of an intercontinental missile."

"They named their missiles Merv?" asked Harper.

"Uhh, no." Cliff laughed. "The military loves acronyms. MIRV stands for Multiple Independent Reentry Vehicle. It's a nuclear missile with a bunch of little missiles in the warhead instead of one big bomb. When it gets close to the target area, the outer nosecone breaks off, and all the little warheads inside fire and go to wherever they're programmed to go." He tilted the four-foot-long hunk of metal side to side, then dropped it. "This probably came from the big missile that sprinkled its load all over Denver."

Harper stared at the mangled piece of metal. It felt like she'd found a knife used to murder her parents and everyone she knew.

"Can you tell where it came from?" asked Logan. "Like what country."

"Nah. Not enough here to guess what type of missile it was... and it's pretty scorched up." Cliff stuck his boot under the fragment and flipped it over. "No markings. Only thing I can say for sure is it didn't come from North Korea. They could barely build a rocket that flew to South Korea. No way would they have a MIRV... unless they got it from Russia."

"So, it's either Russia or China?" rasped Harper.

Logan took her hand. "It's just a bit of metal. Nothing to be worried about."

"I'm not worried. This piece fell off the missile that destroyed my home. This piece of metal could've been *inches* away from the warhead that blew up over Lakewood for however long it took to fly from whatever country." She squeezed her fists, stuck between heartbreak and rage.

"Russia and China are the two most likely to have MIRVs and use them on us." Cliff rubbed his chin. "Pretty sure Iran had missiles... though I'm not sure about MIRV warheads. Also, I don't know if their missiles could reach Colorado. France had MIRVs, but they wouldn't have used them on us. Based on the size of that section, it's too big for a submarine-launched weapon. I'd say sixty percent chance it's Russian, forty Chinese. Hell, it might even be ours if a computer glitch—or hacker—started the war."

"You can tell from a hunk of metal?" Logan raised both eyebrows.

"Nah. I'm not a nuclear weapons technician or from military intelligence." He chuckled. "Just a Ranger."

"Just," deadpanned Harper.

Cliff winked at her. "I'm basin' it on politics. China made so much money off the US, it wouldn't make sense for them to lob nukes our way. 'Course, I don't remember seeing anything in the news about a pissing contest with Russia. Usually, when a nuclear war happens, it follows months of growing political tension."

"Usually?" Harper raked a hand up through her hair. "How often have we conducted nuclear wars?"

"You know what I meant." Cliff patted her on the shoulder. "Figure if things got so bad the US and Russia decided to do this to each other, someone would've noticed the escalation on the news. Not like the president of either country woke up in a pissy mood one day, said 'aww, screw it,' and just hit the button. Maybe hackers really did do it. Or a bug."

Logan scratched his head. "What about terrorists?"

"How ya figure?" Cliff raised an eyebrow. "Nuclear control sites are some of the most secure places in the US Military."

"Gradually infiltrate over a couple years, pretending to be loyal soldiers. Get into positions where they could access the launch controls, and once they had enough in place, boom." Logan made a button-pushing gesture. "Maybe a rogue element within the military. Not saying it even had to be our side they got into."

Harper stared at the missile piece. *Nope. Can't pretend we're a normal family out for a day trip in a normal world anymore.*

Other than leaving a lingering sadness in the pit of Harper's stomach, the nosecone fragment ceased being interesting to everyone after a few minutes. She headed back over to where she'd left her pole on the ground. She picked it up and reeled in a drowned worm. Sighing, she re-cast it out into the lake. No longer soaking wet, Lorelei put her dress on, then hovered beside Harper watching her fish.

Madison unenthusiastically reeled in a smallish fish. Once she lifted it out of the water, she made a face at the flapping critter like she'd just murdered a baby.

*Grr. Are we doing more damage to her? She's miserable. We don't have to insist she be the one to kill food.*

Cliff approached and crouched beside Madison. "Not bad. Want to release it back into the water?"

Madison blinked in shock. "Seriously?"

"Yep." He grasped the dangling fish. "This one's too small even to feed Lorelei. We ought to let it have more time being a fish. It's good you're learning what you might need to do if you have to survive. How about we let him go, and you can take it easy for the rest of the day."

"Really?"

"Absolutely." He patted her on the back.

"Umm. How do I get it off the hook?"

Cliff carefully worked the fish free of the hook, then lowered it into the water. Madison hugged him. Harper teared up a little watching him really embrace being Dad instead of just some nice former mall security guard with a heart of gold who couldn't leave a pair of young girls and a boy to fend for themselves. Thrilled not to be forced to 'kill animals' any more today, Madison brightened in an instant. She ran around with Lorelei, exploring the island. Jonathan continued angling, apparently having fun. He and Logan joked back and forth, having a competition for who caught the most.

Harper tried to forget the missile fragment and enjoy the beautiful landscape around her. In light of what happened to civilization, sticking a worm on a hook didn't feel at all like a significant enough tragedy to be worth her earlier hesitation. Carrying bugs alive out of the house instead of smashing them also felt pretty stupid, but she'd still do it. The worms died for a greater good.

They took a break for a lunch of tomato sandwiches. After, they resumed fishing, Carrie taking up the pole Madison no longer used. Madison and Lorelei wandered off to the west, exploring the island's north edge, along the bank of Bear Creek.

"Don't get too far," called Harper... right as a fish tugged at her line.

"Okay, we won't," shouted Madison.

*How many fish does he want to catch? We still don't have power for the fridge. Is he expecting we're going to eat all of them tonight?* She reeled the fish in, held it up to make sure she hadn't caught one too small to keep, and dropped it in the bucket. *All of us plus Renee... yeah, we're probably going to finish it all.*

Lorelei came out of nowhere, grabbing on to Harper and hiding behind her. Madison darted around behind her as well. Instinctively, Harper looked in the direction the kids came from. A shaggy, bearded man in an old-style olive drab Army coat stumbled over a second bridge at the west end of the island, almost a hundred feet away, waving a large kitchen knife around. Wild hair, beard down to his waist, tattered clothes, and a crazy gleam in his eyes put Harper on edge the instant she looked at him.

*Holy crap! If Lore is afraid of someone, he must be the literal Devil.*

Harper put a hand on her sidearm. She'd probably never hit a target at a hundred feet using a .45, but had no way to know if the man had friends who might come out of nowhere and rush at them. With Lorelei and Madison huddling behind her, she couldn't advance into range, so she held still. Jonathan, who'd gone way to the west side of the island for a 'better spot,' found himself in lunging grab range of the man. He scrambled away from the seemingly crazy dude, sprinting toward Logan and Cliff, who set their poles down and faced the approaching weirdo, also resting their hands on their sidearms.

Carrie swung the AR-15 off her shoulder and gripped it, but stopped short of aiming at him.

"That's close enough, friend." Cliff raised his left hand. "Mind putting the knife down?"

The man waved the knife back and forth, jabbing it off to the side while muttering incoherently about Denver, Boulder, a 'green highway' and Elvis.

"He's either extremely drunk or has considerable brain damage," whispered Carrie.

"Didn't really catch that." Cliff pointed the same way the man indicated using the knife. "Are you trying to find somewhere?"

The strange guy jabbed the knife like a pointing device, indicating the direction he'd come from, then left and right. He mumbled too quiet for Harper to make out words, but judging by the look on Logan and Cliff's faces, they didn't understand him either.

"You're looking for someone *named* Denver?" asked Logan.

"Naw!" yelled the guy, flailing his arms and yelling louder. "They said the camp's up at midnight, but there's not a single pole here. All five of them are watching us. Ain't seen no signal flare yet. Think the Moon's been lost, too. Where is waypoint Elvis?"

"It left the building," deadpanned Cliff. "Over that way." He pointed west.

"Wow," whispered Carrie. "He's on Mars. Not sure what the hell he took, but he's dangerously high. Not sure he even realizes he's holding a knife."

The man remained still for a short while, making confused sounds and gestures. As if reacting to an explosion only he heard, he jumped, spun around, and ran off back over the south bridge. Everyone watched him until he disappeared into the woods on the far side of the golf course west of Evergreen Lake.

"Before anyone asks, I don't have a damn clue," said Cliff. "Whatever went wrong in that man's brain is not a minor problem."

"Yeah…" Harper turned to look at the girls. "You two okay?"

Madison nodded once. She didn't look *too* frightened.

"Yes." Lorelei grinned. "You said scary people might wanna hurt us, so if I didn't know someone, I hadda stay safe 'til you said is okay ta hug them."

"Yep!" Harper scooped her up into a hug. "You did great!"

"Think he would've hurt us?" asked Madison.

"Umm. Hard to say." Harper stared at the trees where the guy disappeared, relieved to see no trace of motion. "Maybe not on purpose, but he didn't look like he knew what he was doing... and he's waving a blade around."

Madison shivered. "Great. *Another* crazy guy with a knife."

"Sorry." Harper bit her lip.

"Not your fault." Madison hugged her, too.

Cliff checked the fish bucket. "Looks like we got enough here. Let's pack it in and I'll go over how to clean and gut them."

Madison grimaced.

He smiled at her. "You don't have to watch if it bothers you. Just saying... if things go really bad, it's much easier to feed yourself by fishing than start up a farm all alone."

"Yeah. I know." Madison slouched. "Fish don't bother me as much as other animals. I can probably watch, so I know how to do it if I end up somewhere all alone. I'd still prefer to eat weeds and stuff, though."

*Wow. Lorelei didn't hug a random knife-wielding stranger and Madison is willing to learn how to gut fish. The world has gone crazy.*

Harper gave the girls a quick squeeze, then picked up her fishing rod for the long walk home.

# 15

## SEARCH PARTY

The Wednesday following the fishing trip, Harper awoke to a strange feeling.

She slipped a hand under her T-shirt nightgown to rub her stomach. A general, but mild, sense of ick lurked in her gut.

*Ugh. Is it about time for the monthly visitor, or is this because we've been eating lake fish for three days in a row? Hope the little bastards aren't radioactive.*

She nudged Madison and Lorelei awake.

The girls bounced out of bed, neither showing any signs of being sick, overtired, or in a bad mood. After a quick round of rock, paper, scissors to decide who got the bathroom first, Lorelei ran across the hall. Madison bounced in place. Harper decided to hold it until the kids finished. She threw on a fresh T-shirt and the same jeans she'd been wearing for the past five days. Having to wash clothes in fire-heated water made her cut down on doing laundry to twice a month.

*Please fix the electricity. I'm not ready to go full Wild West.*

Renee mentioned one of the books she'd read about textiles having a story about an old trick of warming rocks over a fire, wrapping them in towels or blankets, and taking them to bed for warmth. Sounded like something they'd have to do come winter if Jeanette and her team couldn't fix the transformer.

She meandered out to the kitchen, still scratching at her stomach —and stopped short at the end of the hallway. The light bulb in the lamp beside the couch glowed. She ran over to it, wiped her eyes to make sure she didn't see things, then let out a scream of joy.

Jonathan ran in the back door from the yard, wide-eyed. "What happened?"

"The power's on!" She pointed at the light.

"Yes!" He jumped around.

Madison skidded to a stop at the end of the hall, looking frightened. "Why did you scream?"

Again, Harper pointed at the light. "We have power again!"

"Sweet." Madison grinned.

Jonathan went back outside.

"Where are you going?" called Harper.

"Was getting firewood. I'm gonna put it back on the pile since we don't need it," yelled the boy.

Harper ran over to the fridge. It had already become cold, suggesting power came back up sometime in the middle of the night... definitely an odd thing to happen from *solar* panels. The town must have some sort of huge battery. Alas, they'd already eaten the fridge empty to avoid wasting food. She'd have cooked eggs due to the power being back, but they didn't have any on hand. She also didn't feel like running all the way to the farm to get some.

True, Rosie lived in a small coop in their yard, but without a rooster, hadn't been laying. Madison already schemed a way to bring home one or two more chickens to keep her company so she didn't get lonely.

"Toast it is." Harper reached for a frying pan.

*Wow. How messed up is it to feel like a millionaire just because the electric stove works?*

"Lore!" shouted Madison from the hallway. "You need more than underpants on."

"Turn around," said Jonathan.

"Aww." Lorelei sighed.

Jonathan entered the kitchen, laughing. "Hey, where's Dad?"

"Uhh…" Harper added bread slices to the frying pan. "Not in his room? He had night patrol yesterday."

"No, he's not in his room." Jonathan dragged a chair over to the cabinets so he could climb up to grab a mason jar of strawberry preserves.

"Strange… not sure where he went. Maybe Carrie's?"

Jonathan set the jar on the table, then darted out the back door.

Madison and Lorelei entered the kitchen. Harper asked Madison to watch the toast while she ran to the bathroom. Her little sister managed not to light the kitchen on fire—or even burn toast—before she got back.

A few minutes later, Jonathan returned. "He's not over Carrie's. Sorry. Now she's worried."

"Hmm. Weird. I'll check with Walter before I start my route today."

The four of them finished off the whole—admittedly smallish—jar of preserves on their toast. After breakfast, Harper walked the kids to the farm, where they'd help out until noon or so, then backtracked into town rather than cross Route 74 into her patrol area. She headed for the militia HQ, specifically Walter's office.

Though he'd gone fully grey, the man wasn't old enough to feel like Harper's grandfather, only having turned fifty-one a few months ago. Still, he had a particular kind of laid-back friendliness that made him feel more like a relative than a boss.

She knocked on the doorjamb as she walked in. "Mr. Holman? Got a quick second?"

"Sure, Harper. What can I help you with?" He looked up from the notebook on his desk, smiling at her.

"It's probably not a big deal, but I can't find Cliff. I know he was on an overnight patrol, but he should be home asleep by now. Wondering if you needed him on a special project or something."

Walter tapped a finger on his desk, thinking. "Hmm. No. I can't think of why he wouldn't be home this morning. No one reported any trouble. He and Roy did go on a 'long patrol' last night. I don't imagine Cliff or Roy would get lost."

*Oh, no...* She fidgeted. A 'long patrol' meant they went several miles out from Evergreen, following an extended border as sort of an early warning of potential threats. While it didn't necessarily mean something bad happened, being miles away from town put them out of airhorn range if they needed help. Even rifle shots might have gone unnoticed from so far away in the middle of the night.

Outwardly, Harper remained calm despite the sudden worry she'd never see Cliff alive again.

"Where did they go?"

"Northwest quarter." Walter got up from behind his desk, waved for her to follow, and went to the outer room with the big wall map. He traced his finger around in a line. "They'd have gone out on Squaw Pass Road, followed it west, then kept going south where it hits 475. Followed it until it intersected Upper Bear Creek Road, and taken that east back to Route 74 by the lake. It's a hair over twelve miles. Four hours if they walked fast. Six to eight if they took their time. Could be, they saw something and stopped to check it out so they might just be running late."

She stared at the map, tracing the route with her gaze. "He and Roy have gone on that walk a few times. He's always back before sunrise. Something happened."

"You've got a look in your eye like you're about to ask what I think of you going out to look for him." Walter set his hands on his hips. "*Saving Private Ryan* moment."

"Uhh, I really hope not."

He chuckled, lifting his gaze off the floor. "I mean, it's a question of how many lives do you risk for two. If something *did* happen to them, it might also happen to anyone who goes looking for them. Or it might not."

"Yeah..." She looked off to the side. "It's wrong not to try."

"Agreed." Walter patted her on the arm. "Little early to assume the worst. It *can* be a long walk if they had to do anything more involved than hiking the roads. But, waiting until it's obvious something's wrong could be bad. If you want to take a search party out after him, I'm not going to object. But... take a search party. Don't go alone."

Harper nodded. "Okay. I won't. Thanks, Mr. Holman."

"Gah, you make me feel old." He chuckled. "Are you ever going to feel comfortable calling me Walter?"

"I suppose it's probably time for me to grow up and stop feeling like a high school kid." *Kids don't blow bad guys' faces off.* "Gonna feel weird but since you keep asking me to, I'll try."

"Stay safe out there. Take two or three with you, not the whole militia. Leave some for the town." He winked.

"Sure thing, Walter."

"There ya go."

She offered a weak smile. Calling a man older than her father by his first name felt surreal. In all the upheaval of the world devouring itself, her turning eighteen and officially becoming an adult hadn't really registered in her mind. Then again, 'official adulthood' lost most of its meaning. Earl gave beer to fifteen-year-olds. No one cared about driver's licenses anymore, and a couple of sixteen-year-olds (Beth and Jaden) effectively considered themselves married. Neither of them had killed anyone.

*Mom always said being an adult would sneak up on me. Didn't quite expect it to happen so soon.*

Harper hurried out of the militia HQ and headed back to the farm. Going off in search of Cliff risked her life, even if it wouldn't take her too far away from town. She couldn't simply disappear on Madison, Jonathan, and Lorelei. If she ran off and ended up dead or worse, kidnapped, they'd never know what happened. She also couldn't simply wait and hope Cliff merely stopped for a nap. If he needed help, he'd get it. After everything he'd done for them, she more than owed it to him.

MADISON, JONATHAN, AND LORELEI LOOKED UP AT HER, FEAR IN their eyes.

She'd gathered them from their respective farm chores for a meeting beside the chicken barn, but stumbled over how to explain the situation to them. The kids apparently took her hesitant silence as a worst-case scenario. Jonathan appeared ready to cry, perhaps expecting her to say they'd found Cliff dead.

"Dad and Roy went on a long patrol last night. Means they walked out a couple miles and went in a quarter-circle around northwest Evergreen. They aren't back yet, which worries me."

"Uh oh," whispered Lorelei.

Madison's expression turned somewhat grim, almost a 'here we go again' look.

"What now?" asked Jonathan, his voice teetering on the edge of tears.

"Hey, don't panic yet." Harper pulled him into a hug. "Maybe they just found a cabin or something with a stash of supplies or walked unusually slow. We don't know anything bad happened to them. I'm going to grab a couple more militia and go retrace the route they followed last night."

"Okay." Jonathan exhaled. "Please be careful."

"Don't let the bad guys get you." Lorelei hugged her.

"You promised not to die," said Madison, avoiding eye contact.

"I did, and I intend to keep my promise." Harper hugged Madison, though her sister didn't unfold her arms. *Crap. She's angry with me.* "Going to take a couple militia with me and it's not far. We'll be back in a few hours. Not like we're marching a week to another town. It's the area right west of Evergreen."

"Okay," muttered Madison.

*Ugh. Am I being stupid for doing this or is she being needy?*

"You three be good, and stay safe." Harper tried to project confidence so the kids didn't sense how worried she'd become about Cliff. "The farm can be dangerous."

"Yeah. Kyle had a metal blade stuck in his leg the other week." Madison stared down at her sneakers. "They carried him right in front of us."

"Ack. Why didn't you say something?" Harper blinked.

"Because I've seen more blood when you shot the jerks in Lakewood. Kyle getting hurt was just an accident." Madison offered a blasé shrug.

Harper delayed for a moment or two more, reassuring the kids she'd be absolutely careful. Finally, they appeared willing to go back to their tasks. *Maybe I shouldn't treat Maddie like a glass faerie so much. She's tougher than I give her credit for.* Grumbling mentally at herself for being too sensitive, Harper fast-walked away from the farm, intent on finding some militia willing to go with her.

"Harp?" called Logan.

She stopped.

He jogged over. "You look like something's wrong. What's up?"

"It's Cliff…" She explained the situation. "Going to grab a couple people for a search party and trace the route."

"Cool. I'll go."

"You've already been shot once." She poked him in the side. "Don't want you to get shot again."

"Not my plan." He took her hands, staring into her eyes. "We're family, right? Gotta stick together."

"You don't have to impress me to get into my pants. I've already made the decision."

Logan flashed a roguish smile. "I'm *so* looking forward to it. Wish we had more time together."

Perhaps she had been nervous about the idea and not exactly making time when she could, but she'd address the issue once the current crisis ended. "Okay. Not going to stand here and argue when Cliff might need help fast."

They hurried down Route 74 toward town. At the approach of running footsteps coming up behind them, Harper looked back—to find Madison sprinting down the highway.

*Crap. Here it comes.*

Rather than burst into tears or cling, Madison stopped a few paces away, her expression determined. She seemed a little winded from the run, but kept her voice controlled. "I'm going with you. He's our dad now and I don't want to lose him, too. I gotta help."

Harper's lip quivered. She hadn't quite realized how attached her little sister had become to Cliff. Losing him could easily send her straight back into the semi-catatonic state she'd been in for weeks after their parents died. A small glint of worry in her kid sister's eyes said she also feared Harper disappearing, too.

Hearing Madison say she didn't want to lose *another* father stabbed Harper in the feels. "I'm sorry, Termite."

"No way. I'm going." Madison pushed at her. "Go. We're wasting time. Walk."

"Not that. I'm sorry Dad died. I choked."

Madison stopped trying to shove her and stared for a moment. "It's not your fault."

"I choked. I could've shot the Lawless f—bastard."

"No, Harp." Madison leaned against her. "You can't even step on bugs. Even Dad didn't think you'd be able to shoot a person. He gave you the Mossberg because it's so big and loud you'd scare people away just by pointing it at them."

Harper sniffle-laughed. "I'm pretty sure he didn't want me to just wave it around."

"Well, Dad also knew you could shave a mole off a pig's backside at thirty feet with a twelve-gauge." Madison winked.

"Termite, I don't know if I can protect you out there and do everything else. It's so stupid for you to go out there away from the protection of town."

"I know," said Madison. "But you're my big sis and we are gonna stay together no matter what, okay? I *can't* sit here being scared when I don't know what's happened to you."

"What if there's something dangerous out there? Cliff's way better at this soldier crap than us. I don't want you to die."

Madison narrowed her eyes. "I don't want you to die, either. Why don't *you* stay home and let the other militia people look?"

*It's just a long walk around town. I don't have time to argue with her.*

"All right. Fine. C'mon."

Madison's expression said 'wow, really?' for only a second before she again put on a look of pure determination.

Logan gave Harper side eye.

"Yes, I'm serious," muttered Harper as she resumed fast-walking down the highway. "It's not far and we're wasting time. I make her stay and she's worried sick about both of us. She's got every bit as much reason as me to go after Cliff."

"She's ten," said Logan.

"Kids her age fought in the Civil War."

He exhaled hard. "Doesn't make it right."

"Umm," said Madison. "I'm not fighting in a war. We're trying to find Dad."

Harper put an arm around her shoulders. "If you're scared, you can stay in town. I'll find him."

"Not scared. What makes you think I'm scared?"

"Thought it took you a bit to work up the nerve to follow me. You could've asked to go right away."

"Umm, I didn't want to say it in front of Jon and Lore. They'd both want to go, too. And you'd never have let all *three* of us go. You'd have asked Jon to keep an eye on me and left me behind."

Harper chuckled nervously. "Probably."

She rushed back to their house on Hilltop Drive long enough to grab a spare Beretta 92 from Cliff's room. After checking it to make sure it was loaded and on safe, she stuffed it in a nylon holster and put the belt on Madison.

"Whoa." Logan pointed. "Are you seriously giving her a gun?"

"No. I'm letting her borrow it," muttered Harper. "It's not a gift."

Madison laughed.

"C'mon, you know what I mean." Logan rested a hand on Harper's shoulder.

"Bad enough she's going with us outside town. I won't leave her totally helpless. She went to the range with me and Dad all the time... just never loved shooting enough to do competitions. This is the same type of pistol she used before. Hell, I didn't *love* shooting either, but it made Dad so happy."

"You didn't hate it." Madison smiled.

"No... I didn't hate it. Yeah, I enjoyed it even, but it wouldn't have broken my heart to stop."

Madison lowered her arms to her sides once Harper finished securing the gun belt around her waist. "I won't touch it except for an extreme situation."

"What's an extreme situation to you?" asked Logan.

Harper headed off down the hall.

Madison rushed after her. "A bad guy or bear finds my hiding place and no one is able to stop them from hurting me."

Logan grumbled, but followed.

They headed down Hilltop and back to the militia HQ. To avoid having to explain to Walter why Madison carried a handgun, she waited outside while Logan went to requisition a rifle for the search party.

While they waited for him to return, Deacon exited the building. Predictably, the sight of Madison wearing a holster attracted his attention, so he walked over. "'Sup with the kid packin' heat?"

"Mental health day." Harper sighed, then explained the situation regarding Cliff not being home in the morning. "We're going to look for them. Walter said I should bring a few people for backup. Speaking of which, you're basically half the militia…"

Deacon laughed. "Yeah, I'll go along. Not sure it's a good idea to bring the little one though."

"I'm not *that* little. And I have to help our dad. He's been there for us."

Logan emerged from the HQ building carrying an AK47 and wearing a black hip bag he didn't have before, probably containing a spare magazine or two. "All set. By the way, Walter said Madison should stay at the center of the group and take cover if anything happens."

*Crap.* Harper's face burned hot the same way it did when Cliff nabbed her for shoplifting at fourteen. *He's seriously not storming out here and yelling at me? Guess he thinks it's fairly safe.* She exhaled. *We're not going far from town.*

She hurried north up Route 74, propelled by worry.

Ken Zhang, Leigh Preston, and Darnell Buck staffed the bus barrier at the big intersection where Lewis Ridge Road crossed the highway. Harper paused there long enough to explain the search party. She didn't expect any of them to join, owing to the need to keep up defenses at the buses, but Leigh decided to go with them, probably to help protect Madison.

"You sure?" asked Harper. "Don't you need to stay here?"

"Technically, I ought to, but this M-16 doesn't have a scope."

Leigh patted her rifle. "Mostly here to help out if the snipers can't pick off threats before they get too close... or if someone who looks harmless pulls a weapon after approaching to talk. Help is an air-horn away. You need at least one more body along, especially if you're going to bring Maddie."

Madison's expression gave off guilt and hesitation, but she didn't change her mind.

Neither Darnell nor Ken looked terribly keen on the idea of bringing a kid out on a 'long patrol,' but they both knew her well enough to understand what Harper hoped to do in regard to her sister's mental health.

Before she changed her mind and started a long argument with Madison, Harper thanked Leigh for coming, and started down Route 74. Though hazy, the sky promised reasonably clear weather for a search party.

*Please don't be too bad a scene. If he's dead, let me find him before she sees him.*

# 16

# HELPING DAD

T hey headed north along Evergreen Parkway, also known as Route 74.

Harper barely glanced to the right at her usual patrol area as they passed it. A little bit north of the residential neighborhood sat a small shopping center in front of a fire station and an elementary school farther in from the road. As best she knew, no one had been in any of those buildings since the initial scavenging the militia carried out before she arrived in Evergreen.

Not far past the shopping center, Route 74 became a pair of bridges spanning a shallow valley. A formerly nice two-tone brown and beige building stood beside the nearer of two lakes to the right. Minutes after crossing the bridge, they reached the intersection with Squaw Pass Road. At the corner on the right stood a long three-story building resembling a huge alpine ski lodge. She assumed it to be a former hotel until noticing a tattered blue banner hanging on the banister of the second story porch closest to the highway: 'Saint Anthony Health Center.' Another sign on the north-facing side read 'Tuscany Tavern.'

*Oh… it's a shopping center. Weird they made it look like a giant log cabin.*

She headed left, retracing the route Cliff and Roy would've taken last night after dark.

Squaw Pass road followed a low spot among the hills. The hilly terrain on both sides stretched for miles. trees occasionally dotted the landscape, but the woods remained far enough off the road not to make her worry *too* much about danger hiding among them. Plenty of open land between the road and woods made an ambush unlikely, though a lone wacko lying in wait with a sniper rifle could be an issue.

As Walter suggested, the group arranged themselves protectively around Madison. Harper, walking at the lead, occasionally looked back to make sure her kid sister handled leaving town okay. Madison appeared calm, though her eyes couldn't get any wider. She didn't swing her arms much while walking, and kept looking around — pretty much the way she used to act crossing parking lots at night before the war. Fortunately, she didn't make any move to reach for the Beretta on her belt, almost behaving as if she'd forgotten entirely about having it.

*She's afraid of bad guys but not freaking out.*

They followed Squaw Pass Road for a little over an hour, finding no trace of Cliff, Roy, or anyone else alive or dead. Gradually, the wide-open spaces on either side of the road closed in. To the right of the highway, the ground fell into a treacherous downhill slope. On the left, an equally steep incline covered in dense trees came within mere feet from the edge of the paving. The narrow, straight trunks had no branches close to the ground, making them useless as hiding places. They provided *some* cover, but in the daylight, anyone could see thirty feet or so deep into the forest up the hill. Unless they had on a bush suit, anyone lurking in the woods would be obvious.

The road curved gently to the left, leading into a sharper rightward bend where the forest on either side became much thicker. A piece of spent 5.56 rifle brass sat on the pavement ahead near the center of the ninety-degree curve. Harper stopped short about twenty paces from it. The brass could've come from Cliff's rifle, but tons of people had AR-15s or M-16s, not exactly a rare ammunition.

*Still sorta shiny. It hasn't been there long.*

She froze still, moving only her eyes to scan the woods on either side of the curve. The shadowy forms of people in hooded jackets trying to stand still lurked amid the dense foliage—three on the left up the hill, two on the right. As best as she could, she tried to act as if she didn't notice them. If any of the people in hiding had rifles, they kept them pointed down, hidden behind trees or perhaps laid flat on the ground. The two on the downhill side had a mild disadvantage of lower ground, far enough away from the road their heads sat below the level of the pavement. To the left, the three had roughly twenty-five feet of fairly steep, overgrown hill to cover before reaching flat road. Despite having an elevated position, their footing looked far from stable. They wouldn't be able to charge or move out of their cover fast without a high chance of falling.

"Three left, two right," whispered Harper.

Deacon, Logan, and Sadie aimed their rifles into the woods. Madison dove to the ground on her belly, right on the center paint line. Harper pivoted to aim at the people on the right.

"Not looking for a fight," called Harper. "What are your intentions?"

"Easy," said a man from the uphill side. "Just defending our territory."

Harper risked a quick glance toward the voice. Two of the three figures she'd spotted crouching on up the hill stood before descending to the road, grabbing trees on their way to steady themselves. One man made no effort to move. She redirected her focus to the men to her right. Both eased themselves upright before walking up the hill. Neither had rifles, though she didn't trust them not to be hiding handguns or knives under their Army coats.

*Who wears coats in August?*

Still, as they didn't point weapons at her, she lowered her aim. She also didn't trust them, so she lowered it only a little.

"Defending your territory?" asked Deacon. "By laying an ambush?"

"Just observing. I'm Bill," said a thirtysomething dude in serious need of personal grooming. "What are you folks up to?"

"One still hiding," whispered Leigh. "Watching him."

"Looking for some friends who went missing." Logan pointed his rifle at the trees. "Few bullet holes in the woods there look pretty new."

Harper flicked a glance at the lighter brown spot on the trunk. *Dammit. I should have seen those.*

"Get the occasional bear or mountain lion out this way. Decent eats." Bill chuckled.

*Those hits are pretty high up the trunks to have been shooting at animals.* She squeezed the Mossberg's pistol grip a little tighter imagining a black bear coming out of nowhere. *Bears do stand up on two legs sometimes, right?*

The two men coming up the downhill side reached the edge of the road. Both wore similar, relatively thin olive drab Army style coats and fatigue pants. They also appeared about a year overdue for a shave.

"Can't say I have." Bill shrugged. "Not many people out this way lately."

"If the road's so empty, why are you hiding here?" asked Harper. "Kinda implies you saw us coming and planned to ambush when we got close enough."

"Nah, we're just a bunch of survivalists trying to get by." Bill ogled Harper's chest. "You all got a place to sleep?"

"We do." Deacon stepped closer to Bill. "Mind where ya be starin'."

Bill held his hands up, flashing an insincere grin. "Heh. Sorry. Been a while since we had a lady around." He flicked his right hand forward into a pointing gesture at Deacon. "No trouble, big man."

A second later, Leigh fired into the woods. A man's wail of agony followed.

Chaos erupted.

The four 'survivalists' on the road all sprang into motion at the same time.

Bill lunged to grab Harper

Man Two pulled a handgun from his coat pocket.

Man Three (on the downhill side) drew a machete and charged Logan.

Man Four (also on the downhill side) rushed at Leigh from behind her.

*Gun!* Harper aimed for the narrowing gap between Bill and Deacon, squeezing off a shot at the last second. Man Two ate a faceload of buckshot. His pistol went flying as he crumpled over backward. Bill's lunge at her ended to Deacon walloping the butt of his rifle across the man's jaw. Logan hastily ripped a burst of automatic fire at the machete-wielding man running at him, barely controlling his AK-47, which spat the last two bullets almost straight up. Man Four abruptly changed course, grabbing Harper from behind instead of pouncing on Leigh. He seized her in a bear hug, squeezing her arms into her sides and picking her up off her feet. She kicked around and thrashed to no avail. Leigh fired twice more at the screaming man up the hill in the trees.

"Let go of her!" shouted Madison. "I mean it."

The guy holding Harper spun, swinging her around.

Deacon's gun went off behind her, likely ending Bill.

Madison stood in the middle of the road, holding the Beretta in a two-handed grip, legs wide like a rookie Hollywood cop on her first day.

Harper couldn't move her arms or maneuver the Mossberg. She let go with one hand, hammering her fist into his balls—but he had a Kevlar cup or something under his pants. The harder she hit him, the more he seemed amused by her struggling. She switched tactics and rammed the heel of her hiking shoe into his shin.

He grunted, stumbling to the side. "Do that again and I'm gonna—"

Madison spun to her right, firing a single shot into the trees on the downhill side.

A man yowled in pain.

Harper caught a brief glimpse of a guy in a ghillie suit, right arm up over his head. Blood sprayed from his elbow. A throwing hatchet tumbled from his raised hand, falling to the ground behind him with a dull *thump*. Deacon one-hand grabbed the guy holding Harper around the neck. The man squeezed her so hard in a desperate attempt to save himself from Deacon, she expected a rib or two to crack any second. A shot rang out from far up the hill an instant before the high-pitched *ping* of a bullet ricocheting off the road came from *way* too close. Madison shrieked and darted to cover on the downhill. Logan fired twice at the man who tried to throw the hatchet, finishing him off. Madison hit the dirt behind some trees, out of sight below the road. Harper wobbled around as Deacon tried to peel the man off her. Another shot came from high left. The bullet whistled past Harper's head, far too close for comfort.

*They're trying to kill Deacon but leave me alive… oh shit.*

Fueled by terror at ending up someone's pet, Harper thrashed in a wild frenzy, loosening the man's grip around her.

Leigh fired a rapid barrage up the hill. A male voice grunted an instant before another body came tumbling down the incline.

A sickening *crack* came from behind Harper's head; the arms wrapped around her went limp. She clenched her jaw tight and shoved her way free. Deacon flung the dead guy to the road.

"Hey now," said a man to the right in a saccharin tone. "You're not going to shoot me, kid, are you?"

Harper whirled.

A second man in a crude ghillie suit made from a green poncho, duct tape, and tree branches, had gotten close enough undetected to grab Madison's left ankle. It appeared he tried to drag her into his grip but she'd rolled onto her back and put the Beretta under his chin, causing a stalemate. The glint of a knife concealed in his other hand caught Harper's eye.

Logan pointed his AK at the man. "Let go of her, now!"

*Maddie!* She couldn't see her sister's face, but the shaking hand proved the girl couldn't kill a man.

Harper aimed at his head. "She won't shoot you, but I will."

The instant her little sister cringed away, Harper fired. The man's face burst into a spray of blood. He collapsed, sliding down the hill. Madison curled up against a tree, refusing to look.

Logan blinked at Harper. "You shot him."

"Guy had a knife behind his back. Didn't want him to use it on Maddie."

Deacon spat to the side. "Most likely would'a just held it to her neck to threaten us."

"Still." Harper frowned.

"I mean…" Logan pointed at the woods. "The guy was like three feet away from Maddie and you shot him."

"Yeah. I know." Harper flicked the Mossberg's safety on and off repetitively. "It's stupid, but I thought more about not wanting her to watch than firing over her. I had a clean shot."

"Damn," whispered Logan. "Clean to you and clean to me aren't the same. Then again, I barely know what I'm doing with this thing."

"Clear left," said Sadie.

Harper scanned the downhill side. The only motion came from the dead man in the sad ghillie poncho continuing to roll-slide away. "Looks clear on the right."

"What the ffff—," Leigh scowled.

"You can say it." Madison climbed back onto the road, faintly trembling. She glanced down at the Beretta, flicked the safety on, and re-holstered it. "I just watched like a bunch of men die and shot one of them. I don't think hearing a bad word's going to be worse than that."

"Looks like you got that one." Deacon clapped Logan on the shoulder while eyeing the corpse of the machete guy. "Six or seven times."

"Didn't realize it was on full auto." Logan fiddled at the selector lever. "Sorry for wasting ammo."

Harper glanced left at the first guy Leigh shot, the one who didn't leave the trees when the others first revealed themselves. He'd tumbled to the bottom of the hill, face pressed to the road. Blood still poured liberally from a large bullet hole above his left eye. A flap of skin-covered skull, a foot or two of silvery hair still attached, hung off the side of the exit wound at the back of his head. Unlike the others, he looked to be at least fifty, maybe even sixty years old. Under his Army-green plastic rain poncho, he wore the filthy, stained polo shirt of a FedEx delivery driver. Blood-soaked bandages and a splint braced his left leg below the knee, suggesting he'd been injured recently. *He probably didn't move because it hurt too much.*

Leigh climbed the hill into the trees.

"Where are you going?" asked Harper.

"Other guy dropped a rifle. Going after it. 'Bill'—if that was really his name—gave the dude kissing the road a signal to shoot Deacon. Soon as he lifted the rifle, I aerated his skull."

"Much obliged." Deacon laughed, then patted Madison on the head. "Damn fine marksmanship, kid. Hittin' the elbow like that. Careful though. Being fancy can get you killed."

"I was aiming for his chest," said Madison, her voice toneless. "But I guess I didn't want to kill him."

Harper brushed a hand over her sister's head. "I don't *want* to kill anyone, either. The world just keeps putting me in situations where I don't have a choice. Are you okay?"

"Kinda," said Madison. "I couldn't do it. Not when the man was right there in front of me, looking at me."

"Termite..." Harper gripped her sister by the shoulders, staring into her eyes. "Trust me, I know exactly how you feel. Taking a life isn't a thing that's supposed to be easy for people. I'm *so* glad you're still normal enough to hesitate. I hope you never wind up being put in a situation where you have to take someone's life. I... already broke that seal. Let me do it."

Madison bowed her head, tears gathering but not falling. "I can't even stand killing fish. Yeah, I shot the one guy but didn't even think about it. Just a reaction. Maybe I could do it if someone was about to kill me or hurt you, but it's stupid of me to be out here when I don't have to be. I'm sorry. I shouldn't have demanded you bring me along. It's like I made you choose between me or Dad. I'm still too small to do this. A bullet bounced off the road like *right* next to me. You're right. I should stay in town. The best way I can help you help Dad is to stay where it's safe. I'll go home if you want."

Harper hugged her. "You can stay in town for the next crisis. We're too far out for you to be alone. I can't send you on an hour-long walk by yourself."

"Sorry for shooting. I jumped when the bush turned into a guy and started to throw an axe at me. Then another guy came out of nowhere. I'm gonna have nightmares about bush monsters now." Madison gave an uneasy laugh.

Harper gasped. "At *you*?"

"Uhh. Looked like it." Madison fidgeted. "He popped up so fast with an axe up in the air, I just wanted to stop him from attacking us. Didn't really look at him much before shooting. Maybe he was gonna throw it at Deacon, but he looked right at me."

"Does sound kinda silly to sacrifice surprise and lose his hiding spot to attack a little kid, even if she did have a gun pointed at one of his buddies." Deacon shook his head. "Probably meant to take me or Logan out. Got the feelin' those dudes had other plans for the ladies."

Harper shivered. "Other plans... yeah, right. I'm sure they did. Exactly why I let her carry a weapon."

"What is *wrong* with people?" yelled Madison, shaking her hands in the air. "The world burned. We should all be trying to help each other."

"Dudes could be crazy. Maybe criminals before the war, or just the sort of people who always wanted to do illegal crap but were too afraid of jail to bother. Now, ain't no jail." Deacon kicked Bill's corpse. "War didn't make these fools do dumb crap. The itch was always in 'em."

Leigh half walked, half slid down the hill carrying a bolt action rifle in her left hand, the M-16 in her right hand. "Looks like a .308. Not in bad shape. Worth bringing back. Saw a light on in a small house a little up the road from here. Probably where these idiots lived."

"A light?" Harper blinked. "They have electricity?"

She nodded. "Gotta have solar panels."

"Do we have time for scavenging?" asked Logan.

"No, but we do have time to make sure these creeps didn't kidnap any other women." Harper searched the man she shot in the face, recovering a few handfuls of .40 caliber pistol ammo plus collecting the Sig handgun, which landed a few yards away from the body.

Leigh rummaged the pockets of the FedEx guy.

"Damn, that's nasty." Deacon walked up beside Harper, wincing. "Why'd you shoot homeboy in the kisser?"

"Baggy coat. Didn't know if he had Kevlar on under it." *Faces are the same size as plate targets.*

"You okay, kid?" asked Deacon in a lowered voice. "Getting' that thousand-yard look in your eyes."

She exhaled. "Yeah fine. Just bad memories. Well, not bad memories, but they feel kind of psychotic now."

"Wanna talk about it?"

"Nothing too crazy. Just thinking about being thirteen and going to the range with my dad, shooting plates out of the air and thinking it was super fun. Laughing, cheering, the first time I hit one... never even thought it trained me to kill people."

"Ahh."

"The twisted part is my brain associating how happy I was to get to a point where I could reliably hit flying targets and imagining my younger self cheering and laughing over blowing some dude's head out like a hollow egg."

"Ick," said Madison. "Can you please talk about something else?"

# 17

# MARKSMAN

A short distance farther down the road from the ambush site, Leigh led them up a tree-studded hill toward a house on the south side.

"I don't think Cliff and Roy could've gone past here and not run into those guys," said Logan. "Wood around those bullet holes looked newly exposed."

Harper stared down. "Yeah. I know." She couldn't bring herself to say she also wanted to search the house for Cliff or Roy's possessions… or bodies. Didn't make sense those 'survivalists' would bring bodies home unless they'd gone *way* off the deep end into cannibalism.

The light Leigh mentioned in the window appeared to be a fairly weak electrical light inside the house, undoubtedly powered by solar panels on the roof. Assuming she didn't find anything in this place too disgusting, she made a note of it. Jeanette and her people could come out here and grab the panels for Evergreen. The group crossed the flat pavement of a long, switchback driveway twice on the way up the steep incline. At the end, the asphalt expanded into a bit of a courtyard where a huge separate garage stood catty-corner to the main house, a massive two-story structure.

*Whoa. Whoever lived in this place had a lot of money.* She whistled in awe, mentally. *This is like one of those houses they use for murder mystery movies.* "Okay... time is short. Not here to go crazy and tear the place apart looking for stuff. Just search for victims, maybe ammo..." Harper sighed. "Maybe Cliff and Roy's stuff."

Everyone fell quiet.

"Sorry," whispered Harper. "The guy with the sniper rifle didn't shoot himself in the leg. Who else would've gone past those jackasses recently?"

Logan held up a finger. "But, no blood on the road. Could be a good sign."

Deacon cupped his hands around his mouth and bellowed, "Anyone here? If some crazy sons o' bitches grabbed y'all, we here to help."

Silence.

Leigh headed over to the garage and peeked in via a normal person-sized door at the corner. She recoiled after only a moment. "Ack. It's a bloody mess in there. Six dead. Doesn't look like anyone familiar."

"How can you tell so fast?" asked Logan.

"They're all laid out in a row, naked on the floor like someone was preparing them for burial... or maybe cremation. Doesn't smell *too* bad in there, so they all died pretty recently."

Harper shivered. *Please be burial and not butchering.*

Deacon led the way to the house, nudging the front door open with the tip of his rifle. "Hello? Anyone in here? If you're bein' held against your will, speak up and we'll get you out."

"We're not trying to trick you," yelled Harper. "I know he sounds scary, but he's not."

The crying of a small baby started.

"Aww, shit," whispered Deacon.

Leigh and Logan headed upstairs while Harper and Deacon rushed from room to room on the ground floor, rapid-clearing in search of armed threats or prisoners. Madison remained in the living room, watching the door in case anyone tried to sneak in behind them. The lump sitting in Harper's throat shrank little by little the more she looked around and didn't see any items or clothing belonging to Cliff or Roy.

*If they did get into a shootout with those idiots, where are they? Did they chase the idiots away or did the idiots chase Cliff and Roy into the woods, wounded? Are they buried out there?* She grumbled to herself. Ranger and ex-cop or not, two on six, eight, fifteen, or however many there'd been the other night didn't make for wonderful odds. Their sniper had been wounded in the leg, not killed. But they had a sniper. Did the guy manage to hit Roy or Cliff before they got him in the leg? Logan pointed out a lack of blood on the road. It didn't seem at all likely these fools would've cleaned any up.

*Yeah... I'm sure Dad saw the ambush coming. Probably opened fire right away. People with good intentions don't set up a crossfire ambush.*

In a back bedroom, Harper located the source of the crying: a maybe-one-year-old boy in a makeshift pen. From the looks of it, the 'survivalists' hadn't bothered with diapers. The baby wore only a coating of his own runny poo he'd evidently been frolicking in for some time.

"Oh, gawd." She coughed at the rancid sour-milk smell, then checked the last bedroom.

Fairly certain the ground floor contained no threats, she slung the Mossberg over her shoulder and headed to the bathroom to test the faucet. It produced a weak trickle of water. *Gotta be a ground well... maybe an electric pump. The lights aren't too bright. System's not producing much power.* She left the sink filling and crossed the hall to collect the baby from the foulness he'd been stuck in. Holding her breath, she gingerly reached down to grasp him under the arms. The instant she touched him, he stopped screaming, staring up at her in awe.

"Hey, little guy. You don't belong here. Oh, my. You have a bit of a poo situation going on."

He emitted happy baby noises.

"All right, squirmy. Sit still. Let's get you cleaned up." As if transporting a small crucible of radioactive waste, she held him at arm's length while carrying him across the hall. "Sorry, kiddo. But a pooptastrophe of this magnitude is more pressing than a lack of hot water. It's not *ice* cold, but the water heater is apparently having mood swings or an existential crisis at the moment."

Predictably, he squealed when she plonked him seated in the tepid water.

Deacon poked his head in. "Aww, man. What the hell?"

"They left him alone when they ran out the door to ambush us." Harper washed the boy as fast as she could. "Maybe they wanted to grab me or Leigh to deal with him."

"Yeah, right," muttered Deacon.

She closed her eyes under the weight of a sudden guilt crash. "Crap. Please tell me we didn't just kill his parents."

"If we did, just the dad. No women around." Deacon made a silly face at the baby.

"One of them could've been the father." Harper sighed.

"They shouldn't have tried to kill and kidnap us then," said Madison from the doorway. "I'm not saying it's good they died, but it's not our fault. Besides, they probably stole him from someone. *Parents* would take better care of him."

Harper exhaled out her nose. "Yeah. Good point. He looks way too healthy—as in fed properly—to have been here long."

"Doubt any of those dudes were breast feeding him." Deacon chuckled.

"Eww," said Madison from the bathroom doorway.

Harper raised an eyebrow. "What do you expect mothers to do now? Run to the store for formula and Gerber?"

Madison rolled her eyes. "Not eww-ing at the idea of breast feeding. I'm eww-ing at the idea of a *man* trying to breast feed a baby." She stepped into the bathroom, holding up a purple bundle. "Here, I found a big towel."

"Give me a minute… he's got poop everywhere. It's in his damn ears." She glanced sideways at Deacon. "I'm surprised you're not retching. Most guys can't handle baby poop."

Deacon chuckled. "Saw plenty o' things in the joint way, *way* worse than this little dude. I'll spare ya the details. You don't wanna know."

"Eww." Madison cringed. "Umm. I should really go back home. I'll take him with me. It's not *that* far."

"No way, Termite. I don't want you running off alone." Harper twisted toilet paper into an improvised ear-cleaning device. Miraculously, the baby tolerated the cleaning, amusing himself by gripping Deacon's finger. "Aww, such a good boy. You know. You don't want poop in your ears, do you?"

He cooed.

"But he's just a baby," said Madison. "We can't take him with us on a mission."

"You're not going off alone. Carrying a baby is still alone. We stay together like you said, right?" Harper spun the boy around to clean his left ear.

Madison gestured at him. "You want to bring a little baby to wherever Dad might've gotten hurt?"

"Kiddo, that's how your sister feels about bringin' you along here." Deacon ruffled Madison's hair.

"He's a little small to carry a gun," deadpanned Madison. "I can sorta defend myself if I get cornered. He's completely helpless."

Deacon shook his head. "Dunno, Harp. I ain't at all comfortable sendin' a ten-year-old and a baby off alone."

Harper looked over at her sister when the girl *didn't* point out she'd turn eleven in two months. Madison stared glumly at the floor. *She thought it. Definitely thought she's 'not really ten' anymore. Dammit. She's going to have a hard time on her birthday. I think we both are. How am I going to keep her mind off Mom and Dad for a whole day?* Harper drained the sink, refilled it with clean water, and rinsed the baby, pouring cups of water over his hair a few times before lifting him out of the sink. *She didn't even notice her tenth birthday. We were all still too numb from everything.*

Madison wrapped the boy in the huge towel. "Hey there, little man. What's your name?"

The baby made a face at her. Harper pictured him thinking 'who the heck is this bitch' based on his expression, and cracked up.

Madison responded to the silly face with a sillier face. The boy smiled, laughing.

Deacon shook his head. "Well, you two got the baby situation under control. Gonna keep checkin' the house."

*Ugh.* Harper dried her hands on the towel. *Cliff's not going to like me bringing Maddie out here. Now a damn baby, too?*

She and Madison returned to the living room, where Logan and Leigh searched a collection of metal Army style boxes.

"Not a crapload, but some ammo we can use." Leigh looked up smiling, but gawked when she spotted the baby.

Logan gestured at the stairs. "House is clear. No prisoners or dead here."

"The bodies in the garage... were any of them women?" asked Harper.

"Nope." Leigh poured all the bullets from different ammo cans into one. "Someone's going to get stuck sorting these later, but I'm not carrying eight cans for three-quarters of one can's worth of ammo."

"So... baby." Harper glanced at Logan. "Cliff's going to ream me out already for putting Maddie in danger."

"Maybe, but there's more than physical health to think about. We're not in the same world we grew up in. She's going to inherit a totally different reality. Hiding from bad guys and foraging for food instead of sleepovers and cheer practice."

Madison scoffed. "I am not a cheerleader. You mean sleepovers and dance class."

Logan laughed.

*We just got into a shootout where she shot a man and she's making jokes about dance class. Either she's coping really well or on the train to crazytown. Hell, we're all on the train to crazytown. I shot a dude in the face without batting an eye, but I won't step on a stupid beetle? Yeah. I'm totally sane. Not.*

"Maddie's learning important skills." Logan patted her on the shoulder. "Any person from a normal world would think it's crazy to bring her along, but it's good she's getting a little learning on this messed up reality we're stuck in."

"You could've said the trip was educational and I'd have stayed home." Madison smiled for a moment, then looked sad. "Sorry. I should've stayed so you didn't worry about me."

"It's all right. I should've been firmer about insisting you stay safe… but I'm worried about you."

"Obviously." Madison poked her in the side.

"I mean up here." Harper tapped her head. "We have to stick together."

"Yeah. I'm good. Not going to start talking to dead phones again. I'm… adjusting." Madison looked over at Leigh. "Any 9mm in there? I'm short one."

Logan and Deacon chuckled.

Leigh stared at her in disbelief.

"All right, guess I'll carry the little guy." Harper reached for him.

Logan intercepted, grabbing the baby from Madison. "Why would it be your job?"

"Oh, come on. You're not that dense. Leigh and I are the only women here and she's already carrying ammo cans and two rifles. Maddie's a little small to lug a one-year-old baby for miles."

"You're also a way better shot than me." Logan winked. "I got him. Just need to bundle him a little better."

The instant Logan unwrapped the towel, the baby shot a stream of pee into the air, hitting him close to square in the left eye.

"Gah!" Logan pivoted, aiming the stream off to the side.

Madison and Leigh cracked up. Harper covered her mouth so she didn't laugh quite as obviously.

Deacon's baritone laugh vibrated the walls. "Looks like Harper's not the only marksman in the room."

18

# NO SIGNAL

Once confident the house contained no kidnap victims or any items belonging to Cliff or Roy, they left to resume searching the patrol route.

Harper cut down the hill to the longer section of driveway, following it to the road. Logan moved to the middle of the group, right behind Madison, since he carried the baby. Deacon advanced to walk beside Harper up front while Leigh had rear guard.

A FEW MINUTES SHORT OF AN HOUR LATER, THEY REACHED A split where the highway forked from Squaw Pass Road to *Old* Squaw Pass Road on the right and Colorado 103 on the left. Based on her notes, she headed left. Minutes later, she spotted an elevated dirt road veering uphill to the left from Route 103. A metal swing gate somewhat blocked it off. No signs indicated what the trail was, but it definitely did not look like Route 475, so she kept going.

"Let me carry him," said Madison. "If we find more bad guys, they're not gonna realize you're holding a baby and shoot you."

Logan sighed. "All right. I could use a break. He may be small, but he's heavy after an hour. Be careful. He's not a doll."

"I'm not an idiot." Madison smirked.

"Hope he don't get hungry," said Deacon. "He starts crying, it's going to be a siren telling everyone where we are."

Leigh scanned the area. "Good thing we're not in the middle of enemy territory. Figure most people we run into aren't going to be an immediate problem."

"Explain those other idiots." Madison collected the baby from Logan. "Oof. Yeah, he is a little heavy."

"One pack of morons doesn't mean everyone out here's got their heads up their asses." Deacon grinned. "Only a few of those fools had guns. Compared to most out here, we are too heavily armed to mess with."

"Yeah, even the innocent little girls are armed." Logan ruffled Madison's hair.

"Ha. Ha." She bounced the baby. "I've got the heavy weapon. I'll just point his butt at bad guys and give him a squeeze."

Harper chuckled. "He's out of ammo. Used it up already."

Madison gagged.

They continued walking along Colorado 103, looking around for any signs of a shootout or fight. The total emptiness—not a single abandoned car—made everything seem unreal and dreamlike, as though she merely had a nightmare of being among the last people alive on the planet.

*Little too close to reality.* She squeezed her grip on the Mossberg. *Hope we're just some of the last people alive in the* country, *not the world. Did anyone nuke Australia or New Zealand? Wonder if people down there are still going on like normal.*

Hours later, they reached a rightward bend in the road with a sizable dirt clearing on the inside of the curve. Up ahead lay the intersection with Route 103, where she needed to go.

*How the hell do they navigate this at night without getting lost? Maybe they* did *simply get lost? Made a wrong turn?*

A hint of motion came from her right, farther along Squaw Pass Road.

Harper held a hand up in a warning signal, then crouched, squinting at a group of people walking into view where the gradually curving road emerged from thick trees a couple hundred feet away. Everyone lowered themselves to one knee. Logan, who'd been carrying the baby for the past hour or so, handed him off to Madison again before pulling the AK-47 off his shoulder. Harper kept the Mossberg ready but not aimed. Buckshot wouldn't work too well at long range.

Cliff taught her the human eye seeks motion. Sitting still in the middle of the road protected her more than making a mad dash for the trees on the left. Of course, such tactics worked better at night. Even the most oblivious person would notice a group kneeling out in the open. She considered moving left into the woods, since the dirt lot and open field on the right offered zero cover or concealment.

However, it soon became apparent the people at the front of the approaching group were children. Four tweens about Madison's age walked ahead of a woman and four men. Everyone except for two of the men wore a variety of shredded, grimy pre-war clothing that looked like they got into a fight with a lawn mower and lost. It took her only seconds to recognize the man in a blue police-style jumpsuit as Roy Ellis and the man in green camo as Cliff.

Her heart nearly exploded from joy and relief.

"It's them!" shouted Harper, then whispered, "Stand down."

"Dad!" yelled Madison. "Daaaaad!" She handed the infant back to Logan so she could jump up and down while waving her arms.

Even from here, Cliff's 'WTF is she doing out here' stare was obvious.

Leigh, Deacon, Logan, and Madison relaxed and moved closer to Harper, waiting for the other group to move up to their position.

A minute or so later, the ten-or-eleven-year-olds at the lead stopped short a safe ten or so paces away. All filthy, they had to have been living rough in the same clothes ever since the war. All had long hair. Harper guessed the two kids whose hair stopped at their waists —instead of hanging down past their knees—were boys, but couldn't tell for certain. The blonde girl, a willowy twelve-year-old, wore shoes so mummified in duct tape Harper could only guess actual shoes lurked under the tape. The others, except for one man, went barefoot. The oldest of the strangers, a black guy in his later forties, wore sandals made from license plates and foam padding likely taken from a car seat, held on by wires. Harper tried not to breathe too much as the people all gave off a fairly rancid smell. They looked one strong windstorm away from not having clothes at all—which she would consider an improvement purely from a health standpoint. If bacteria could be knitted into garments, this group wore it.

Cliff approached Harper, eyebrow up. "Fancy meeting you out here."

"Holy shit," she exhaled more than said, then collapsed against him. "You didn't come home last night. I got worried."

"We bumped into Randall and his daughter Rylee last night"— Cliff gestured at the dude in sandals, also wearing a shredded AC/DC T-shirt and some scraps of denim pretending to be jeans —"some fools back up the road were taking pot shots at him, so Roy and I got involved."

The youngest kid, a pale, brown-haired girl about ten whose dress consisted more of duct tape than fabric, hugged Randall while smiling adoringly up at Roy and Cliff.

"Please tell me your last name ain't 'Flagg,'" said Deacon, chuckling.

"No sir. Randall Greene." He laughed.

Roy gestured at the people. "Evergreen's expanding again. Randall led us back up into the hills where he and these folks had been living rough."

"Real rough," whispered Logan.

Cliff eyed the baby in Logan's arms. "Dammit. We weren't gone *that* long. You two aren't wasting any time, huh?"

Harper blushed so hard she couldn't speak.

"Uhh…" Logan laughed. "We found him in a house."

Leigh pointed back over her shoulder. "We ran into a little trouble by a bend in the road a ways back. Probably those same guys who gave you trouble. Looked like they'd been in a shootout already."

"Aww hell." Cliff spat to the side. "I told ya we should've cleaned 'em out. Now, we're going to have to go deal with them."

Roy gestured at the girl whose dark brown hair almost reached her ankles. "We had a kid with us."

"Yeah, I know, but." Cliff pointed at Madison. "So did they."

"Uhh, pretty sure we already dealt with them." Harper exhaled hard. "I did see them before they could spring the ambush. A piece of 5.56 brass on the road gave it away."

"Idiots," muttered Cliff. "What are you doing out here?"

Harper took a deep breath, bracing for the scolding. "You didn't come back by morn—"

"I was talking to you, little lady." Cliff gestured at Madison.

"Umm. I demanded to go, not thinking Harp would say yes. Then, when she did, I guess I was dumb and went. It wasn't fair to Harp, and I won't do it again until I'm older. And…" Madison flung herself into a hug. "I was really worried about our Dad."

Cliff wrapped one arm around her, scratching at his eyebrow with his other hand. "Surprised you didn't bring Jon and Lore, too."

"Ehh." Harper winced. "I wasn't planning on bringing any of them. She kinda followed me away from the farm."

"Carrie's looking after them, and Jon doesn't have my mental issues." Madison clamp-hugged Harper. "I'm super clingy and needy." After a few seconds, she laughed, announcing she meant it as a joke.

Roy introduced the others. Kip West, a prematurely grey-haired man in his early thirties, appeared to be the father of Tristan. The woman, Krystal Tucker, looked pretty young, not far past twenty, and didn't resemble any of the children. The three adults had collectively adopted Allie (the blonde girl), Rylee, and Elliot who all thought of both Randall and Kip as 'Dad' and Krystal as Mom despite being only about ten years older than them.

*Gee, that feels familiar.* Harper mentally hugged Lorelei.

"We decided to head on back and give them an escort to Evergreen," said Cliff. "Sorry for not calling to let you know we'd be late. Can't get any cell signal out here."

Harper chuckled.

"Faster to double back the way you've been walking," said Roy. "This is about the one-third point, distance wise."

"Works for me. The faster we get home, the better." Harper made an 'after you' gesture at Cliff and Roy, relieved to no longer feel responsible for everyone's safety.

Madison wasted no time before talking to the other kids about what Evergreen would be like. Allie, Rylee, Tristan, and Elliot shared stories of sleeping out in the woods, trying to avoid bears, clinging to each other to get through the cold winter, and eating mostly random plants, berries, and even bugs Randall and Kip thought wouldn't kill anyone along with the occasional treasure of canned goods. From the conversation, it didn't sound as if the three adults had any romantic connections, merely working together to help keep each other alive.

Krystal kept sneaking glances at Roy as if she had a crush on him, or maybe his police jumpsuit seemed too clean and modern to believe. Kip and Randall chatted about their eagerness to rejoin something close to civilization. Other than seeming a little quiet and fearful, the kids didn't strike Harper as overly traumatized or feral. Given a bath, haircuts, and clothing not at the verge of disintegration, they'd appear normal. When Rylee announced it would be 'amazing' to go to the bathroom without having to dig a hole, Harper almost cried.

*Kids shouldn't be as thrilled over working toilets as getting a new PlayStation for Christmas.*

At least seeing people who'd been living as uncivilized as possible *not* being crazed marauders gave her hope for the future of humanity. She allowed Cliff and Roy's presence to reassure her enough to suspend hypervigilance for a few minutes and collect her emotions. Finding them alive, okay, and merely helping out some people who needed it made her feel like she overreacted, even if she had no way to know *why* Cliff hadn't been home in the morning. Eventually, she accepted she did the right thing. Brushing aside the idea of freaking out over a non-issue bothered her far less than dealing with the guilt of doing nothing and he never came home.

*Better safe than sorry... our new national motto.*

# 19

## DINOSAUR PASTA

Days later, Harper let go of her anxiety someone would yell at her for the search party.

No one even made a joke about her overreacting. She'd been expecting to hear complaints about leaving her patrol route undefended, risking the safety of Evergreen. Admittedly, things had been fairly calm for a while. It's not as if the Lawless or some other large, organized gang made frequent raids. If the town suffered multiple attacks every week, she might have been more hesitant to rush off after Cliff without a stronger feeling he needed help, and she definitely wouldn't have brought Madison.

Harper spent most of the previous day, August 15th, feeling like some kind of prairie farm daughter in the kitchen with Carrie teaching her, Madison, Becca, Eva… and sorta-teaching Lorelei how to bake a cake not only from scratch but using nonstandard ingredients. The last package of boxed cake mix in the United States had probably grown legs and walked off to find a quiet cave to lair in.

Lorelei tried to pay attention, though no one expected an easily distracted just-turned-seven-year-old to become proficient at cake making from a single day, or even remember much. Carrie had one of those plastic cake protectors, which they used to keep it safe until today... August 16th. Renee's birthday.

Since her friend no doubt expected some manner of 'event' made of the day, Harper didn't bother trying to surprise her, and simply informed Renee to come over directly after she finished up working on fabric. Her team had finally managed to produce useful flax cloth and a few basic children's dresses — or tunics depending on how one looked at it. The people of Evergreen might end up looking like medieval villagers in another few years, but at least they wouldn't go tribal. Harper considered herself fortunate not to live in a region known for hot weather. If it never became cold enough to be uncomfortable, survivors might not bother going to the effort of learning how to make clothes, living like rain forest tribes or something.

The morning passed in routine normality. After finishing her patrol time, she picked the kids up from the farm and walked them home. Madison carried a relatively young rooster she'd gotten permission to adopt. She'd initially wanted to name him 'Pecker' because he had a habit of repeatedly pecking at pebbles, mistaking them for feed. However, when Harper burst out laughing, Madison realized the error of the idea and changed her mind, naming him Mr. Cluck instead. She'd probably take home another hen at some point as well, but hadn't yet decided on which chicken to 'save.'

Upon arriving home, Harper made some sandwiches for lunch while Madison set Mr. Cluck out in the backyard coop with Rosie. The face she made when she sat at the table to find a chicken sandwich waiting for her almost made Harper laugh.

"Seriously?" Madison sighed. "I just spent five minutes introducing Rosie to her new friend."

"If you want to swap the chicken out for jam, go ahead." Harper gestured at the fridge. "We don't *have* to use up an entire jar in one shot now... at least until the power goes out again."

Madison made sour faces at her plate, pondering the 'tragedy' of a dead chicken. "This is like eating babies."

"Oh, come on." Jonathan rolled his eyes. "Stop being melodramatic."

"What's melon dramatic?" asked Lorelei.

"Her." Jonathan pointed. "Chickens aren't babies."

Madison looked *just* like Mom when she stared at the ceiling in frustration. "Not literal babies. But I just spent all morning taking care of chickens, carrying Mr. Cluck home to be safe, and then I go inside and I'm going to eat chicken. It feels wrong... but this one's already dead. Shouldn't waste it. Allie said sometimes she only got to eat once in three days."

"Yeah." Jonathan squirmed. "Was like that for me before Cliff found me. But I found a donut store once. Totally epic. They weren't even too stale yet."

Lorelei looked up with a 'you guys had food at all?' expression, but didn't say anything.

"We all got super lucky." Harper sat at her place. "I know you hate the idea of meat. Sorry, I should've given you a tomato sandwich."

"Dad's right. Wolves don't eat tomatoes. Eating meat isn't 'wrong' according to nature. My problem is really with the cruel way they used to treat the animals in the big farms." Madison sighed, then took a bite of her lunch. Once she finished chewing, she shrugged one shoulder. "I guess it's worse to kill a chicken and waste it. Pretty stupid of me to be mad at having food because it's not the right kind when people are starving."

"I was so hungry I would have even eated vegetables," said Lorelei.

"Eaten," whispered Harper.

Lorelei laughed.

"She knows. She's saying it on purpose to be cute so people hug her." Jonathan smiled. "Same reason she says 'fwea' when she knows it's flea."

"I like hugs!" Lorelei thrust her hands in the air.

The front door opened. "Hey, it's me," called Darci.

"In the kitchen," replied Harper.

Darci entered, wearing a simplistic brown off-the-shoulder dress. It stayed on courtesy of a tie string at armpit level, but essentially looked like she put a skirt on *way* too high. It hung a bit short for

Harper's taste, but for Darci, counted as fairly modest. Elijah, the five-year-old she'd adopted, trailed in behind her. The boy looked around at everyone, no particular emotion on his face. He also looked like an actor from a medieval ren faire, wearing a man's T-shirt like a tunic, complete with a bit of rope tied around his waist as a belt.

"Are you dressed up as a lamp?" asked Jonathan.

Darci gave him the finger. "It's new. They made it here in town. I'm still going to be able to fit into it when I'm a blimp."

"Darce, by the time you're seven months, the baby bump is going to lift the curtains away from the stage," said Harper. "I think you're confusing a little girl's dress with a maternity garment."

"Hah. It's not *that* short." Darci 'modeled' the dress. "I'm not gonna get *too* big, am I?"

Harper gestured at the living room. "Stuff one of the couch pillows under it."

"Okay." Darci darted out.

Elijah stood there looking at everyone.

*I wasn't serious...*

The kids laughed.

"Wow," called Darci a moment later from the living room. "Yeah, this might be a bit too short for me when I become a gravitational anomaly. There's definitely a breeze where a breeze shouldn't be."

"I think the idea is you get a bigger dress when you need it. That one's for early pregnancy." Harper laughed.

The math finally clicked in Madison's head; she nearly choked on her mouthful of sandwich. "Holy crap! Darci is pregnant?"

While Harper adored seeing her little sister happy, several minutes of sustained gleeful squealing almost gave her a headache. After lunch, the kids headed out to the backyard, staying close to home because they knew cake would happen soon. Lorelei collected Elijah, leading him by the hand outside. Harper hung out in the living room with Darci, mostly talking about her relationship with Lucas Garza. According to Darci, he'd been depressed over going from rich celebrity to 'ordinary guy' overnight. Not that he'd been a Hollywood A-list actor, but he had like twenty million or so in the bank and decent residuals coming in from television reruns. She didn't describe him as a douche who couldn't handle not having money, more he missed the whole 'scene' of being an actor, getting in front of cameras, being around people, having fun with his role, and bumping into fans who recognized him. Unlike many in his position, he hadn't lived huge or bought overly expensive cars. Also, after starring in a pirate-themed network show for several seasons, he ended up being a reasonably decent swordsman. The idea such a skill might prove useful in the real world again blew her mind.

"We just totally clicked," said Darci. "He says performing used to be his passion and reason for living, but now, it's me."

"Are you sure he's not just acting?" Harper grimaced.

"Yeah. He didn't start off hitting on me or anything. We were both having a blue day."

Harper took Darci's hand. "I didn't know you were depressed."

"Pff. Come on. Everyone died. I ended up in a hell camp for weeks. I'm not as tough as you, Harp. Besides, I was depressed for years before the war. Why do you think I started doing drugs so young? Just trying to escape."

"Sorry. You seemed normal from the outside. Nice neighborhood, great house, good Dad. I'm sorry, it just didn't seem like you'd have any reason to be sad."

Darci stooped forward, head in both hands. "Harp, depression isn't 'being sad.' It's brain stuff out of my control. People can be depressed for no damn reason anyone can see. My mom had it, too."

"I never met your mother."

"Right. Most of my friends didn't. She, uhh..." Darci exhaled. "She killed herself when I was seven."

"Oh my God," whispered Harper. "I'm so sorry. Always thought she had cancer or something."

"She dropped me off at my grandparents' house, said I was going to spend the day with them, and she'd see me later." Darci twirled a lock of black hair around her finger. "I figured she'd pick me up after lunch. Maybe after dinner. Never knew 'later' meant in the afterlife. Dad never told me *how* she did it. My head's full of all these 'could be' images. No one knew anything was wrong with her. She didn't say a word." Her voice faltered. "Mom kept up a smile for the world to see, but it was all an act."

Harper rubbed Darci's back. "I'm sorry."

"She left a suicide note. All it said was, 'This is no one's fault but mine.'" Darci exhaled as if breathing out a deep hit from a joint. "Look, it's 'Nee's birthday. I don't want to shit all over it."

"Don't feel that way. Like you said, it's not just being sad. Talk to me whenever you want about whatever you want, okay?"

Darci glanced sideways at her for a second, then smiled. "I would've told you the truth a long time ago, but I didn't want to make you cry. You're so sensitive, I thought it would mess you up for good. Letting everyone think Mom just got sick years ago ended up being the lazy way out."

"Maybe it would have messed me up if you told the old me." She laughed mirthlessly. "I'm actually kinda worried because I'm *not* having nightmares about shooting people."

"You're a lot tougher than you think. I'd never have survived watching people shoot my dad right in front of me."

"*Survived* might be a strong word there. I'm coping."

They sat in silence for a while, listening to the kids playing out in the yard.

"Okay, enough." Darci took in a deep breath. "It's Renee's birthday. Let's try to stay upbeat for her. She's been a little off lately."

"Yeah. Everyone's going to be a little off on the first birthday they have where most of their family is gone." Harper idly swished her feet back and forth over the rug. "We just gotta be there for her, yanno."

"Right."

Grace arrived, carrying a box.

"Oh, crap." Darci flailed her arms as she struggled to get up off the couch. "Damn. This is getting serious. In another month, I'm going to need help to move."

"You're not at all that big yet." Grace laughed.

"Yeah, but I'm a twig." Darci headed for the door. "Be right back. I forgot to get her a present. You okay watching the little guy for a few minutes?"

"Sure. I think Lorelei stole him though. Might be tough getting him back later." Harper laughed.

"Hah!" Darci rushed off.

Harper sighed out her nose, got up, and moved to stand in the back doorway, watching the kids kick a ball around the yard. Becca, Eva, Mila, and Christopher had arrived at some point over the past few minutes.

*Ack. Good thing we made a big cake.*

Cliff and Carrie showed up a short while later, soon followed by Renee.

As soon as Renee walked in, Cliff deadpanned, "Surprise."

"Thanks, guys." Renee smiled. "Surprised, not surprised."

"Since it's a birthday and all, figure it's a worthy occasion for coffee." Cliff headed into the kitchen and opened a high cabinet.

"Whoa, we still have some?" Harper gawked at him.

"Yeah. Like three bags… been saving it for important occasions. Damn shame the stuff won't grow in this climate. Might as well use it before it goes bad." Cliff grabbed a bag.

"It's *already* gone bad," whispered Grace. "Coffee doesn't last for a year."

"Didn't they build a greenhouse at the big farm?" asked Renee. "Aren't they trying to grow coffee in there, and like oranges?"

Harper headed for the living room where her friends congregated.

"Trying is the operative word." Cliff glanced at her as she passed. "It's stale. Stale and bad aren't the same thing. As long as it ain't furry, it's good to drink. Hell, considering this is the last coffee I'm likely to ever see in my lifetime, I'd probably drink it even if the beans got furry."

Harper, Grace, and Renee all shivered.

Darci swooped in the front door carrying a box, did a pirouette, and handed the box to Renee. "Happy birthday, 'Nee."

"Aww, you didn't have to get me anything. We're grown-ups now. Birthdays aren't about presents." Renee laughed. "They're about sitting around, drinking wine, and complaining over getting old."

"That doesn't start until thirty." Carrie laughed.

Darci wagged her eyebrows. "I would've gotten you a bob as a gag gift, but there are kids here, and well... no batteries."

"Bob?" asked Harper before it clicked, and she gasped. *Battery operated boyfriend.*

Renee didn't react much. "Damn. I could've really used one."

"It's not battery operated," deadpanned Darci.

Grace got the giggles, her face reddening. "You did *not* give her a dildo for her birthday."

"Wow..." Harper couldn't help but laugh at the concept of Grace, who'd grown up extremely sheltered, knowing that word. "I'm not sure I dare ask how you know what one of those things is."

"Even the former princess made friends at school." Grace fussed at her hair. "No way would my parents let me have an actual boyfriend, so I had to... take matters into my own hands."

Harper gawked.

"Gotcha." Grace pointed, laughing. "My mother would've sold me to a convent if she found one of those things in the house."

Renee opened the box and looked in. "Oh, sweet! This is way too big for me though."

"Oh. My. Gawd." Harper looked away.

"Chill out." Renee pulled something out of the box.

Grace and Carrie burst into laughter.

Harper risked a peek, relaxing once she realized Renee held a Funko Pop doll, not a sex toy. "All those things look the same to me. Who is it?"

"Jayne from *Firefly.*" Renee hugged it, then hugged Darci. "Thank you! He's adorable."

Darci smiled. "You're welcome... wow the weird stuff they decided to bring back from Walmart, right?"

The kids came in from the backyard, finally noticing Renee's presence.

Lorelei led the charge, first into the living room. "Can we please have cake now?"

Harper laughed.

"Might as well. Went to all the trouble of making it." Carrie headed for the kitchen, retrieved the cake, and carried it out to the dining room table.

As with Lorelei's birthday, they lit one candle—which remained lit for less than a minute before Renee made her wish. No sense wasting a candle when the lights worked. Cliff distributed the pot of coffee he made among small mugs so everyone who wanted got a fair portion. A few minutes later, Logan arrived, looking exhausted from a long day at the farm. He'd apparently rushed right over without going home to clean up. Fortunately, the weather had become a little cool, so he didn't smell. Without a word, Cliff handed him a mug he'd set aside.

"Thanks." Logan sniffed. "Oh damn. I haven't had this stuff in a while."

"Yeah. Same. here. Been two whole months filled with indescribable suffering," deadpanned Cliff.

Conversation over cake and coffee—Harper figured it had been too long since she had coffee because it didn't taste stale at all—generally involved Renee and her efforts at making clothing. At least she appeared to enjoy doing it. She joked about being happy not to have the pressure of studying for college or getting accepted by a school good enough for her to get a serious job in the fashion industry, then working her ass off chasing deadlines with the constant threat of being fired for small errors. She'd always daydreamed about going into fashion, but hated the high-pressure world of it.

Renee seemed a little somber, certainly the least enthusiastic she'd ever been for a birthday before. Of course, their crew came up three short. Christina's random giggling never went off in the background. Andrea wasn't there to constantly crack jokes or trip over things. Veronica didn't once say 'the hell is wrong wit' you' or end up laughing so hard at something Renee said she couldn't breathe. The absence of their three other friends made the 'party' feel more like a wake. Harper didn't mention them, fearing it would kill the mood, but the way Renee and Darci acted, she figured they also thought about the others.

Grace, who they'd only met after arriving in Evergreen, didn't know anything about their old hangouts, habits, jokes, or the life they had before the world burned. Harper simultaneously envied and pitied her. The girl used to live with extremely demanding, controlling parents. Sure, they'd been 'kinda rich,' but Grace had zero freedom, not even to make decisions about her own future or education. They'd even decided on her college major for her.

*How bad does it have to be for nuclear war to kill your parents and you feel relief?*

Harper couldn't even imagine having zero love for her parents. As far as she'd come to understand, Grace didn't *hate* them as much as had no feelings toward them at all beyond a sort of 'ugh, go away and leave me alone' distaste... plus a healthy amount of fear. She'd never have defied them when they'd been alive.

*She'd been so messed up, she didn't even realize the world stopped. Thought she'd get in trouble for missing school.*

"Hey..." Darci nudged Renee. "You okay? Seem a little down."

"Yeah. I'm dealing. I got all the sobbing out of my system when those creeps had me locked in a room. Being here is about as awesome as it can get. Only thing better would be a rewind button for time and no war."

Darci looked at her small coffee cup. "Yeah. Need something a little stronger than coffee, but gotta be good for at least another like six months."

"Welcome to the start of birthdays sucking." Cliff held his mug up in toast toward Renee. "It's all downhill from eighteen."

"Not twenty-one?" Carrie clinked her mug with his.

Harper, Darci, and Logan joined in as well. Renee passed on the coffee, but she clinked her water glass.

Cliff raised both eyebrows. "No drinking age anymore. Suppose eighteen doesn't really matter much, either."

"Doesn't matter how old you get, cake is awesome." Renee smiled. "Birthdays are only going to start sucking when we run out of cake mix."

Carrie chuckled. "We already did."

"But..." Renee pointed at everyone standing around eating. "Cake?"

"Yes." Carrie folded her arms. "Believe it or not, people made cake before Betty Crocker."

"How?" Renee stared at her like an Amish seeing a car for the first time.

"Wow." Madison whistled. "Holy blonde moment, Batman."

"Augh!" screamed Jon, overacting anguish.

Everyone looked at him.

"Little young for a moment of sudden existential crisis." Cliff stuffed a forkful of cake into his mouth.

"Jon?" asked Harper. "You okay?"

He grinned. "Yeah. Maddie just made me think about my comics. I used to have a lot of them. Like a serious lot. Some collector ones. No, I don't want to go back looking for them. Just being funny."

"You could always draw new ones." Harper patted him on the head.

"Ooh." Jonathan lit up. "Yeah!"

"Sounds fun." Grace bit her lip. "But is it really practical now? I mean, it takes a lot of time to learn how to draw."

Cliff wagged his fork at her. "People need art and entertainment. If we don't have a reason to smile anymore, what's the point of surviving, right?"

"Maybe he does it in his spare time?" Carrie scratched her head. "People have to be alive to enjoy art. Survival's gotta come first."

Darci flailed her arms. "What the hell is it about art? Why does everyone always act like it's not a real job or real career?"

"Hate to say it, but nothing's a 'real job' anymore." Cliff sectioned off another bit of his cake onto his fork. "Which might actually be a good thing. An artist contributes to the overall health and wellbeing of the town. At least now, they don't have to worry about money for food or rent."

"Seriously, though. How did you make this without mix?" Renee nibbled on a bit of cake. "This *is* cake, right?"

Darci held her plate up to eye level. "Looks like cake. Smells like cake. Must be cake."

"Honey…" Carrie put an arm around her. "We need to spend

some kitchen time together. Since I'm kinda-sorta your mom now, I should get to work."

Cliff seemed to be forcing himself not to eat his entire piece in four bites. "This is the best cake I've ever tasted. A lot of stuff we had—like cake—simply became easier and faster to produce with technology, but was possible before. Except for weird crap like dinosaur-shaped pasta."

Everyone laughed.

"It's probably the first sign of the downfall of a civilization," muttered Cliff before eating his second-to-last bit of cake.

"What is?" Harper raised an eyebrow.

"Dino pasta." Cliff exhaled, acting overly serious. "When the vast resources of a first world nation have the spare time to make little noodle tyrannosaurs and triceratops, it's a giant red flag resources are being misallocated."

Harper nodded. "Right. Didn't you say sneakers with lights in them heralded the downfall of civilization?"

"Them too," mumbled Cliff around the last of his cake.

The kids ran outside to play again, tossing their plates and forks in the sink on the way.

"Should start up a betting pool. How many minutes can they go unsupervised before there is screaming, crying, an explosion, or spontaneous unexplained streaking?" Cliff chuckled.

"Bad bet." Harper headed for the back door. "Because I'm not leaving them unsupervised."

Renee, Darci, Grace, and Logan followed. They sat around the back porch talking, mostly about random things like being bored, missing movies or television, and so on.

"They say people back then had lots of kids to increase the odds of a few living to adulthood." Grace scratched her head. "I think they had lots of kids because there wasn't anything else to do for fun."

Renee laughed.

"Truth." Darci patted her stomach. "The universe is cruel."

"How so?" asked Renee. "I mean, beyond the obvious. What do you specifically mean?"

"This baby exists because of weed, but I can't have weed until I hatch."

Renee and Harper chuckled.

"You jonesing for it?" asked Logan.

"Not really. I miss feeling relaxed more than being high. Not sure they're different." Darci chuckled. "But I can't exactly feed a baby pot-laced breast milk, so I might end up being sober way longer than is healthy for people I interact with."

They all laughed.

Harper leaned against Logan. "People back then must have come up with some way to entertain themselves other than constantly having sex. I mean, no one in those days had the time to invent dinosaur-shaped noodles."

Mila punted the ball across the yard, trying to score a long-distance goal. Elijah strayed into the path and ate it square in the side of the head. Despite it being a relatively soft blue ball and not a legit soccer ball, it still knocked him over sideways.

He wailed.

"Ack! Sorry!" yelled Mila.

"Screaming!" called Cliff from inside the house. "Twelve minutes. Longer than expected."

Elijah scrambled to his feet, dodged Mila's attempted apology hug, and ran straight to Darci, wailing.

Cliff poked his head out the door. "Any blood?"

"Nope," said Harper. "Ball upside the head."

Mila, holding the offending rubber orb, approached the porch. "Sorry. Didn't see him."

"It's okay, kiddo." Darci patted the boy on the back. "I saw. Just an accident."

"Fuzzy!" yelled Lorelei.

Harper's blood practically froze in her veins. She looked left toward the girl's voice, dreading what she'd see. *Please be a rabbit. Please be a rabbit.*

A black bear poked its head over the rear fence, sniffing at the chicken coop.

Lorelei waved. "Hi, Mr. Bear!"

"Don't eat those chickens!" yelled Madison. "They're not food chickens."

Time seemed to grind to a standstill. Harper gripped the .45 on her belt, unsure if it would be effective or simply piss the bear off. Shooting a bear in front of Madison would not go over well either, but she'd rather deal with an upset sister than a mauled one.

Everyone stood still—including the chickens. A moment later, the bear lost interest and dropped out of sight behind the fence.

The kids all continued staring at the fence where the bear appeared for another two minutes. All at once, they seemed to forget entirely about the bear and resumed playing their odd version of soccer—except for Madison, who went to comfort Rosie and Mr. Cluck.

*Now I know we're all messed up in the head a bit. A bear just poked its nose into the yard and we didn't all scramble inside and shut the door.*

"Looks like you have things under control." Cliff smiled. "Carrie and I will be next door for a bit, trying to figure out something fun to do."

Harper blushed slightly. "Okay."

Darci whispered, "Someone's getting lucky tonight."

*Really?* Harper's blush deepened.

Cliff retreated into the house, humming merrily to himself.

"Okay, awkward." Renee coughed. "So... umm, poorly disguised attempt to change the subject. What's it like having chickens in your backyard?"

## ALL THE WAY

The following day, Harper brought her compound bow along on patrol.

She had no intention to use it in a real situation yet, mostly because she still only had a bunch of practice arrows. They hadn't worked too well on the escaped convict gang, sticking in and being more annoying than deadly. Relatively blunt tips made them about as effective as stabbing someone with a pencil. When the day came she ran out of bullets, she'd carry razor arrows instead. Hopefully, by then, she'd feel as comfortable firing a bow as she did using a shotgun.

One of the houses on Interlocken Drive had a wooden tool shed in the backyard, well on its way to total collapse. No one lived in the house, and the shed could only be useful at this point as firewood — or a target.

Harper leaned the Mossberg against the fence near the sidewalk, stretched out her arms to limber up, then picked an arbitrary dark spot on the facing wall of the tool shed to use as a bullseye. She'd brought eight arrows along in a nylon hip quiver. Dennis Prosser, another militia person who lived in the house directly behind theirs, came by to chat weeks ago when he saw her practicing. He apparently had been a huge fan of bow hunting as well as a history geek. According to him, the 'Hollywood' quiver on the back was total nonsense. 'Real' combat archers wore hip quivers, which made for smoother, easier drawing plus didn't make the arrows bounce out all over the place when running.

She'd never worn a quiver on her back. Usually, when she practiced, she'd stick the arrows in the dirt nearby. The hip quiver worked well enough, so she proceeded to get herself used to it. Every eight shots, she walked to the tool shed to recover the arrows and do it all over again. They penetrated the particleboard wall only a few inches, and—for the most part—didn't give her much problem coming back out.

After putting in about an hour of practice—the driveway allowed her to shoot at longer ranges than her backyard without the risk of a stray arrow hitting someone—she resumed walking her route. Silence turned her thoughts somewhat glum over the news Jeanette and the electrical team expected their cobbled-together transformer would probably last only a year, if that. Even if it survived longer, the solar panels would progressively deteriorate over time. Within two to four years, Evergreen wouldn't have a stable, long term electricity source unless they figured out a wind-power solution that didn't require a large, centralized transformer.

Electrical engineering made less sense to Harper than someone shouting in a foreign language. She could only keep her metaphorical fingers crossed they got it working *and* trained some people so skills didn't evaporate.

Randall, Kip, Krystal, and the four kids with them passed their health screening—as in they didn't have contagious diseases—and had become official residents. Harper smiled as she passed the house Anne-Marie assigned them to at the curve in Inverness Drive. The seven of them considered themselves a family already, no sense breaking them up. Harper smiled to herself, thinking about the day she and Darnell showed them to the quartermaster, then took them to the house. The kids were so thrilled to have an actual house again, they cheered and ran around like primitives who'd gone through a time machine, never seeing modern construction before.

Tegan declared the baby in good health, proving he'd only been with the survivalists for a day or two at most. They'd brought him to Doreen Mack, who took care of a handful of other babies and toddlers. She'd formerly run a day care center prior to the war and had, perhaps, the most experience of anyone in Evergreen in taking care of extremely young children. A small group of women helped out nursing the smallest. Doreen made baby food from crushed apples, mashed-up hard boiled eggs, and even watery bread. No one could say the kids had variety of tasty food to choose from, but it kept them alive and healthy. Madison wanted to name him Chance due to the slim odds of their finding him at all, but Cliff said he'd be teased about some old Jean Claude VanDamme movie, so they decided to simply go with Oliver as a reference to *Oliver Twist*.

*It's four days away from being a year since the nukes fell on our heads. Only a year. Why does it feel like a whole lifetime ago?*

HARPER LAY IN BED, MADISON BESIDE HER ON THE RIGHT, Lorelei on the left.

Normally, she found it comforting to have her sisters close at night. Not only did they reassure her the way a pair of warm teddy bears might, having them right next to her made it so she didn't have to worry about them. Also, lazy bonus: if Madison had a nightmare, Harper didn't have to crawl out of bed in the middle of a freezing night to go comfort her. She kind of felt bad for Jonathan having his own room. Boys his age had it rough for nightmares, or at least responding to them. It seemed weird to let him sleep in the same bed as her and the girls. The kind of weird that made people give disapproving stares if they heard about it. It also didn't feel right for him to share a bed with Cliff and even more awkward for him to crawl in bed next to Carrie. People would probably think it a little strange for Harper to continue to share the bed with her sisters when they turned into teenagers. Grace mentioned in medieval times, 'family beds' had been quite common. She didn't think it strange at all for Harper to share a bed with the girls given society had reverted.

Alas, the house had only so much room. At most, they could cram one more bed in here, which still meant two of them had to share. Maybe Cliff would build a bunk bed for Madison and Lorelei at some point to make better use of space.

Jonathan didn't have nightmares too often anymore, but when he did, they hit him hard. Fortunately, he handled bad dreams pretty well for an eleven-year-old. Once he realized he'd only had a dream, a few minutes of hugging Harper allowed him to sleep again in his room — unlike Madison who remained clingy for the rest of the night.

Her nightmares had lessened in frequency. Compared to Jonathan, she had them way more often, but nowhere near as terrifying. Madison generally didn't have one bad enough to shock her awake unless something happened to her during the day or she went to bed hungry.

On most nights, Harper loved cuddling her two 'teddy bears.' Tonight, however, she tried to avoid becoming entangled — so she could slip out once they fell asleep. Lorelei wouldn't be a problem. Once the girl passed out, it took high explosives to wake her up. Madison had never been a truly heavy sleeper, but since the nukes, the girl would wake up to a mouse farting.

Harper figured she'd never be able to get out of bed without Madison noticing, and didn't really want to lie to her about going to the bathroom. Granted, she didn't feel right telling her the truth either. At least, not all of it. Madison might've been a month short of eleven, but she'd probably figure out pretty quick what Harper wanted to do with Logan after dark.

Sure enough, when he appeared in the window and Harper tried to get out of bed, Madison opened her eyes.

"Bathroom?" whispered Madison.

"Not exactly. Gonna have a little date with Logan."

"Oh. Okay. How long are you gonna be out?"

"I dunno. Maybe an hour? Maybe less. Can't stay up too late. Got patrol in the morning."

Madison nodded and closed her eyes.

They'd already planned everything out, so she knew she wouldn't have to walk too far. Given the intended activity, Harper didn't bother getting dressed. She plucked her handgun and holster off the night table, stepped sockless into her hiking shoes, and went down the hall to the kitchen in the long T-shirt she used for a nightgown.

Logan met her by the back door, took her hand, and walked with her around the house to Hilltop Drive. They hurried past Carrie's house to the east, cutting left on a dirt driveway adjacent to her property, which led north to two smallish houses. Neither had an official occupant yet, so they planned to use the nearer, smaller one for 'the big night.'

Her stomach knotted up in anticipation. She dreaded and couldn't wait in equal parts. How much different-slash-better could it be compared to all the other 'not quite intercourse' things they'd done over the past several months? After finally getting past her embarrassment and talking to Carrie, she expected the first time would include a bit of discomfort. Most of her dread came from not knowing if it would end up being 'uncomfortable' or 'painful.' It surprised her when Carrie said she might not even bleed at all. Speaking of 'Carrie,' Harper had been expecting her first time would be like throwing buckets of blood everywhere.

All the not knowing got her hands shaking by the time they reached the empty house.

To be on the safe side, Harper crept in first, gun ready but not pointed. She cleared the house the way Roy instructed. Tactical entry while in a 'nightgown' seemed ridiculous.

"I feel so damn stupid right now," whispered Harper. "Like I'm the sex police or something."

Logan snickered.

"Seriously. I'm only wearing a T-shirt and sneakers, going room to room with a gun so we can do it in here."

A small, fast-moving shadow bolted toward her from the back corner of the kitchen.

She bit back the urge to yelp, fumbling to get the gun out of the holster. Fur brushed the side of her leg. A critter, probably raccoon, zoomed into the living room. It climbed the walls in a frenzy for a few crazed seconds before discovering the front door and escaping the house.

"Holy crap." Logan pressed a hand to his chest. "Scared the shit out of me."

"Just a critter." Harper slouched.

Logan felt around the wall until he discovered a light switch. Surprisingly, it worked. After the flea incident with the kids, Harper didn't feel terribly comfortable going into an untested house. Even though the place appeared to be in decent shape, an itchy tingling crept up her legs. Most likely, someone at the 'bug house' had dogs or something before the war and it got out of control. She crouched to examine the carpet. No sign of bugs—the itching came entirely from her imagination.

They headed to the bedroom. After a brief inspection for mold or bugs in there turned up nothing, Harper finally allowed herself to relax. She set the gun on the floor next to the bed, kicked off her shoes, and pulled her shirt up over her head.

Logan turned the light on in the bedroom, hurried down the hall to shut off the living room light, then returned, hastily stripping. "You'll never believe what I found."

"Dare I ask?"

He crouched to fish something out of his jeans pocket, then held up a foil packet.

"Is that what I think it is?" Harper suppressed a nervous giggle as she lowered herself to sit on the edge of the bed.

"Yeah. Found it in a house down the street from where I'm staying."

"Umm. Is it still good?"

Logan chuckled. "It's a piece of latex. Don't think it goes bad."

He set the packet on the nightstand and sat next to her.

"Wow. Why am I blushing at the sight of a packet?" Harper raked her hands through her hair. "I can't even say the stupid name of it."

"I dunno. Something about them. Felt like I had to keep it hidden." He chuckled and put a surprisingly warm arm around her back. "Do you still want to do this? You're shaking."

"It's a little cold." Harper took a few calming breaths. "And the jump scare from the raccoon."

Sitting together holding hands soon became kissing, nervousness fading with each passing minute. She reclined on her back. As they'd done countless times before, Logan ran his hands over her body, still kissing her. She drank in his scent, his warmth, inhaling deep until she could taste his presence.

The more he touched her, the more revved up she became. It seemed like an eternity of bliss before he stopped kissing her neck and shifted to look into her eyes.

"Is this a good time?"

"*Yes!*" whispered Harper, clawing at the bedding. She writhed in pleasure, yearning for more.

He reached for the packet. "Sorry if this isn't exactly a fairy tale moment... first time for me."

Harper clung to his back, kissing along his spine. "That makes two of us."

"Oh, this is weird. Never put one of these on before."

She bit her lip.

"Aha. There we are."

Harper scooted back. He climbed up onto the bed, hovering over her. She closed her eyes, waiting for it. Logan resumed kissing her on the chest.

"What are you doing?" she rasped.

"Trying to make this perfect for you. Don't want to go too fast."

"How do you know that if it's your first time?"

"I can read." He gently raked his fingernails down her front.

Harper shivered from the sensation. "My, what sort of books do you read, Mr. Ruiz?"

"Interesting ones."

She grabbed fistfuls of bedding on either side of her body, barely able to resist screaming in pleasure at what his touch did to her. More than the physical contact, having him be so concerned to make this moment with her as perfect as possible lit a spark deep in her brain. She could no longer envision a world in which she didn't have him in her life.

When something made contact down below, she gasped.

"I love you, Harper."

She reached up, threading her arms around his neck. "I love you so much. I can't even say how happy I am my first time is going to be with you, Logan Ruiz."

"Moment of truth. You sure?"

She felt nothing but trust and love for this boy—no man—embracing her. All the fear and anxiety this new world brought with it made living in the moment the only way to exist. If anything happened to him, she wouldn't bother with another boy ever again. She wanted to stay with him for the rest of whatever time the world let them have.

"Yes," whispered Harper. "I want to do this with you."

Logan leaned down to kiss her.

She held him tight... closed her eyes, and waited for the most special moment they ever shared.

Harper cuddled against Logan, out of breath, her brain still swimming in ecstasy.

Other than being mildly sore, she'd never experienced such world-shaking pleasure. She wanted to fall asleep in his arms right there, naked as the day she was born, without the first care who might find them. Alas, she couldn't. Madison would freak out if she didn't go home.

For the first time since the war, she found herself looking forward to the day Madison outgrew wanting to share the bed. She even looked forward to living in a house just with Logan, but didn't know if it would happen any time soon. Most likely, the two of them would end up sharing a room in a house also occupied by her family, like people did years ago. That didn't bother her at all, as long as they had a room for privacy. Not only did it make sense from a food-preparation standpoint to have larger groups eating together, after losing her parents, she wanted to keep what family she had now as close as possible.

Still, she had to force herself out of bed—probably grab a super quick shower—then return to her sisters.

"You were amazing… I never imagined a man could be so gentle and caring."

"I never imagined a woman could be so… perfect."

She cuddled him, groaning in overacted annoyance. "I hate to say it, but I have to get home before Madison freaks out."

"Yeah. She seems like she's doing well. How are you right now? Feeling all right?"

"Way more than all right."

"Good. Wow, I haven't seen that much blood since the last time I played hockey."

Harper laughed. "Stop. I didn't bleed at all. Didn't even really hurt much."

He grinned. "Teasing. Seriously, though. You're good?"

"Yes. Little sore, but you were amazing and so gentle and wow… did that really just happen?"

"That is exactly what I've been wondering for the past, oh… however long we've been in this house. Being with you is so perfect, I keep waiting to wake up."

Harper moaned. "Ugh. I want to sleep here with you."

"It's all right. Maddie is still emotionally brittle. She'll grow out of it soon. We're only eighteen. We have plenty of time."

*Yeah, until some crazy son of a bitch decides to shoot us… or we cut ourselves on a farm tool and catch a horrible disease.* Harper exhaled out her nostrils. *Good thoughts. Think good thoughts.* "Yeah. Plenty of time."

# 21

# THE NOTEBOOK

H arper caught herself lost in her thoughts rather than paying attention to her surroundings on patrol.

Her mind had been spinning in circles ever since she returned home last night. Lorelei hadn't even noticed her absence, sleeping too deep. Madison, however, clung to her as if she'd been afraid never to see her again. True, the desperation might've come only from Harper's imagination, but she still ended up staring at the ceiling trying to collect her feelings.

She didn't hate or even dislike sharing the bed with her sisters, but she also wanted to have more time with Logan. However, as much as she loved him, Madison had to come first. As long as her little sister needed her, she would be there for her. It didn't make her feel too guilty to hope Madison might hurry up and grow out of being afraid to sleep alone. Worst case scenario, she'd go straight from wanting to sleep with Harper to finding a boyfriend and sharing a bed with him. Well, not really. *Worst* case would be a grown Madison still wanting to cling to Harper all night long. Didn't seem likely, though. Her little sister had mostly recovered her former personality. Considering they'd both witnessed their parents' deaths, had the world blown out from under them and lost everything they once considered normal and safe, the girl had made remarkable progress. Perhaps in another year or two, she'd fully deal with everything.

"Argh," whispered Harper. Random screams of frustration tended to make people nervous in a tomb-silent neighborhood.

The idea of Madison and boys hadn't even occurred to her once in the year since the bombs fell. How would she handle it when—if—her kid sister became interested in a boy? Madison's emotional state made her highly vulnerable to manipulation. The wrong sort of boy could say the right things and talk her into doing whatever he wanted to satiate her need to feel protected, loved, and wanted. Would Madison resent Harper hovering over her and getting a read on any boy she brought home?

*Maybe I should talk to her now, just explain she has to be careful emotionally, so she understands later.*

Harper turned a corner on the road, eyeing the houses in the area for signs of anything being abnormal. In the morning, most of the neighborhood ended up being quiet. The golf course turned secondary farm absorbed many of the adults as workers during the day. Kids spent four or five hours at the main farm learning and helping out before being cut loose to play. Older kids, fourteen and up, spent more time working. Surprisingly, she hadn't seen any of them really complain about it.

*Trying to survive is way different than a stupid mall job... and there's nothing else to do.*

She continued walking her patrol, still glowing from last night's time with Logan. Emotionally, breaking down the last hesitation had been a galaxy-shaking tremor. Physically, she enjoyed it—but it hadn't been quite as weird, different, or mind-blowing as she'd built it up to be. Maybe if they hadn't spent the past few months doing so much other stuff, and she'd gone straight from never seeing a boy naked right to full-on intercourse, it would've been exactly as transcendental as she'd thought it would be.

Honestly, she didn't even truly feel as if he'd taken her virginity last night. Not that she cared much about such a stupid, flimsy, pointless social construct to begin with... but she couldn't exactly pinpoint the moment where it felt like she'd gone from 'innocent' to 'woman.' Had it been when he first touched her down below, the first time she'd gotten off due to someone else touching her? Did the tongue count as losing her virginity or all the 'almost but not quite' things they did that fell short of 'traditional' biological copulation?

Somewhere over the past few months, her 'virginity' melted like a snowman she'd left on the front lawn in early spring. Darci's snowman had been dynamited into oblivion in a supply closet at their high school. Renee made hers out of concrete. Harper chuckled. Her best friend hadn't done much beyond kissing a boy. After her experience with the Lawless, she suspected Renee wasn't in any hurry whatsoever to find a boyfriend.

As far as she knew, none of her other friends had gone all the way yet other than Darci.

Being on the other side of the 'virgin fence' didn't feel as different as she once thought it would. She hadn't experienced a magic moment where she 'became a woman' at the snap of a finger. Well, maybe she *had*—but not due to having sex.

She'd stopped being innocent the instant she'd killed someone to protect Madison.

Harper mulled the idea of having a baby with Logan, but not yet. Probably not for a few years. She wanted to make sure Evergreen remained stable enough, that *she* remained stable enough. She already had Madison and Lorelei to take care of, and wanted them both to grow less brittle before she added an infant to the mix. Before she rolled the dice of fate and risked dying in childbirth, Madison had to become old enough to take care of herself if need be. Of course, she had Carrie and Cliff and Jonathan to look after her, but losing Harper so soon after their parents would destroy her.

Besides, she'd promised Madison she wouldn't die.

She had no control over some random idiot shooting her, but she could make the choice not to risk her life to pregnancy yet. Harper's mood swung back and forth. One minute, she wanted to shelter with Madison and slow it down with Logan for the time being… the next, she couldn't wait for the next chance they had for sex. *Damn my raging teenage hormones.* Maybe she could gently suggest Madison have a sleepover at Becca's so she could see how it felt to spend an entire night in bed with Logan… like a married couple.

*Oh, ack. The M word. Are we too young for that?*

She smirked, thinking of Beth and Jaden. She'd caught them doing it—well, barged in on them after the fact—in an abandoned house when Beth had been sixteen, Jaden seventeen. Months later, Beth turned seventeen. The two considered themselves married already. Harper mentally committed herself to Logan, but referring to it as 'marriage' still sounded weird… as if marrying at eighteen meant she threw away college and a career for the sake of a man.

*Hah. As if.*

Vestiges of the society that burned still haunted her with the 'shame' of being a high school dropout. Friday, September 7th, 2018… she'd only gone to school for about a week into her senior year before it all went to hell. She'd never earn a high school diploma even. Even though she realized *no one* in the United States would be getting an official high school diploma ever again—at least, not for a long time—she felt as if she'd failed. Irrational notions of screwing up didn't care about logic.

"Wow, my hormones are going crazy." She sighed hard, raking her hands up through her hair. "The hell am I caring about graduation for?"

To distract herself from the emotional crapstorm going on in her head, she thought back over various minor incidents she'd handled or helped deal with. By most people's opinion, Evergreen had become a fairly ideal post-apocalyptic hamlet. However, 'fairly ideal' in the wake of nuclear war didn't mean Mayberry. People fought. People got drunk. People hit their romantic partners. People got *really* drunk and wandered around naked peeing on things they shouldn't pee on.

Well, okay. Not 'people' in that case, just Mr. Hodges.

The man spent more time unconscious in the road than awake. Earl had to ration him at the brewery, which naturally caused a scene. Fortunately, he'd only screamed and threw things at the wall. Mayor Ned hadn't yet decided to kick him out of town.

Harper mentally rehearsed the hand-to-hand techniques Cliff

taught her as well as the 'police tactical' stuff Roy shared with the militia. It felt beyond ridiculous to think of herself as a cop, so she didn't, preferring to compare herself to a 'rebel soldier' from *Star Wars*, here to protect the town and everyone in it from outside threats.

Of course, she also had to protect the people from inside threats, but compared to pre-war police, the Evergreen Militia was highly laid back. For example, they didn't care too much about things like theft since no one used money. Also, pretty much everyone in town essentially stole their houses. Besides, no one really stole from each other anymore since the food situation had stabilized.

*Is it because everything's basically free no one steals, or is it because none of the really expensive stuff works? Weird how nuclear war rearranges value. Food and clothes are a hundred times more precious to us now than a $4,000 computer or a fancy car.*

One of the houses she'd been to while exploring with the kids had a massive flat-panel television, easily more than a hundred inches... and there it sat untouched, in a house with a wide-open door. No one even tried taking it. Here in Evergreen, it hadn't even been EMP-fried. All sorts of electronics, expensive artwork, jewelry, cars, and whatnot sat around as ignored as chunks of rock on the side of the road. They'd even found a Lamborghini in a garage at one place. At least the kids played in it as a pretend spaceship, the only useful purpose it would ever serve again.

*That massive television would probably kill our entire power grid by itself.*

She chuckled, and resumed patrolling her route.

Whatever happened with Logan, Madison, and her future would happen. No point stressing out over it.

Civilization ended in nuclear fire. Nothing else should even rate on the stress scale.

SEPTEMBER 7TH WOULD ARRIVE IN A MERE TWO-ISH WEEKS whether Harper wanted it to or not.

Some people in town discussed the idea of holding a formal

ceremony to commemorate those killed one year ago. Mayor Ned thought it still a bit too soon, wounds a bit too raw, to forcibly call everyone's attention to it yet. Sitting around talking about people's memories of the day sounded like a horrible idea to her. Harper still didn't want to relive it, especially the first few hours her family spent in stunned silence after all the noise stopped.

Despite her best efforts to distract herself, Harper randomly thought about sitting in the basement, staring wordlessly at her parents, having no idea what had happened other than all hell broke loose outside and the power failed. They hadn't even noticed the giant chunk of concrete debris in Harper's bedroom until two weeks later.

The amount of food they lost from the deep freeze in the basement made her feel sick.

Dad stocked up 'for emergencies,' but didn't plan on said emergency involving the immediate loss of electrical power—or the end of civilization.

Lorelei didn't show any sign of understanding the significance of the impending date. Both Jonathan and Madison seemed quiet and more reserved than usual, though neither cried or acted overly sad. Harper suspected her sister would fall to pieces if she said anything at all about their parents, home, or the past, so she triple-checked every thought in her head before letting it reach her mouth.

At least until lunch one day when Madison asked, "Are ghosts real? Is there an afterlife?"

"I don't think so." Jonathan shook his head. "Or we'd know for sure by now. So many people died, there should have been tons of hauntings. Even ghosts appearing just once to say goodbye."

Harper cringed from heartache.

"Could be backed up." Cliff bit off a piece of carrot. "Gotta be some damn long lines at the check-in desk for wherever spirits end up. They probably haven't even gotten to last names starting with D yet."

Madison and Jonathan stared at him, seemingly confused if they should laugh or cry.

"Dunno, Termite," said Harper, her voice a little raspy from grief. "Nobody really knows for sure."

Carrie waved a slice of cucumber around. "I think it's a difficult thing for people to do, to confront the idea of no longer existing. Humans have such a strong survival instinct, we create theories and stories about continuing to exist in some way after the body dies. Some of us simply can't fathom the concept of an end."

"I hate ends." Lorelei stuck out her tongue. "Like when we have to stop swimming, or gotta go to bed, or the cake is gone."

"Maybe." Harper shrugged. "I kinda think ghosts might be real. Seen some stuff that's really hard to explain. Andrea's house... whenever we had a sleepover, we'd hear someone walking around in her attic at night. And it *always* felt like someone or something watched us if we went into the front room after dark."

"They say it's the restless souls stuck wandering the Earth." Cliff smiled at Madison. "If you aren't seeing ghosts, it must mean they are at peace and know you're safe."

Madison let out a long, slow breath. "Yeah. I miss them."

"Me, too," said Harper, her voice faltering.

Everyone stopped talking—even Lorelei.

Once the spontaneous moment of silence passed, it felt as though heaviness lifted off Harper's shoulders. Acknowledging their parents had the exact opposite effect she worried it would. Madison's somberness lessened.

*Tegan's right. Burying stuff won't help. Guess I'll let Maddie lead the conversation at her pace.*

THE KIDS BOUNCED BACK FROM THE SOMBERNESS OF MORNING, but Harper's friends struggled talking about the upcoming anniversary.

Without the haze of marijuana in her head, Darci spent most of the afternoon into the evening crying on her shoulder. Renee alternated between sadness and silence. Grace, at least, stayed calm. After all, she didn't really miss her parents much. Harper decided to stab the white elephant right away and started talking about their other friends who'd disappeared, people from school, teachers, parents, and so on... diving headfirst into everything they all missed.

Somehow, being the choreographer of the conversation kept Harper's emotions on an even keel. She'd tamed her heartbreak and sadness over the loss of her parents, acknowledging it without letting it rule her anymore. Darci hadn't gotten there yet. She'd spent the past year hiding behind a pot curtain, blurring reality into a manageable, distant haze. Renee still acted shell-shocked, having buried her emotions for the most part.

They sequestered in Harper's bedroom while she played referee for Renee and Darci, letting them get a year's worth of crying out of their system.

"How are you so calm?" asked Darci a few hours into their reminiscing session.

"I am a raging storm of grief and anger inside," said Harper in a deadpan tone.

Renee laughed.

"Seriously, though." Harper squeezed Darci's shoulder. "All the emotions, disbelief, and shock hit me right away. I've moved past it... admittedly faster than I'd have liked to. Didn't have a choice. Madison needed someone there for her. Don't take my lack of tears right now as anything more than me having dealt with things already... as much as anyone can deal with things like this."

Darci wiped her eyes. "Yeah..."

"Hey, remember that time Christina nearly blew up the entire chemistry lab?" asked Renee.

"Holy crap!" Darci snickered. "Yeah. Sophomore year. Epic."

"Remember seventh grade," said Harper. "Food fight. Andrea whipped a burger at that annoying kid with the big ears. He ducked, and she hit Mrs. Connors in the face."

Renee, Harper, and Darci burst into giggles.

Heart-wrenching grief turned into teary, but therapeutic laughter. Talking about all the goofy, stupid, or hilarious stuff their friends did made it seem as though they hadn't gone away forever.

By the time Cliff poked his head in to announce dinner, Harper's stomach hurt from laughing so much.

ON THE SECOND SATURDAY OF AUGUST, THE EXPRESS RETURNED to Evergreen.

For two days leading up to it, the militia had an unusual, new (albeit temporary) job: they went door to door to inform people about the Express office. Appropriately enough, Mayor Ned suggested they take over the former US Post Office on Route 74 next to the Shell station. Unfortunately, being so far south from the solar farm meant the building had no electricity, but it didn't matter.

Letters, verbal messages, or small packages didn't require refrigeration and sending letters could wait for daytime.

Harper might've been annoyed at the Express office being almost a mile south from Hilltop Drive, but it's not as if she had distant relatives she needed to stay in contact with on a regular basis. Her grandparents on Dad's side lived about a mile from her old house in Lakewood. The first time he'd ventured outside after the strike, Dad made the grim discovery their house had simply ceased existing. A nuclear blast wave had turned it—as well as all the other houses around it—into toothpicks. Considering the grandparents would have been asleep at the time of the attack and they hadn't seen them since, Harper and her family assumed they'd died instantly, perhaps even vaporized in their sleep.

Mom's parents lived in West Texas, Fort Stockton specifically. She had no idea if they'd survived the war, or the year after it. Even if they had, the Express didn't carry messages over such long distances—at least not yet.

The Express sent a small group, including eight horses, to help get the office set up. According to them, Evergreen appeared to be among the safest and most well-established settlements in the immediate area. Consequently, they'd asked Mayor Ned if they could relocate their primary horse-breeding operation here. Granted, they didn't exactly have a large operation yet.

In exchange for taking up enough land to breed horses, the Express would share the animals with the militia when needed—once people learned how to ride. A few had experience already, not Harper. The closest she'd ever been to riding a horse involved a coin-operated amusement outside a grocery store as a six-year-old. She preferred mountain bikes, but admittedly, without the industry to support machining new parts, they wouldn't last forever. Horses could also go places bikes could not. She didn't particularly look forward to having to learn how to ride.

*How's the girl who saves bugs from the bathroom afraid of horses?*

Only one of the Express people, Adriana Rodriguez, planned to remain in Evergreen as the official representative. She'd be managing the office and taking on a few locals as assistants, likely training a few to become couriers. Once they established enough additional farming capacity to feed more horses, more Express people—and horses—would arrive, but likely not until next season.

Madison immediately announced her desire to work there, taking care of the horses. She'd never been one of those girls obsessed with horses or even displayed any particular fondness for them, but a role where she got to take care of animals not destined to be killed for food thrilled her. Alas, she had to wait a few years, but hoped to talk them into letting her 'apprentice' as early as thirteen. Then again, a month from now, she might decide the chickens would miss her too much.

Once Sadie showed up to relieve her, Harper gave in to curiosity and headed down Route 74 to the old post office. Rafael used the former Shell station for his mechanic shop. He didn't have much to do lately in terms of repairing cars, since civilization had long since run out of usable gasoline. For the past six months or so, he'd been working on a biodiesel project to somewhat limited success. Most of what he'd gotten to work involved adapting mechanized farm equipment for alternative fuels. Consequently, the increased output and stability of the farm resulted in more raw materials to work with from which to develop more reliable biodiesel. His next project beyond farm tools would likely be getting the tractor-trailer running again. The odds of successfully scavenging usable stuff from far away diminished with each passing week. Retrieving anything from a long distance became infinitely more plausible if they had a working motor vehicle. By now, most food would be iffy at best. Some canned goods might be usable, but would likely be gone to other scavengers. Tools, solar panels, clothing, soap, or cleaning products might also be found... but none of it seemed worth the effort and risk of driving fifty, a hundred, or more miles away. Too much could go wrong, not even taking hostile people into account.

Harper waved to Rafael, presently tinkering with a naked engine hooked up by clear hoses to a tank of strange brown liquid. He smiled back at her, gave a thumbs-up, and resumed working.

*Not sure what we're going to do with it if he gets a working truck, but I guess it's better to have one if we can than not have one and discover a reason to want one.*

The dirt lot to the rear of the post office and a little north contained horses. Farther behind the post office, where a tree service place used to be, they'd constructed a rudimentary stable to give the horses shelter from weather. The 'new' building made from pieces of other buildings, fences, and scrap metal looked bizarre.

*Good grief, we're really turning into Mad Max, aren't we?*

She paused at the side of the post office building, staring at the stables and horses for a few minutes. The animals looked much larger in person than she'd imagined, setting off a tingle of nervousness in the pit of her stomach. She didn't fear them out of worry they'd deliberately attack her. Critters so big and heavy could crush her without even realizing it. Harper knew only one thing about horses: don't sneak up on them from behind. She'd seen enough YouTube videos of people being kicked into next week.

Shaking her head, she went inside.

For the most part, the place looked pretty much like she expected a post office to look, including all the old signs advertising stamps, PO box rentals, Priority Mail, and so on. Only one change to the room looked out of place: a thick spiral notebook on the counter, as though some random college student forgot it there. Five or six people from the Express milled around the back of the office, rearranging furniture and shelving.

Adriana Rodriguez, up front at the counter, took her attention off a much smaller book she'd been jotting notes in to smile at Harper. The woman appeared roughly Carrie's age—mid thirties. She exuded an air of friendliness, but also looked like the sort of person who tended to solve her own problems with the help of a .357 magnum. Perhaps the feeling came from her fringed cowboy-style shirt.

"Hi," said Adriana in an unexpectedly cheery tone, while offering a hand. "Don't think we've met before. Adriana Rodriguez."

"Harper Cody." She shook hands.

"Need to send something or just stopping by to check the place out?"

"Mostly checking the place out." Harper pulled her hair off her face, hooking it behind her right ear. "Don't really have anyone to send stuff to. Everyone I know is here, except for some friends who I haven't seen since... you know."

Adriana offered a sympathetic sigh. "Hear that story all the time, hon. Lot of people who gave up hope before Debbie got the idea to do this Express thing."

"Oh, right. The guys who showed up a couple weeks back said something about a list of names."

"Yep." Adriana pointed at the fat notebook. "There it is. Welcome to look through it or add your name if there are people you think might be trying to find you out there. If you do decide to add your name, let me know so I can add it to the update sheet. That way, it goes out to all the other offices. Just sneaking it into our book here won't do anyone any good."

Harper looked at the ordinary five-subject notebook. "Hope it lasts a while. At least until someone remembers how to make paper and books."

"For sure." Adriana laughed. "For some reason, no one thought notebooks worth taking. We got a nice stash of them in Granby."

"Right? Can't eat them. Can't wear them." Harper sighed. "Amazing what nuclear destruction does to priorities of what's valuable."

"So, how's this work?"

"What's that, hon?" asked Adriana.

"Sending mail. I mean, do you charge postage or anything?"

"Ahh, no." Adriana leaned on the counter. "Some settlements have taken to using money again, some—like here—don't. We don't charge any fees for transporting messages or items small enough for a person to carry on horseback. Basically, we just ask for some space and maybe enough food to get by. All of us have to work together to help the country get back on its feet."

Harper meandered along the counter to the right, stopping by the notebook. "Cool. Sounds nice. Are there many people sending mail?"

"Not so much yet. It's only been a year since things went to hell, and three months since Debbie started the Express. Lot of folks are still sort of in a fog over the whole thing. Like you, they don't know who might even be out there they'd want to send a letter to. At the moment, we're more focused on helping people find each other and establishing lines of communication. Year or two from now, we're expecting the need to run letters and such back and forth will pick up. Maybe we'll even wind up carrying cargo. One town produces a bunch of wool or something like it, but the people best at making clothes live somewhere else. Already have a couple in Granby working on a newspaper type thing. They got an old printing press running and are sending friends out to various settlements looking for interesting stories."

Harper opened the big notebook. "Cool."

"Want to add your name?" asked Adriana.

"Yeah, sure... maybe some of my friends ended up somewhere else and are alive." *Worth a shot, right?* "Can you add Logan Ruiz, too?"

Adrianna grabbed a small piece of paper and a pen. "How old are you, hon?"

"Eighteen. So's Logan. Why? Do I have to be eighteen to add myself to the book?"

"Nope. Just another piece of information to avoid confusion if multiple people have the same name. Say someone's looking for their father named Bill Smith, and they see ten Bill Smiths, but only one of them is over twenty..."

"Oh, right. Yeah, that makes sense."

"Where did you live before here?"

"Lakewood." Harper looked back at the book.

Small strips of paper stuck out the sides, marked with letters—an alphabetical index. She opened it at the beginning. Each letter-marked section contained a vertical handwritten list of names, ages, location, and a column marked 'orig,' which also contained a city name.

"What's o-r-i-g?" asked Harper.

"Short for origin. Where someone lived before the bombs."

"Ahh."

Harper flipped to J, searching for Veronica Jackson. She found the name, but her friend was not forty-three years old. She skipped ahead to M. No Christina Menendez at all. The list of O names failed to include any Andrea Ortons or even a single person named 'Orton' at all. Even though she hadn't expected to find her friends in the book, not seeing them still broke her heart. She mechanically kept turning pages, staring at them more than reading, until her gaze fell on a line that shocked her out of her sorrow:

*Luisa Ruiz – Age: 15 – Settlement: Fairplay – Orig. CO Springs.*

She stared at the page for a moment, then covered her mouth.

"Hon?" Adriana walked up on the other side of the counter. "Are you okay?"

"H-how is this possible?" She pointed at the line. "Colorado Springs evaporated."

Adrianna turned the book half toward her so she could read the line. "It's only as accurate as the information people give at the office. I haven't been to Colorado Springs since the war, so I can't really say one way or the other what kind of shape it's in. Even if it did end up entirely leveled, a person being from there doesn't mean they *were* there during the strike."

"But she's only fifteen. Where else would she be?" Harper blinked. "Logan was up in Denver for a school hockey game…"

She scanned the R page for more people named Ruiz. A handful looked about the right age to potentially be Logan's parents, but he'd never told her their names. However, none had 'Fairplay' listed as their settlement or Colorado Springs as their origin.

"Uhh…" Harper bounced on her toes. "Be right back. He really needs to see this."

"I'll be here." Adriana smiled. "Anything else I can help you with?"

Harper stopped short three steps from the door. "Umm. My little sister wanted to know how old she has to be before she can like get a job here helping to tend horses."

"Any experience?" asked Adriana.

"No… she's never been within forty feet of a horse before. But she's only ten."

Adriana grinned. "Plenty of time to learn then. She's welcome to stop by to get a feel for things whenever it's okay with your parents. Far as joining the Express as whatever passes for an 'employee' these days goes, not until she's at least fifteen."

"Yeah, figured. Thanks. Again, be right back." Harper rushed out the door.

# 22

# THE SMARTER OPTION

Clicking from the gears of Harper's mountain bike as she coasted made Logan and several other men look over at her.

Logan carried a large basket of potatoes toward a large pull cart they'd use to lug them down the road to the quartermaster. She came to a stop next to him as he set the basket on the end of the wagon and gave it a shove.

He wiped his hands on his shirt. "Hey."

"You gotta see—!"

He kissed her. "Couple more hours to go here. Gotta get this stuff in off the field before it rots."

Harper stared at him. Logan didn't seem too worried about losing food to rot. Not like he rushed frozen perishables from the trunk of a car to the freezer in the house. "Umm. Can I borrow you for like fifteen minutes? You really need to see this."

"Wow. Umm." He brushed a hand over her cheek. "Must be important. Yeah, sure. I can slip away for fifteen or so."

"Hop on." Harper swung her bike around, then stood on the pedals.

Logan somewhat awkwardly got on behind her, grasping her hips to steady himself. "I will never get tired of having your butt in my face."

She blushed. If not for the storm of emotions in her head over the possible discovery of his little sister still being alive, she'd have made a joke.

"Okay, this must be serious if you're not saying anything."

"Umm. It could be. I don't know yet." She pedaled off the farm to Route 74.

After a quick stop at the militia HQ to grab a second bike for Logan, she led him roughly a mile down the road to the post office.

"The Express?" called Logan from a little behind her. "Seriously? This couldn't wait."

Harper rode her bike almost into the wall, jumping off it to jog alongside for a few steps before coming to a full stop. "Nope. Couldn't wait."

"Ooo-kay." He got off his bike, then leaned it against the wall. "I trust you."

She grabbed his hand, and basically dragged him inside, straight over to the notebook. "Before I freak out... read this."

"So, umm, mail? That's like the last thing humanity should be worrying about yet." He looked where she pointed... and most of the color drained out of his face.

"Yeah... that's about how I felt."

Logan wrapped his arms around her from behind, staring at the notebook in silence. The only sign of his emotion came from how tightly he squeezed her.

She reached up, grasping his hands in front of her chest.

"What is this?" asked Logan, his voice a touch louder than a whisper.

"They have a list of people in other settlements who are trying to find family or friends. I added us to the book in case anyone we know might end up in a settlement somewhere with an Express office."

Logan shifted his stare from the book to Adriana. "Is she still there?"

"That, I can't say. The only way we would know to change or

remove an entry is if someone told us." Adriana drifted over behind the counter, peering at the notebook. "Fairplay is a reasonably organized settlement. Not as big as here. No militia to speak of, but seemed fairly safe."

"Can't be her." Logan fought back tears. "Springs is dust. There's no way she could've gotten out."

"I'm sorry." Harper twisted around in his arms to face him.

"What are you apologizing for?" Logan bowed his head against hers.

"I didn't even think it might be someone else and not your sister. I know you've had a really hard time dealing with losing your family. But what are the odds of another girl from Springs with the same name and age?"

"Springs is dust," whispered Logan.

"So they say." Adriana raised both eyebrows.

"Let's go look." Harper squeezed him back.

"How far is it to Fairplay?" asked Logan.

"Sixty…" Adriana walked sideways to where she'd been standing before, picked up a little notepad, and flipped some pages while muttering 'Evergreen to Fairplay' repeatedly under her breath. "Sixty-two miles fastest route."

Harper nodded. "Not too far."

"Not too far when we have cars." Logan chuckled. "It's a hell of a walk."

"About thirty hours on foot, give or take." Adrianna tossed the notepad back to the counter. "You're talking about a roughly four-day trip each way, camping out in the sticks at night. That's assuming you don't run into any problems or bad weather."

Logan looked down. "She might not even still be there. Or maybe it isn't even her."

"Why not send a letter?" Adrianna smiled. "That's kinda why we're here. Rider can make that trip in two days without punishing the horse. One day is possible, too, but it's a little mean to the animal without good reason."

"So, we'd know in four days if it's my sister or not?" asked Logan.

"Not exactly four. Takes a while for a rider here to be scheduled to go down that way. Plus, however long it takes her to write a reply then have a rider bring it back here. Probably safer to expect a full week to two weeks to get an answer." Adrianna pulled a sheet of paper out and set it on the counter in front of him.

Harper nudged him. "Umm, yeah, that's a really good idea. Much better than running off like an idiot."

"You're not an idiot." Logan squeezed her hand. "Just have a tendency to think with your heart before your brain can engage."

She laughed. "Yeah... guilty."

"I dunno." He flicked at the blank piece of copier paper. "I'm not sure how to handle this. I'd accepted she was gone. What if it's someone else with the same name? I think that would hurt even more than thinking she evaporated in a nuclear fireball before she ever woke up."

"Lo..." She threaded her arms around his neck. "You've already seen the book. You'll never stop thinking about it if you don't try. I can't imagine not wanting to know for sure."

"You're going to write to her if I don't, aren't you?"

"Thinkin' about it," she said in an overacted innocent tone.

He glanced at Arianna offering a pen.

"Send a letter and we'll see what happens. If it isn't her, better we find out this way than spend a week going down there." Harper rubbed a hand up and down his back. "What if it *is* her?"

"Yeah." He reached for the pen, a lone tear creeping down his face. "You're right. I have to know."

# 23

# SIXTY-TWO MILES

L ife continued in Evergreen, normal in every way except for a constant nagging thought teetering between hope and dread.

Not an hour went by Harper didn't contemplate what a potential response from Fairplay would do to Logan. He hadn't wanted to talk much about it, nor had he been too interested in romance, or even making out since writing the letter. She knew he wasn't angry with her. He'd been at the house every chance he got, being with her, cuddling, holding her... everything short of kissing or getting sexy.

His pain and worry practically scrolled across his forehead on a marquee.

Harper did her best to be there for him to lean on without pushing him to talk about the obvious topic hanging over them. She didn't even pester him to stop thinking about it. Sometimes, she read too much into sideways glances, wondering if he blamed her for ripping open an emotional scab. It would be like someone saying her dad didn't die after all, merely appeared to... but when she got there, she realized they made a mistake and some dude simply looked like him.

Then again, Harper *watched* her father get shot. No one in

Evergreen had seen Colorado Springs since the attack. Countless people told stories about it being vaporized, but always second-hand. People heard from someone who heard from someone. The problem with stories was they often turned out not to be true. A lie—or an exaggerated tale—didn't become any truer because many people believed it.

Monday, August 19th started off pretty much the same as every other day for the past two weeks—except for an unexpected bizarre chill and a light dusting of snow appearing overnight. Lorelei made Madison squeal by running barefoot out into the yard. Harper shivered at the sight of the girl frolicking in a half-inch of snow with no shoes on. Fortunately, the cold *did* eventually reach Lorelei's brain after about a minute, and she listened to Harper and Madison yelling at her to come inside.

Walking patrol during the colder months in a high-elevation town like Evergreen sucked in ways a girl used to a comfortable suburban life couldn't have imagined before experiencing. It hadn't yet become truly cold, but she still wrapped herself up in a scarf and would have worn ski goggles if she had them. Hopefully, no one's house would catch fire from November through February. It would be too tempting to merely stand there and warm up rather than throwing water at the flames. They had precious little leeway in terms of fire, anyway. It didn't take too long for a burning house to pass the point of no return where a bucket brigade couldn't save it.

She figured she'd get a few more years out of her warm boots before they disintegrated. Her winter coat would perhaps make it another ten or fifteen. Mom had a coat she wore on *really* cold days for as long as Harper could remember. The raspberry-colored thing had to be twenty years old.

Next time she saw Renee, she'd try to talk her into learning how to make winter boots. Off the top of her head, she knew Evergreen had twenty-two kids just in the north part of town, not counting the babies and toddlers at the 'orphanage' run by Doreen Mack. She had to be watching at least seven *little* kids. By the time Evergreen's juvenile population grew up, they wouldn't have winter shoes at all unless someone here made them from scratch. Harper didn't have the first clue how to go about making warm boots, but figured it would likely require wool, or maybe bear fur.

Those who hunted meat for the town killed mostly deer and rabbits, but bagged the occasional bear as well. Harper couldn't say exactly which meals had been bear meat, deer meat, or beef. They'd saved the fur from the bear kills, though. What happened to it, she couldn't say. Maybe someone in town knew how to process it into leather. If not, they might've 'Google searched' it, which meant hunting the library for a how-to book.

Harper returned home by way of the quartermaster's to pick up their food allotment. After packing stuff away in the cabinets, she got started on dinner. To stretch supplies, she and the kids had a simple lunch of jammed toast and berries. Some of the fresh vegetables she brought home went into a large pot along with the rabbit meat they gave her. Fortunately, since the power came back on, the quartermaster workers dealt with the ugly parts—skinning and cleaning. If she didn't say anything, Madison would probably assume they ate chicken, unless she recognized the bones.

Having soup without noodles in it no longer felt strange.

While cooking, she randomly cried at the thought kids might never again cheer about finding spaghetti on the table for dinner.

*Dammit. Please tell me my hormones aren't going crazy. We only did it once and he had a condom on.*

The kids, plus Becca, Eva, Mila, and Christopher appeared in the yard, and promptly proceeded to have a snowball fight—or attempt to given the relatively light coating. Carrie and Renee showed up a few hours later, right about the time the soup/stew seemed done enough to eat. The rabbit had kinda broken up in the broth, so maybe it could pass for chicken. She'd only gotten enough meat for one meal and decided to use it right away considering the sketchiness of the electrical power situation. She didn't like to keep a stockpile of meat sitting around in the freezer and risk a repeat of what happened at home in Lakewood.

Few things smelled as bad as a deep freeze cabinet thawing out and rotting with sixty or so pounds of various meats and frozen vegetables in it. Her parents tried to cook and use as much as possible, but four people, one a kid, could only eat so much... and Dad only stocked so much charcoal for the backyard grill.

She, Renee, and Carrie chatted about clothing, specifically winter boots, for a little while until Cliff arrived back from his patrol shift, bleeding from a small cut above the eye. Both Carrie and Harper went into 'mom mode.' He dismissed their worries, explaining a drunken idiot wearing a fat gold ring mistook him and Roy for 'Russian invaders.'

"Here, let me..." Carrie dabbed at Cliff's head with a cloth.

"It's fine." He retreated to take a seat at the dining room table while she kept trying to fuss over him.

Harper couldn't help but smile at the two of them 'arguing.' Finally, Cliff sighed and relented, staring at the ceiling while Carrie wiped blood from around his eye.

Renee cringed. "Doesn't it hurt?"

"Nope."

"Guess you're pretty tough from being a former Ranger, huh?" asked Renee.

"Nah. Mall cop." Cliff heaved a sigh. "A man doesn't know the true meaning of pain until they've been forced to listen to *A Barry Manilow Christmas* on repeat for eight hours a day over two months every damn year."

Harper, Renee, and Carrie laughed.

Due to the size of the soup pot, Harper didn't try to move it off the stove, instead ladling out portions and carrying them bowl by bowl to the dining room. Before long, Madison, Jonathan, and Lorelei headed inside to eat while their friends raced off home. Madison stopped the instant she entered the kitchen, giving Harper an 'I smell meat' sideways glance. Before Harper could say a word, Madison smiled.

"Kidding. I know... I know..." Madison frowned. "I'll deal."

A few minutes into dinner, Logan burst in the front door and ran to the dining room. He slumped against the wall at the transition where living room became dining room, too out of breath to speak. He didn't look hurt, merely sweaty, so Harper held off panic.

"Soup's good, but it's not come running from all the way across town good," said Cliff. "I suspect something else is on his mind."

Logan wheezed.

"Hungry?" Harper stood. "Let me grab a chair from the kitchen."

He waved a letter-folded piece of paper at her, wheezed again, and gasped, "Reply."

"Awesome," whispered Harper, mostly because he didn't look broken, sad, or angry. Even though he couldn't speak at the moment, his expression—like he'd just won the lottery—said all she needed to hear about what the letter contained. She rushed over to him. "You ran here all the way from the post office?"

"Yeah."

"I'll get him some water." Renee got up and hurried to the kitchen.

Logan handed over the paper, then pulled her into his arms. She unfolded it to reveal the telltale cutesy-florid handwriting of a young girl.


OH MY GOD, YOU'RE ALIVE!

Lo, I'm sorta okay. Ended up in a place called Fairplay, but I guess you knew that since you wrote me a letter. Express guy said you're in Evergreen. I'm not sure how to get there or even where it is. The Express won't carry people. Maybe I could ask for directions, but I'm scared to leave town alone. People at the bar tell stories about wild animals, crazy people, and whatever 'highwaymen' are.

Maybe I shouldn't tell you this in a letter, but it feels wrong not to say something. Mom and Dad didn't make it. I haven't heard from Ana or Luis. Please be real and not someone playing a mean prank.

-Luisa


"OH, SHIT," SAID HARPER.

"Yeah," rasped Logan.

"Have some soup," added Cliff.

Renee handed him a glass of water. "Here. You look ready to pass out. You should sit down."

"Thanks." He chugged it.

Harper pulled him around to her seat, pushed him into the chair, then hurried to the kitchen.

"It's okay." Logan got up and followed her. "You don't need to bring me food like a waitress."

While he ladled himself out a portion, she dragged a kitchen chair into the dining room and sat close enough to lean against him.

"I get the feeling the news is positive?" Cliff raised both eyebrows. "No one's in tears yet."

"The night is young," said Jonathan.

Harper bit back a laugh. "Yeah. His sister somehow survived and got out of Colorado Springs. She's in Fairplay."

"Weird." Renee scrunched up her nose. "Is there another town around here named Cheating?"

Logan chuckled. "Ugh. I don't know how to process this. I thought she was dead... letter says our parents didn't make it. I should be more upset."

"You thought they were all dead and grieved already." Harper took his hand. "Finding out Luisa is alive... I've never seen you so happy."

"Coach would be proud of me. Ran the mile in record time." Logan exhaled. "Went to the post office like I'd been doing the past couple days to ask if any reply came in. When Adrianna handed me the paper, I almost couldn't open it. Came right here after I read it."

Cliff stirred his soup. "I'm gonna go out on a limb here and assume the two of you are going to want to head over to Fairplay."

Madison stared at Harper. "I understand. You'd go there to find me."

"Yeah." Harper exhaled in relief. "His sister is afraid to travel alone."

"Don't blame her." Cliff stood. "Hang on a minute." He headed off down the hall toward his bedroom.

"What's going on?" asked Lorelei.

Harper ate a few quick spoonfuls of soup while holding up a 'one sec' finger. "Logan's sister is still alive, and in another town pretty far away. We're going to go there so we can help her come back here and stay safe."

"Okay." Lorelei smiled. "Is it gonna take long?"

"Probably a week or so." Harper cringed, glancing at Madison, who stared down into her lap.

Cliff returned carrying a paper map. He sat back in his chair, unfolding the map beside his soup.

"Eat." Harper nudged Logan. "I know you're excited. But you need food."

"Nervous more like." He chuckled, but picked up a spoon.

"Hmm." Cliff studied the map. "Sixty some miles. Thirty-one hours walking at two miles an hour. Twenty hours if we can hold three miles an hour. Could do it in ten hours on bikes, roughly."

Harper cringed. "Do you think Walter will let us take bikes all the way to Fairplay? If we break a chain or something happens, it's toast. No one here can make new parts."

"Good thing they're bringing in horses." Renee snickered. "Do you remember Paisley Ross? She'd go nuts."

"Oh wow. Haven't seen her since eighth grade, yeah. She had horse stickers on *everything*." Harper forced herself not to think about her old classmates. Otherwise, she'd go down a miserably depressing road of trying to guess how many survived. "I mean, we might as well use the bikes while we have them. If we don't use them, they're going to rust and fall apart anyway. None of us can ride horses and we don't even have many here. Not sure the Express would even let us ride them so far off. The agreement with the militia sounded like they expected us to use them only for patrolling inside town."

Cliff drank the last of his soup from the bowl. "Yeah. They're not going to be too happy with the idea of us riding horses sixty miles away. Less happy given none of us know a damn thing about how to take care of them."

"So, we're looking at a three-day walk each way." Harper cringed internally at the idea of being away for so long, but it had to be done.

"Three days?" Madison gawked. "It's just like the next town over."

Cliff chuckled. "The world was a much bigger place before cars."

"If we do take bikes, how are we going to manage bringing an empty one along for Luisa to ride back to Evergreen?" Logan glanced at Harper, then Cliff. "Harp gave me a ride from the farm to the militia building, but doing that for ten hours a day? Ack."

"Suppose we could bring Lorelei along to ride the spare bike down." Cliff winked. "She's little enough one of us could wear her like a backpack for the return trip."

Lorelei giggled.

"No." Harper shook her head. "She's too young. She's gotta stay here where it's safe. Besides, her legs are too short to reach the pedals on a full-sized mountain bike."

Cliff grinned.

"Yeah." Harper biffed herself in the forehead. "I know. I messed up bringing Maddie out to look for you and Roy."

"Ehh." He waved dismissively. "Not like you were expecting to go on a long trip, or even a dangerous one. Extended patrol's only a few miles outside town. Those idiots couldn't have been there more than two weeks. Last time we walked the route, no sign of anything out there."

Madison bit her lip. "I'll go if you want me to. Just put one of those kid seats on the back of Harp's bike for the trip back. I don't want you guys to be gone for a whole week."

"Hmm." Cliff made a face of contemplation.

*Holy crap. Is he really considering bringing Maddie?* "Uhh…"

Cliff glanced at Logan. "How big is your sister?"

"I dunno, umm…" Logan fidgeted. "She's the exact opposite of my older sister, Ana. Luisa's skinny and real short. Haven't seen her in a year, so she's probably taller now. Unlikely she got fat."

"Maybe we can rig a second seat on a bike for her." Cliff made a silly face at Madison. "You have an important job. Stay here and be safe."

Madison exhaled, her expression strange. Harper couldn't tell if her little sister was relieved or disappointed.

"How long is it going to take us to get there on bikes?" Logan drank the last of his soup.

"Depends on terrain and pace, but between ten and twelve hours. Figure we'll average out to roughly nine miles an hour on a bike. Can cruise much faster than a person or horse can walk. One day there, one day back… assuming nothing goes wrong." Cliff looked over the map again. "Let me talk to Walt in the morning. I want to make sure he's of the same mind about us taking the bikes. He'll appreciate the overall risks are much lower the faster we get back."

"Wait… you're going with us?" Harper sat up a little taller.

"Damn right." He folded the map up. "Not about to let my daughter go sixty miles away into unexplored territory without doing everything in my power to make sure she comes home. Besides, I kinda like my son in law. He makes you smile. Gotta help him out, too."

Logan coughed.

"Uhh, Dad, we're not married." Harper's face heated up.

"Yeah. Neither am I and Carrie." Cliff leaned left and gave Carrie a peck on the cheek.

Madison, Lorelei, and Jonathan exchanged confused looks.

"Are Jon and Mila married, too?" asked Lorelei.

Jonathan melted straight down out of his chair and hid under the table.

Madison cracked up into giggles. "Did we miss a wedding?"

A moan came from under the table.

"I meant Dad," said Madison.

"He's saying formality has nothing to do with reality." Grace rolled her eyes. "Guys, come on. Don't be dense."

Lorelei shifted her eyes left and right. "I don't understand. Can I have more soup, please?"

"Absolutely." Harper leapt to her feet and grabbed the child's bowl before she could change her mind.

"I've seen grief eating and boredom eating before." Cliff laughed. "First time for confusion eating."

*She's hungry!* Harper didn't think a girl her size *could* eat too much more, so she put one ladle's worth of soup in the bowl and brought it to her.

"Thank you," chimed Lorelei.

Renee coaxed Jonathan back into his chair. The boy's face remained bright red. She whispered something in his ear that earned her a 'wow really?' stare, and he appeared less mortified.

"Right." Cliff patted the map. "I'm going to assume you want to do this as fast as possible."

Logan took a deep breath. "Please. I'd like to bring her here before it gets cold and we get a nasty snow."

"Where are you going to put her?" asked Renee.

"On the extra seat if Cliff can rig one." Logan scratched his head. "If it doesn't work, maybe we can take a bike for her apart and sling the parts over our backs."

Renee rolled her eyes. "I mean, where is she going to live? Aren't you sharing a house with like six single dudes?"

"Five, but... umm, yeah." Logan cringed. "Ugh. That's not going to work."

"I've got the space," said Carrie. "Got two rooms not doing much of anything right now. One of them is kinda small, though."

"She could share my room," said Renee. "If you want to avoid the tiny one."

"Thanks." Logan smiled. "There's a little house right up the dirt road from you. Maybe Luisa and I could go there."

*You want to live with your sister in the house we had sex in?* Harper blushed. *Well, it is close... suppose it's not too cringey as long as* he *takes the bed we used.*

Cliff patted the table like a judge banging a gavel. "Done, then. I'll pester Walter first thing in the morning. Get a good rest. If he's on board with us using the bikes, we're leaving as early as possible tomorrow."

Madison looked up from her lap at Harper. "Will you play Uno with us tonight?"

"Yeah. Definitely." Harper forced herself to smile despite feeling guilty. *She wants to spend every last minute of remaining daylight with me in case I don't come home.*

# 24

# FORAGING

**W**ind made Harper's long, red hair trail behind her like a pennant.

She cruised at an alarming speed down a hill on Route 285. The nice — somewhat — blue sky, indistinct clouds behind the haze of dust, and reasonably good weather didn't register much in her mind. Other than concentrating on not crashing her mountain bike into the occasional abandoned car, fallen boulder, or random piece of debris, the major thought going on in her head involved how much it was going to suck to pedal back up this hill on the way home.

Route 285 had loads of room, two lanes in either direction, dead space between them as wide as a travel lane sometimes paved, sometimes grass, and generous shoulders on either side. A scattering of partially melted vehicles as well as still-intact ones littered the road, though not in any great number. She imagined an ordinary amount of traffic for almost six in the morning on a Friday melting where it happened to be at the time the nuclear bombs created a premature sunrise. The more intact vehicles looked as though they'd been abandoned when they'd run out of gas, likely driven days or weeks after the strike. Many of the melted cars had gone off the road or crashed into oncoming traffic, a fair number nothing more than twisted metal on charred patches of ground. Harper cringed, picturing people being blinded or vaporized by the unexpected blast and their still-moving cars going out of control.

Harper white-knuckled the handlebars while swerving around wrecks. Downhill runs helped cut the time it would take to reach Fairplay. She had to be doing thirty or forty miles per hour, way faster than possible on foot. Alas, the burst of speed lasted only for a short stretch before the ground leveled off. Going uphill slowed them, but they still moved at least as fast as walking, so the bicycles didn't turn into a handicap.

Harper couldn't stop yawning. Cliff pulled her out of bed before sunrise.

Ever since they'd settled in Evergreen, she'd been more or less waking up with the sun. Before, in the normal, boring, ordinary life of an average suburban teenager, she didn't get along well with dawn. Left to her own devices, she'd have stayed up until one or two in the morning and crawled out of bed around ten. Unfortunately, the people who used to run the school system disagreed with such a schedule, insisting on starting stupidly early for some unknown reason. Dragging her ass out of bed before she wanted to move had been standard procedure for her entire life... at least from about age six on.

Nowadays, she woke naturally with the sunrise, and didn't suffer the same foot-dragging listlessness as before when the alarm clock kicked her out of bed. The oddity of it struck her as confusing. How could she get up so early without a problem when all her life she hated mornings? Maybe because she generally went to sleep when the sun went down—especially when the electricity didn't work. She no longer had tons of homework to do before morning or the internet to keep her up late. She, Renee, and Grace—before Darci arrived in Evergreen—had a long conversation about the effect electrical light and industrialized society had on the human circadian rhythm, forcing people to function on sleep-wake schedules the body couldn't adapt to.

Renee liked the 'natural' alarm clock of dawn. Harper kinda

agreed with her, but wouldn't have unless she'd lived it. However, Cliff smashed her routine by waking her up an hour before sunrise. While she'd always had to wake up early for school, and she'd been getting up at dawn recently, she'd only woken up *before* the sun a handful of times in her life. Two had been to hit the road with Dad to attend shooting competitions out of state, one to catch a plane for a family vacation to Florida. In those cases, she only needed to be awake long enough to go from house to car before she could sleep again.

Apparently, Cliff decided to revert to his military ways and woke up at the time Darci used to go *to* sleep—roughly four in the morning. By the time he returned to the house to wake Harper and Logan, he'd already talked Walter into letting them use the bikes as well as attached a 'rear' seat to one. The thin black steel frame and red padded cushions made her think the chair came from a pizza place. He'd cut the legs off and turned them into a frame, which he'd bolted to a cargo shelf already installed on the bike.

For sake of thoroughness, Harper ended up testing the seat while Logan pedaled around in circles. It felt secure enough, so they'd deemed the add-on seat a success and left Evergreen at sunrise. Her Mossberg rode in a sheath made from a soft nylon rifle case strapped to the side of the bike, in easy reach should she need it. Cliff and Logan had similar hook-ups for their AR-15s. When Walter suggested they bring a fourth person along for increased security, Ken Zhang volunteered to go. He borrowed one of the scoped .308 rifles in case they ended up having to deal with a sniper problem.

Madison got out of bed the same time as Harper, shadowing her for the hour and a half they spent awake before leaving town. Surprisingly, her kid sister didn't throw a fit or even act overly emotional when they started riding. Knowing Madison, it didn't seem likely the girl buried her feelings to have a meltdown once they'd gone out of sight. Perhaps hearing Cliff talk about the route being tremendously simple eased her mind: south down Route 74 to the end of Evergreen, hook around a curve onto Route 73 and take it to Route 285, which they'd stay on all the way to Fairplay. They didn't have to remember any tricky turns hours from now and, in theory, couldn't get lost.

The bicycles might also have helped eased Madison's fears. If another group of 'survivalists' or a gang decided to cause trouble, they'd have a more difficult time catching people on bikes than on foot. The Express riders made the trip back and forth to Fairplay more than once, reasonable evidence the route ought to be mostly safe. Since gangs, bandits, wild animals, and weather didn't exactly follow predictable schedules, everyone remained vigilant.

Harper and Cliff started off the ride discussing tactics in the event of an unexpected ambush. Straddling a mountain bike didn't make for a great position in a gunfight. He suggested ducking down and riding hard to the nearest cover, even if it meant a ditch on the side of the road and taking a spill off the bike. Eating dirt wouldn't hurt anywhere near as much as eating a bullet. Their response would, naturally, depend on the nature of threats. No point crashing into a tree on purpose if an idiot fifty feet away threatened them waving a hatchet.

They all wore backpacks of the type she once used for school. Instead of textbooks, they carried water jugs, raw vegetables, and some bread—enough food to last four days if rationed. If they could obtain a meal at Fairplay, all the better, but Cliff didn't want to depend on it. Despite planning to find shelter in town for the night, everyone also packed a blanket in case something went sideways and they had to camp outside.

Back on flat road at the bottom of the hill, Harper pedaled along, cruising faster than anyone could walk, but didn't kick her butt to maintain. Someone had spray-painted doomsday messages in black on an all-concrete overpass up ahead. Everything from 'doom is the price of capitalism' to 'death are the wages of sin' to a simple 'we are all f***ed', using skulls and crossbones to censor out a few letters.

*Unbelievable. The world's on fire and someone still has a problem with curse words. Did my mother write that? What's wrong? Billions dead isn't shocking enough, but some survivor might be 'offended' at an F-bomb? People are so damned stupid.*

She gazed at various strip malls, gas stations, and little towns on either side of Route 285 as they rode by. No one even suggested stopping to check any of them out. By now, everything usable had either been looted already, rotted in place, or would be too bulky to carry on bicycles. Even if they *did* find good stuff, anything they kept would have to fit in their backpacks.

A few minutes after passing a blue sign reading 'In Memory of James R. Ellison, Please Drive Slowly,' they discovered a rather unexpected sight for a highway: a huge debris field apparently from a crashed aircraft. Based on the section of tail and the remains of only one engine lying in the middle of the road, she figured it had been a military jet of some kind.

"Whoa," said Ken. "Someone missed the runway."

"Just a bit." Logan whistled. "One of ours?"

Cliff made an appraising noise. "Ehh, jets aren't my thing, but the tail looks like it came from an F-16. Possibly out of Peterson AFB, or maybe Buckley. Those boys would definitely have known the nukes were incoming. Could be, they tried to intercept the missiles. Can't think of any other reason they'd have been in the air during the strike."

Harper looked down. *At least they tried.*

"You're sure the plane was flying when it happened? Maybe they went up the next day to survey damage?" asked Ken.

"Ehh, don't think so." Cliff exhaled hard. "Military airfields would've been primary targets. Any planes on the ground would've been vaporized."

"Carrier?" asked Harper.

"Not an F-16." Logan smiled.

"Huh?" She shrugged. "I dunno anything about military planes. Those aren't on carriers?"

"Nope." Logan shook his head.

Harper swerved around pieces of former aircraft in the road. However it ended up here, she offered a moment's silence for the pilot, thanking them for trying to protect people. Only a hint of 'fuel smell' hung in the air, a good sign the crash occurred quite a while ago. Above, the dust haze swirled in alternating bands of darker grey, making the sky look like a rumpled satin sheet.

*How long is it going to take all that dirt to come back down? I shouldn't complain. At least we didn't have a nuclear winter.*

One hour melted into the next. They rode along the wreck-strewn highway, surrounded by picturesque scenery, an ever-changing panorama of wide-open land, trees, forest-covered distant hills, rock faces, valleys, and steep canyon walls.

Another blue sign read, "In Memory of Stephanie Webb, Levi Sanford." Beyond it to the right, a garage type building and several dump trucks stood at the base of a huge rocky hill. Up ahead, Route 285 entered a canyon with a rock wall on the left and a tree-covered mountain on the right. A fence of thin steel cables and knee-high posts divided the highway in half. Everyone veered to the right, perhaps out of subconscious habit not to drive into the oncoming lane.

It had been a few hours since they started the trip, so when Logan asked about stopping for a pee break, Cliff groaned, as did Ken. Harper cringed, going from 'fine' to 'bladder crisis' in an instant. Her desire to get home in one piece as fast as possible stomped on any sense of embarrassment. She calmly pulled her bike to the side of the road, hopped off, and stepped over the guardrail, intent on watering the ground right there. Despite a mild blush, she forced herself to lower her jeans and squat out in the open. Not only had Cliff been in the Army, served in combat zones, and seen it all before, he'd totally become Dad—so she felt confident he wouldn't look. Logan had already seen all her secrets. Ken would probably be more embarrassed than her, so she ignored her emotions to get things done and back on the road as fast as possible.

Without a word, all three guys stepped over the cable fence to pee on the rock wall on the left side of the highway, standing with their backs to Harper. Logan peeked over his shoulder at her every few seconds. Once she had her jeans back up, he muttered something and the guys returned to where all the bikes leaned on the guardrail.

They took a short break to drink some water and munch on raw string beans, carrots, and potatoes. Not the ideal snack, but they didn't exactly have trail mix on hand, nor anything else suitable to bring on the road. No one in Evergreen had bothered making beef—or venison—jerky. In between bites of potato, Harper suggested they look into making some since it would be a way to preserve meat in the event of a loss of refrigeration. Sounded like a great idea until Cliff and Ken told her jerky only lasted a week or two.

Soon after they resumed riding, they reached the town of Pine Junction. The streets in sight from Route 285 looked empty, though Harper swore she saw figures moving around, ducking for cover behind a long, rustic-looking building, apparently the 'Someplace Else Saloon' according to the sign on the roof. Another guy darted out of sight through a gap between the bar and two-story brown structure somewhat stylized to look like a giant log cabin. A big, oval wooden sign attached to the railing of the second-story porch identified it as 'The Log Building on Hwy 285'. It appeared to be some kind of shopping center containing a thrift store. She got the sense people inside it watched them, but no one called out, showed themselves, or shot at them.

Harper kept peeking at the parking lot in front of the place until they'd gone far enough off not to be able to see it anymore. *Guess they're scared of outsiders. Better that than hostile.*

"Something catch your eye?" asked Cliff.

"Thought I saw some people back there. Whoever it was ran like hell as soon as they saw us."

Cliff chuckled. "Fine by me. Rather be run from than shot at."

"Same here." She smiled.

"Problem on the way back?" asked Logan.

Cliff made a so-so hand tilt. "Gonna be at least tomorrow before we come by again. Probably catch them off guard and be out of sight before they can do anything... and they have no reason to expect we'd be coming back anyway."

"Right..." Harper exhaled.

They rode on.

Here and there, they passed buildings or small towns, some little more than a gas station and a Subway shop in sight from Route 285. Harper looked straight up as she rode beneath a set of power lines crossing the highway, astounded to see them intact. The deeper they'd gone into the hills away from the Denver area, the fewer wrecked cars existed. By about three or four in the afternoon at her estimation, the few cars and trucks they encountered appeared abandoned, not melted. Most sat in parking lots, only a handful on the road.

"It's so eerie out here." Harper stared at the red-and-white awning over the gas pumps at a Loaf 'N Jug as it went by on her right. "Nothing looks destroyed. It's like all the people simply disappeared."

"Yeah total *Night of the Comet* stuff," said Ken.

"Huh?" asked Harper.

"Old movie." He chuckled. "People just disappeared into dust."

"Yeah." Logan whistled. "Where did everyone go? No nukes hit this far up in the mountains."

"Not around here anyway." Cliff chuckled. "Imagine the locals went wherever they thought they might be able to find food. Could be hundreds of little tiny settlements out there, just a family or three living together on the same farm. Anywhere they managed to survive."

Harper stared into the distance on her left. Fields, hills, and more trees. She'd never before even considered the idea small groups might be out there fending for themselves on family farms, and spent a while trying to come up with reasons ancient humans decided to live in towns and cities. 'Mutual protection' made the most sense, so if people didn't have an outside threat to be afraid of, they might stay isolated. Not like grocery stores, doctors, dentists, or malls existed anymore to draw people in.

AT THE TOWN OF BAILEY, ROUTE 285 SWUNG AROUND TO THE right, going from southerly to due west. A building with a green roof and bare wood siding marked 'Rustic Station' appeared to have been the scene of a war. Four square windows facing the highway had all been broken out, the walls around them pockmarked by bullet holes. At the far end of the lot beyond, a big sign on the roof of a larger building read 'Alcohol Tobacco Firearms' between a pair of green plus signs.

"Everything the post-apocalyptic badass needs," said Cliff.

"What do you think happened here?" Ken raised an eyebrow.

"Oh, probably the first group of locals came here to grab some guns and booze, then spent the next few days defending their stash." Cliff waved dismissively at the little shopping center. "Probably used up all their ammo, got overrun, and killed. Or they effed off into the hills."

Logan stood on the pedals, staring left as they cruised by. "You sure they're not still in there?"

"Yep. No one's shot at us." Cliff laughed. "And there aren't any bodies lying about. Someone cleaned up after the big mess."

Up ahead, a large white box truck had crashed into the side of a convenience store-slash-car wash at a Conoco station, missing a cage full of propane tanks by inches. Cliff pulled over to the truck and hopped off his bike.

"Guess we're scavenging." Harper stopped beside him.

"Just curious why no one's popped the door on this thing. Unmarked white trucks this big always make me suspicious." He grinned, drew the crowbar from his North Face pack like a barbarian yanking a sword from a back sheath, then attacked the lock.

Logan stopped on Harper's left. "He's looking for coffee."

"Damn straight." Cliff popped the padlock, stuffed the crowbar into the backpack, and flung the truck door upward.

The cargo area contained multiple stacks of large cardboard boxes marked only with cryptic numbers, no brand logos or anything obvious. Cliff pulled his knife and began a hasty examination of the contents. Ken climbed up into the truck to help. After a few minutes, Logan, too, muttered something about making it go faster, and also entered the truck to assist.

"Anything?" Ken looked up from a box. "This is all cheap dollar store bullshit."

"Yeah," muttered Cliff, sounding disappointed. "Not even *good* toys. Chintzy knockoffs like He Person dolls or GI Jim."

"I got some Sailor of the Moon toys." Ken laughed.

Logan whistled. "Wow, they're not even trying hard to pretend these aren't rip offs."

"Hah." Harper shook her head.

"I'm serious." Cliff pulled something out of a box and held it up. "GI Jim figures. Looks sorta like a drunk guy drew GI Joe characters."

"The derpy cross-eyes totally make it." Ken laughed.

"Get some spatulas," deadpanned Harper. "Those cheap stores always have spatulas."

Cliff, Logan, and Ken rummaged boxes for another minute or two before Harper's right butt cheek mysteriously warmed up.

Naturally, she considered this an unusual event.

*What the heck?*

She twisted to look behind her—and came within an inch of wetting her pants.

A full-grown mountain lion had snuck up on her, its nose inches away. The big cat kept sniffing her, its breath warming her jean-covered backside. Staring into the shimmering green eyes of a cat roughly waist high to her took all the strength out of her legs. If not for the bike under her, she might've collapsed.

*Hi, Kitty. Nice kitty. Please don't bite me... please don't make someone shoot you.*

The cat appeared more curious than angry, ears up, eyes wide. Paws bigger than her hands concealed dangerous claws. As majestic as the animal was, she couldn't think of it as a big housecat. In a split second, it could go from beautiful and majestic to deadly. Unsure how to react to having a big furry murder machine's nose so close to her butt, she held as still as possible.

"Uhh, Dad?" whispered Harper. "Got a little problem out here."

"Whoa! Shit!" yelled Logan a second later.

The cat twitched, backing up a step when he shouted.

"Oh, he's a big one," said Ken. "Niiice kitty. Go on. No food for you here."

"Do not run away. His instinct is to chase. Stare him down. Act intimidating." Cliff pushed past a box, making his way to the back end of the truck. "They go for the necks of their prey. Stay upright. If it becomes aggressive, scream, make noise, fight back. Don't show fear."

Harper did *not* like being stuck straddling a bike with her back to a cougar. She kicked her left leg out, swung it over the bike, and spun to stand close to the truck bumper, hand on her .45. The clatter of the bike falling over made the cougar twitch again and back up. The cat made no move to lunge at her, so she allowed herself to calm somewhat. "I'm starting to be less scared of him and more hoping we don't have to hurt him. He's beautiful."

"Okay, Maddie." Cliff jumped down from the truck.

The cougar backed up a bit more.

"Maddie hates the idea of killing *all* animals. I don't have a problem with it if there's a good reason." Harper stared the cat down. "We're not food. Go find a raccoon or something smaller."

Cliff drew his handgun, but didn't point it at the cat yet. "If he doesn't wander off in a minute, I'm going to start yelling. Loud noise usually gets 'em to run."

Logan jumped down from the truck. He walked up on Harper's right, standing partially in front of her, closest to the cat.

She grabbed his arm, tugging him back. "Careful."

"He's really giving us the eye." Ken drew his Glock. "Hope he's not used to eating people."

"Uhh, maybe we just figured out why there's no bodies in the parking lot," said Logan.

"Ick." Harper almost gagged. "You think?"

"Doubt cats would've dragged the bones away." Ken shook his head.

Cliff stepped toward the cougar. "If he *has* tasted human, it's more likely he's stumbled across random dead bodies than attacked a live person."

"Ugh." She cringed. "Yeah, we left a few of them lying around when looking for you and Roy. Is that going to attract cougars?"

"Might." Cliff waved in a shooing motion. "These guys don't usually attack people. When they do, it's little kids they can carry off easy. 'Course, who knows what they'll be like now. Humans are kinda scarce compared to before."

"This is their land, now," said Logan.

"Least for the time being." Cliff took another step toward the cat.

After a long few minutes, the mountain lion lost interest. It broke the staring contest and slinked off into the car wash port, out the other side, and across a gravel lot toward a bunch of small beige houses.

"Let's get outta here before he changes his mind." Logan nodded toward the bikes.

Harper got back on hers. "Yeah."

"Ain't dyin' for a bunch of cheap junk made in… overseas." Cliff slid his handgun back into its holster.

Ken laughed. "It's fine. You can say it. All that crap *was* made in China. Not all cheap junk comes—or came—from China, but that particular cheap junk did. They're not the only country to do everything for the lowest cost possible. We do—or did—it here in America, too… by offshoring manufacturing to China."

Logan and Cliff chuckled.

"You think the last president will consider himself a champion of American jobs since nuclear destruction brought all the manufacturing back to the States?" Ken mounted his bike.

Cliff snickered. "It *would* be just like a politician to say something drop dead stupid like that and be serious."

They continued riding along 285. Not far from the Conoco, a small green pickup had gone into the creek beside the highway. Both doors hung open, the seats empty—proof whoever had been in it got out alive.

Harper groaned mentally, already sick of riding a bike for hours nonstop. She couldn't exactly quit, since going home required hours of riding. In fact, going home would take longer than simply finishing the trip to Fairplay. Despite wanting a break, she didn't ask for one. The faster they got there, the faster they'd be home.

*The trip isn't going to feel as long when we're on the way back.*

Soon, the road curved into tree-covered hills again. Swaths of exposed rock peeked out of the dirt on the right. Ahead on the left, a small dark-brown wooden sign spelled out 'Lynwood' vertically beside a metal sign advertising trout fishing, B&B, and firewood.

*Ugh. This is taking forever. So glad we didn't walk.*

HOURS LATER, THEY APPROACHED A METAL PEDESTRIAN BRIDGE spanning the road.

It connected what appeared to be a high school on the right to an odd brick wall on the left side. A small structure resembling the sort of little trailer offices they used at construction sites at the top of the odd wall bore the words 'Platte Canyon.' Beyond it lay a track around a football field, probably for the high school.

Harper gazed up at the elevated walkway as they rode under it, thinking it pretty cool to have something like it connecting the school to an athletic field on the other side of a highway. Of course, she thought of a few morons in her class who always caused trouble. *How many idiots tried to drop stuff on passing cars?* Seeing a high school made her nostalgic for hers, a little angry at the world for not letting her finish it, and a bit jealous at this school for having a cool pedestrian bridge.

*Guess if you're stuck living out here in the middle of freakin' nowhere, a neat bridge is a small consolation prize.*

She twisted to look back out of curiosity. Once they'd gone a little bit down the road, it became clear the 'brick wall' the bridge connected to was the back end of the bleachers facing the football field/track. The 'office trailer' at the top appeared to be an open-faced covered enclosure, probably containing the controls for the scoreboard and PA system.

The next few hours, they rode mostly surrounded by rolling meadows. Harper had enjoyed looking at the mountainous terrain they'd left behind, but miles of open view on all sides eliminated any fear of ambush.

*Madison's never going to believe I almost got killed by a mountain lion over a truck full of cheap dollar-store toys.* She smiled. *Probably shouldn't put it that way. 'We saw a mountain lion.'*

# 25

# FAIRPLAY

Harper rode along Route 285 surrounded by wide-open fields for hours.

Here and there, signs of former farms or ranches popped up in the distance, the odd barn or house, big equipment, fences, loose cows, goats, and other animals. By late afternoon, more mountains came into view *way* off in the distance up ahead to the right. She'd lost track of how long ago the road shrank from a four-lane highway to a two-lane rural road. Cliff didn't show any hesitation in direction, so she trusted they remained on Route 285.

Soon after they passed a huge pond (or small lake) on the right, they reached a green highway sign reading, 'Fairplay city limit elev 9953 ft.' Behind it, another sign bid visitors to 'visit historic 1880s town' with a photo of a wooden archway straight out of the Old West marked 'South Park City.'

A red, rectangular building a short distance off the road to the right appeared deserted. Not far past it, children kicked a ball around a fenced-in parking lot in front of another building. A small sign near the highway identified it as the Park County Animal Hospital. The kids all appeared to be from eight to twelve years old and dressed in clothes that looked like someone tore up a bunch of prewar T-shirts, jeans, and other garments then re-sewed them back into kid-sized dresses, shirts, and pants. One boy suffered the terrible misfortune of having a Shrek face (from a printed T-shirt) in the crotch of his pants.

The kids looked a bit on the dirty side, but happy. They paused to watch Harper, Cliff, Logan, and Ken ride by on bikes with no more astonished a reaction than neighborhood kids pausing a game of stickball to let a car go past.

Adjacent to the animal hospital, a self-storage garage had been converted into tiny apartments. Sheep and goats wandered randomly around along with some chickens. Cliff continued following Route 285 for a little while before veering right where a sign indicated Main Street. Harper steered after him around the curve, leaving Route 285 behind and riding into downtown Fairplay.

Except for a TBK Bank on the left the locals repurposed into some manner of storage facility, the remainder of the buildings ahead all bore various modifications. The town showed no signs of having suffered direct damage from nuclear attack. Nothing looked scorched or melted, yet for some reason, the locals had added large oil-burning lamps here and there, put up hand painted signs indicating a general store, liquors, eats, tailor, undertaker, and so forth like an Old West town. A small yellow building on the right styled like an old-fashioned Mexican adobe hut—formerly the Java Moose Coffee House—had been renamed the 'Drunken Moose,' as indicated by another hand-painted sign.

Locals, some riding horses, made faces at Harper and the others as if seeing time travelers. Despite it only having been a year, they reacted as if they'd never seen mountain bikes before. Most men wore cowboy hats. All but three people in sight sported gun belts and revolvers. Their clothing didn't look as piecemeal as the kids' apparel, in fact, all the adults' outfits appeared to have been made recently. While not an attempt to recreate 1800s fashion on purpose, the slightly odd design of the handmade clothing lent a strange air to everything, making Harper feel as if they'd not only traveled to a different town, but an alternate reality.

"Wow, are they taking the Old West theme a bit too far or have they gone nuts?" whispered Harper. "It's like we've gone to Universal Studios and the actors are staring at the tourists pretending to be baffled by modern clothes."

"Guys…" Ken pointed. "Check out that sign."

Harper glanced left. In front of a small white and teal building with blinding hazard orange doors stood a free-standing sandwich board style sign. Painted lettering spelled out a warning that anyone discharging a firearm inside the city of Fairplay would be shot dead unless they were defending themselves from someone trying to kill them—or shooting someone for breaking the law.

*Oh, crap. What kind of horrible situation is Luisa in?* She tensed, expecting getting Logan's sister out of here would be a dangerous chore. *Get a grip. The letter said she didn't leave because she was afraid of being alone. But… if someone kept her prisoner, she probably couldn't admit it in writing. Duh. If someone kept her captive, why would they let her write a response at all?* She exhaled. *No. Relax. You've watched too many damn movies.*

"Noted," said Cliff. "Not the friendliest town, then."

"At least if someone shoots us, we'll be avenged." Logan chuckled.

"Why would they all be carrying revolvers?" asked Harper. "I mean, carrying guns, sure. Lots of people back home carry handguns… but all *revolvers*? Takes effort. Think they're following a theme, or is it what they happened to have?"

"Who knows? Maybe they did it on purpose to encourage people not to blow through ammo. I can't imagine they have any more bullets than we do." Cliff coasted to a stop in the middle of Main Street, and leaned on the handlebars, looking around. "Unless they've got a sulfur mine hidden somewhere, no one's making any new gunpowder."

Harper shrugged. "They had gunpowder in the Old West, right? Where'd they get their sulfur from?"

"Back east, I reckon," said Cliff in an overacted accent. "Iron horse brought it in twice a month."

She laughed.

"If the Express spreads out enough, maybe someone, somewhere will start making and trading for gunpowder." Logan waved in greeting at a passing group of men. "Excuse me. Do you know where I can find Luisa? She's my sister."

The men stopped, had a short but pleasant conversation, ultimately admitting they had no clue about anyone named Luisa here. They did, however, suggest asking at the saloon, town hall, or the Express office as 'those folks tend ta know where people are.'

"Thanks." Logan shook hands with the three men.

One grabbed his lapels, nodding in greeting at Harper. "Ma'am."

*What the hell?* She smiled at him despite feeling freaked the heck out. Once the men walked too far away to overhear her, she whispered, "This is too weird."

"Seriously." Logan exhaled.

"It's one way to cope with technology sliding back two hundred years." Ken chuckled. "Dive in headfirst."

Harper scrunched her nose. "Yeah, but are they acting or nuts?"

"Don't much matter," said Cliff, still doing the 'cowboy' voice. "We ain't fixin' ta be in these here parts for long."

She smirked at him. "Please tell me you're kidding and this town doesn't have a mind control device turning everyone into character actors from *Westworld*."

Cliff grinned. "Merely trying to fit in."

They walked up Main Street, past houses, shops, and a quaint little real estate office—the tiniest 'house' Harper had ever seen. Similar signs, essentially warning of a death penalty for anyone firing a gun in town—seemed to be everywhere. Most didn't specify exemptions beyond 'self-defense' while some of the signs specifically mentioned defense against being shot at.

*Would people here blow someone away for shooting at a charging bear because it didn't fire a gun first?*

She whistled to herself. For a town obsessed with telling everyone how fast they'd die for shooting off a gun, the place had no shortage of people carrying firearms. Only a year from the end of civilization, they probably still had a fair amount of ammunition left. Depending on the stock taken from local gun stores, this town might outlast the Evergreen militia in terms of ammo reserves. Following the discussion of the 'sulfur problem' back in Evergreen, Harper asked Cliff if she was correct about bullets going bad if they sat too long. According to him, properly stored ammunition could theoretically remain usable forever when kept protected from moisture. If humanity headed toward a future where no one had guns anymore, it probably wouldn't get there for at least a few years. Also, unless places like Australia, Africa, and various Third World countries unlikely to have been targeted by nuclear superpowers somehow ended up destroyed as well, someone, somewhere would have a reliable source of ammo, even technology. Question being, would it ever show up in the USA or would countries that remained intact cut off all contact with irradiated zones? Better question: *had* any countries remained intact?

*Heh. More likely we'll use the ammo up before it rots. Damn, I hope the Lawless are a one-off and not the norm... though we've seen two sets of prison escapees and both groups became violent gangs.*

She bit her lip, not exactly sure how to feel about convicts. On one hand, leaving them to starve in prison after the collapse of society was cruel and wrong. On the other, setting them loose on unsuspecting victims also sounded like a scary idea. Then again, Deacon had been in prison for bank robbery and she considered him one of the nicest men she'd ever met. Granted, he hadn't stormed in the door waving a gun around. He'd gone in at night when the building had been empty.

*Guess it's a reset button. The ones who aren't bad people have a second chance. The rest get shot. Just feel bad for their victims.*

Harper glanced at a group of women hanging out in front of a large grey building on the left, distant corner of the next cross street. They all wore ruffled, gaudy dresses baring far too much skin for late summer at nine-thousand feet above sea level, especially given the unusual blasts of cold lately. Merely looking at them made her shiver. The women arranged themselves in two groups on either side of the main entrance, a double-door set in the blunted corner of the building facing the intersection. Above a wraparound awning, another hand-painted sign read 'The Mushroom Cloud Saloon' along with a crude rendition of a mushroom cloud. Beneath it, the bottom edge of a normal sign bore the word 'Sports.' To the right, a long green, white-lettered sign advertised 'ski and snowboard rentals.'

"The heck are they supposed to be?" asked Harper.

"Either Las Vegas dancers, prostitutes, or Fairplay is infested with a bizarrely aggressive species of moth." Cliff raised an eyebrow. "I suppose this is what happens when someone hires Luc Besson to do the costume design for an Old West movie."

"None of them are blue." Logan chuckled.

Harper blinked. "I'm not even going to pretend to understand what you mean."

"*Fifth Element?*" Logan nudged her. "He directed it. Blue alien woman singing that weird opera?"

"Ohhh." She eyed the six women. "Yeah, pretty sure we're not on a movie set."

"Aww man," muttered Ken.

Harper looked over at him.

A sizable wad of horse poo lay cut in half on either side of his front bike tire.

"Dammit. Didn't even see that." Ken grumbled. "Great. Now I'm going to smell horse crap the whole ride back tomorrow."

"We're going to have to start learning to keep our eyes on the road. Got horses in town now." Logan gestured at the street ahead of them. "A manure minefield is inevitable."

Cliff patted him on the arm. "Look on the bright side. You didn't step in it."

"True." Ken smiled. "Shall we check the saloon then, uhh, pardner?"

"You guys are so lame." Harper dismounted her bike and walked it over the red-painted railing.

Cliff grinned in the way he did whenever he thought something funny, but not quite worth a laugh. "Another potential source of fuel, though I wouldn't suggest using dried-out horse manure for cooking fires. Lends a rather unusual flavor to food."

Harper gagged.

The prostitutes largely ignored her, openly discussing how cute they thought Cliff, Ken, and Logan were. They sounded fake as hell, clearly trying to sell themselves. Blushing, Harper refused to look at them as she chained her bike to the railing. Logan secured his bike to the right of hers, Cliff on the left, Ken beside him. Evergreen had a pronounced lack of traditional bike locks, so they made do with lengths of tow chain and padlocks. The men collected their rifles from the bikes, obviously not trusting them to still be there later if left unattended.

Cliff paid the women only enough attention to offer a polite nod on the way by. Logan said, "Hi," without looking at them. Ken grinned, allowing himself a moment to take in the view.

Harper stuffed the key in her pocket, then pulled the Mossberg from the lime green nylon sheath. The prostitutes fell quiet, staring at her until she slung it over her shoulder. She didn't bother saying anything like 'relax, don't want to leave it out here,' nor did she make eye contact with them on her way through the door. It annoyed her they didn't react with any worry or concern to the men pulling their rifles. Perhaps she unintentionally gave off territorial jealousy regarding Logan they sensed.

The Mushroom Cloud Saloon stank of strong alcohol, fried meat, and cigarette smoke. Scraps of linoleum paths and bland beige-grey carpet revealed the layout of a former sporting goods store converted into a bizarre approximation of an 1800s-era saloon. They'd turned the former glass sales counter into a bar, and cleared out the rest of the space of shelves and displays. A rickety-looking stairway — clearly not built by a professional — led to a door on the second floor bearing a sign advertising rooms for rent.

*This is so weird.*

Square tables filled most of the room, several hosting active card games or people rolling dice. Gamblers appeared to be placing wagers using pennies, nickels, dimes, and quarters... and even a credit card or two, using them like poker chips.

"Hmm, they're off script," muttered Cliff.

"Huh?" Harper glanced at him.

"Bunch of outsiders just stepped into the town's biggest bar. Everyone's supposed to stop and stare at us like we walked into the wrong place." He grinned. "Feels like any other bar back in the normal world… except for no crappy music playing."

"Wow, they've even got a piano." Ken pointed.

Harper looked over at a small group standing in the back by an upright piano. It had definitely seen better days, but appeared functional. *Wow, they're going all out.* Shelves behind the bar held rows and rows of mason jars containing clear liquid. *That's not water, is it?* She cringed. *Great. Moonshine. Or fuel. Maybe we should bring some of it back for Rafael to put in his engine.* "That's moonshine, isn't it?"

"Probably," said Cliff.

"Feel like having a drink?" Logan playfully elbowed her.

"Not unless I need to strip paint off a car." Cliff winced.

"Uhh, pass," whispered Harper. "Don't want to go blind."

A door at the back of the room swung open as a short, skinny Hispanic girl butt-bumped it out of her way while backing into view carrying a large serving tray. Her dress appeared to be made out of fabric scavenged from at least nine different other garments. Fortunately, she didn't have a graphic in an unfortunate place. While her face, arms, and hair were clean, the dress looked as if its former owner had been used as a giant Q-tip to clean out several old chimneys.

She walked with her head down, eyes hidden behind hair.

Logan squeezed Harper's arm. "That's her."

"Wow… she looks younger than fifteen." Her heart raced from joy and relief.

"Yeah, she's like Mom. Real small." Logan wiped a tear.

Harper nudged him. "What are you waiting for?"

"Her to put the tray down so she doesn't drop it when she sees me." Logan laughed nervously.

As soon as she set the serving tray on a table by two men, Logan called out, "Luisa?"

The girl jumped, spinning as if in response to a firecracker going off. She snapped her head up to look across the room. After a few seconds of staring at Logan, all the strength appeared to melt out of her body. She collapsed to her knees, sobbing into her hands. Logan sprinted over to her.

"What the hell are *you* doin' here?" bellowed a man behind Harper.

*Oh, shit. Here we go.* Hoping it hadn't been directed at their group, since no one in this town could possibly know them, she twisted to look.

Three men had apparently come from a table by the front window, and—for no obvious reason—decided to have a problem with Harper's group. All wore not-quite Old West attire of the recently handmade variety. Each man had a revolver strapped to their hip and the somewhat wobbly posture of mild drunkenness. The shortest looked about twenty, his black hair cut close, nearly shaved. His friends both had to be past thirty, but not by much. A tall blond guy in the middle sported a beard down to his belt buckle, over a rounded belly probably emblazoned with a 'body by Budweiser' tattoo above the navel. The third guy teetered the most, his sorta-clean-shaven face so cut up, Harper wondered if he'd tried to shave using a weed whacker or maybe attempted to tongue-kiss an angry honey badger.

She'd seen similar situations more than enough back home at the Brewery. These men had enough booze to get a bad case of the stupids, but not so much they couldn't walk. Subconsciously, she fell into militia mode, widening her stance and getting ready to defuse a barfight while being ready to dodge a punch.

"What are you rattling on about?" asked Cliff, sounding unimpressed.

Beer Belly Blond pointed at Ken. "You damn Chinese what nuked us. Got a lotta damn nerve showin' up around here."

Harper fumed, from calm to furious in an instant. An image of Jonathan's tearful eyes filled her thoughts. His parents had been killed by idiots like this who blamed Chinese people for what happened.

*Shit. So much for this being a quick and easy trip.*

# 26

# THE MUSHROOM CLOUD

The bar fell silent—even Luisa stopped crying.

Ken glared, though his expression conveyed more a sense of 'here we go again' than anger.

Harper clutched the nylon strap holding the Mossberg to her back, not sure what to do with it if the situation escalated to violence. Would people here wait to shoot her until *after* she fired, or would they riddle her with bullets for simply using the shotgun as a club? Hammering a dude over the head for being a racist mouth-breather might be gratifying, but also, excessive. A shotgun—fired or swung —wasn't the proper response to drunk idiots simply running their mouths... unless she faced a three on one situation and feared for her life.

She couldn't toss it aside either. Someone would surely steal it and run off. Couldn't get into a fight with it hanging on one shoulder either. One of the idiots would grab it. Her backpack got in the way of lifting the strap over her head to her left shoulder so the weapon hung more securely across her back.

*No choice. Can't let this turn into a fight.*

Harper let the Mossberg slip off her shoulder, swinging it around into a two-handed grip, keeping it aimed in a neutral direction—

more or less—in hopes people didn't think she intended to shoot anyone.

The short guy, closest to her, raised a hand. "Easy, girlie. No need for that."

"Not planning on using it." She narrowed her eyes at him. "Unless someone threatens my friend... or calls me 'girlie' a second time."

A collective 'ooh' came from the patrons, making Harper feel like she'd gone right back to high school.

"I'm sorry, but I don't think I quite heard you boys right." Cliff stepped toward the three men, head slightly bowed. "Are my ears playing tricks on me or did you just say you've got the smallest dick in the room?" He lifted his head, staring the taller man in the eye.

"That ain't what I said, you moron." The blond guy glowered. "Who in the hell you think you are, and why you getting' all agitated over a damn Chinese?"

"Me?" Cliff folded his arms. "I'm just a retired mall cop who thinks you're about 150 years too late to use the term 'a Chinese.'"

The man with all the scratches and scabs on his face leaned back, eyes widening for no obvious reason.

"Mall cop huh?" asked the blond guy. "Just what the hell you think you're gonna do here, shake your keys at me?"

Logan walked up on Harper's left side, staring defiantly at the men.

Cliff offered an insincere smile. "Figured I'd start off by asking you politely to apologize to my friend here, but something tells me you'd probably laugh. From there, we move on to firmly applying your face repetitively to any nearby hard object until you have one of those epiphany moments."

"You talk pretty big for a mall cop." The blond man made a 'come here' gesture with both hands. "Let's see what you got."

"Hey!" yelled a middle-aged black man behind the bar. "No fighting inside. Brian, knock that shit off."

"Oh, wasn't planning on fighting." Cliff's smile turned sincere. "Fight implies a contest. I'd just be taking out some trash."

"Uhh, come on, guys," said the scratched man. "Let's go drink somewhere else."

Brian, the tall blond beer-bellied guy, backhand whacked Scratchy on the arm. "The hell you turn chickenshit all of a sudden, Cyrus? Desmond ain't gonna invoke rule six on us over no nuclear Chinese sonofabitch."

"Wow, you really are a total asshole," said Harper.

Ken set his hands on his hips, shaking his head. "Can't even debate stupid of this magnitude. Look, just go have another drink. We'll be gone before you even realize."

"Not bein' a chickenshit, Brian." Cyrus pointed at Cliff's left forearm. "Dude's an Army Ranger."

"So?" asked the short guy. "That's all Hollywood BS."

"Best get your stunt double ready," said Cliff.

Desmond, the bartender, grabbed a bolt-action rifle off the wall behind him. "Warnin' you boys."

Brian's swagger lessened ever so slightly. He glanced sideways at the bar, then glared at Cliff. "Why are you helping the damn Chinese? They nuked us to hell."

"I should slit your throat for being a Russian." Cliff unfolded his arms, letting them fall at his sides.

"You son of a…" Brian took a swing.

Cliff caught him by the arm, swinging him around and drilling him face first into a nearby table, knocking a candle jar over and sending several forks, knives, and spoons crashing to the floor. The surprisingly loud *whud* of face-on-wood and subsequent clatter of silverware brought the room to silence.

Desmond pointed his rifle at them. The short guy lunged at Cliff from behind. Harper intercepted, blocking him with the Mossberg sideways across his chest and sweeping his leg, putting him on the floor. Scratched-up-face guy, Cyrus, took a step, but stopped in his tracks when Ken merely leaned toward him. Logan rushed to stand between the short man and Harper.

"You ain't no Russian?" asked Cliff, a hint of growl in his voice as he squished Brian's cheek into the table by a fistful of hair. "Could'a fooled me. You look just like them. White skin. Blonde hair."

Brian shoved himself up. Lacking the strength to keep the larger man pinned, Cliff shifted into a throw, sending the big guy tumbling into a heap. Desmond kept his rifle pointed at Cliff.

"Aim at him." Harper nodded at Brian. "He threw the first punch."

"Brian missed." Desmond continued aiming at Cliff.

Harper trained her Mossberg on the bartender. "Doesn't matter. He initiated the fight. I don't care what happens to me. If you shoot my Dad, your head is going to be all over that wall. Ever see what buckshot does to a human skull at sixteen feet?"

About eleven people drew revolvers and aimed at Harper. She narrowed her eyes. Inside, she wanted to throw up from fear, knowing she'd never survive opening fire on the bartender. Her life had never before hung on a thread as thin as two millimeters of trigger pull. She kept her face steely, confident acting indifferent to death would prevent anyone needing to pull a trigger. Desmond stared at her in disbelief, then nervousness, then fear. He lowered the rifle.

Harper lowered her shotgun.

A bunch of seemingly disappointed locals put their revolvers away.

*Okay. I don't like this town. They are* way *too eager to shoot people.*

"Ugh." Brian rolled over to sit. "I ain't no damn Russian. Do I freakin' sound like I'm speakin' Russian to you, dumbass?"

"And he ain't no 'damn Chinese.' He's an American." Cliff thrust an arm toward Ken. "Is he speaking Chinese?"

"I don't even know Mandarin or Cantonese," said Ken. "I was born in Colorado. My parents and grandparents were all born in Colorado."

"C'mon, Bri." Cyrus jabbed a thumb at the door. "Ain't worth it. This gonna get real ugly real fast. That li'l redhead there's straight up psycho."

"Psycho is a dozen people muttering in annoyance because they didn't get to shoot a teenage girl," snapped Logan. "What the hell is wrong with you all?"

"Them people's carryin' guns all the time, gives 'em a powerful itch ta use it," said an older guy at a table close to the wall on the left.

"Doubt it." Harper slung the Mossberg over her shoulder. "I've been carrying this howitzer for a year now, and the *last* thing I want to do is have to use it."

Ken offered Brian a hand. "One, I'm not nationally Chinese. Two, we don't even know who hit us."

The big guy stood without accepting Ken's help. He didn't much look at him either, heading for the exit while grumbling incoherently.

*He's going to be a problem later.* Harper crouched to pick up the candle jar Cliff knocked over.

Desmond replaced his rifle on the wall mount behind him.

"What the hell is rule six?" asked Cliff, approaching the bar.

"The proprietor of any bar, motel, or brothel is legally allowed to shoot anyone they deem a threat to the peace due to violence." Desmond leaned on the former sales counter. "Basically, someone starts a fight, I can pop them."

Cliff pointed at the rifle behind the bartender. "You might want something a little less spicy than a .30-06. That'll go right through a man and hit someone else."

Logan hurried to the rear of the room, where Luisa crouched behind a square column still marked with 'bargain' stickers from when the place had been a sporting goods store. Harper figured it safe to leave Cliff unsupervised with the bartender, so she followed.

"You okay?" Logan brushed at her cheek. "Look a bit strung out."

Luisa bowed her head. "Nightmares. I wake up two or three times a night. It's hard for me to sleep."

"C'mere." He beckoned her closer.

"What happened to you, Lo?" Luisa stood and hugged him. "Not here five minutes and you're almost getting shot."

Harper folded her arms. "He honestly had nothing at all to do with that."

"Who's this?" Luisa glanced at her.

"This is Harper. My girlfriend." Logan couldn't quite make eye contact with either of them. "She's the one who found your name in the notebook and suggested I write."

Luisa blinked. "You didn't want to?"

"Everyone we ran into said Springs was vaporized. Like *completely* evaporated." Logan pulled his sister into a hug. "I thought you were gone already. Couldn't deal if it had been someone else, same name."

"It's not *totally* gone," said Luisa in a near whisper. "Real bad, though. Houses were on fire for days around us, but everything else is flat."

"Wow. Lucky." Harper raised both eyebrows.

Logan took a few calming breaths. "The hills... we lived on Seven Oaks Drive. Popes Bluffs is right behind the house. It must have shielded our neighborhood from the worst of it. Wasn't sure where the blast came from. Popes would've only shielded the house if it went off to the northeast."

"Like eight or nine houses in each direction were still standing." Luisa stared down. "Past that, it's all gone. Just open holes in the ground. Like the wind blew the houses away. When the Express guy handed me the letter, I couldn't stop crying for a whole day. I thought you died in Denver."

"Whoa," whispered Harper. *How is this girl not glowing? She looks half-starved but not like she's irradiated. She wouldn't still be alive if she got a big dose... and her hair is way too long to have lost it and grown it back.*

They stood in silence for a few minutes, Logan and Luisa holding each other. He tried to speak a few times but couldn't find a voice. Finally, he managed a weak, "How did you get out?"

"You know how Ma always woke up at the butt crack of dawn?"

Logan nodded.

"She heard on the news about bombs going off in New York and Washington DC. She woke me and Papa up and we sheltered in the basement. The house kinda collapsed on top of us. We got a little banged up, but just some cuts and scratches. Papa wouldn't let us leave the basement. We stayed there for a couple days until the bottled water ran out. He started scavenging for food. When he got too sick to go outside, Ma took over." Luisa broke into tears, resting her head against Logan's shoulder. "They had all these cuts. Papa fell and broke his arm outside. I think it got infected. I don't even know how long it was after the blast… woke up and Papa was dead. He lost all his hair and got so skinny."

The emotional knife of hearing this girl talk about watching her father die stabbed too close to home. Tears streamed down Harper's face.

Luisa took a moment to collect herself back from a sobbing wreck. "Ma… I think she knew but she acted like he was only sleeping. She got sicker and sicker, I think from the radiation. Stopped eating. She wanted to save the cans for me. I told her to eat but she wouldn't. Then, she didn't wake up one day… I didn't know what to do."

"Luisa…" Logan wept too hard to speak.

"I ate one can a day. Didn't go outside 'cause I was scared of the radiation. Stayed there with Ma and Papa, talking to them. I knew they were watching me."

Harper grimaced at the thought of this girl spending days in a smashed basement with two bodies, especially her parents. *No wonder she can't sleep through the night. Holy crap! I'm going to have nightmares just from hearing this.*

"They did watch over you," whispered Logan. "You got out alive."

"I ran out of cans. Nothing to eat. No water. I couldn't stay there any longer. I crawled outside and started walking away from the ruins. Like parts of Colorado Springs far away burned *still*. Little fires all over the place. It had to be over a month. I ran 'cause I didn't want the radiation to get me."

"Four or five weeks, the radiation wouldn't have been anywhere near as bad as right after the blast," rasped Harper. "Sorry. I've got this big lump in my throat right now."

"Damn," whispered Cliff. "Hell of a story. You okay, kid?"

Harper jumped, not having realized he'd walked up behind them.

"Uhh." Luisa stared at him, seeming half ready to run.

"It's okay." Logan put an arm around her. "This is Cliff. Harper's dad. Also, Ken. They've come with us to help you get back to Evergreen."

She relaxed. "Oh. Sorry. Just been so scared all the time for so long."

"Anyone I need to have a little talk with before we go?" asked Cliff.

Luisa blinked.

Cliff leaned close, whispering, "Anyone I need to teach why it's a real bad idea to lay their hands on a young girl?"

"Oh. No." She shook her head rapidly. "No one did that. A group found me wandering alone. Gave me water and food, brought me here. Some are still around, but I guess they think I'm old enough to live without parents now."

"Any idea if you caught much of a radiation dose?" asked Harper. "Have you felt sick or anything?"

"At first when I left the house, I felt a little weak and dizzy... but it's maybe from not eating much and emotional stuff. Lo's probably not going to want to deal with me since I'm so messed up. I didn't think you guys would like *come* here to get me."

Logan shook his head. "You didn't think I'd do whatever it took to find you? I don't care about any arguments or stuff we used to have. None of that matters anymore. We're family... and we just fought over bullshit anyway... like Mp3 players."

She sob-laughed. "Yeah. Just pointless crap like that."

He rocked her side to side. "I still have all the songs you put on my iPod. Couldn't delete them because they're all I had left to remember you by."

Teary-eyed, Luisa collapsed against him, crying. "But I'm so messed up, now. Nightmares. Panic attacks. Sometimes, I even think Ma or Papa are gonna be in a dark corner when I look there."

Harper glanced sideways at Cliff. *Holy crap, this poor kid.*

"Luisa." Logan grasped her face in both hands, staring into her eyes. "I absolutely want you to come back to Evergreen with us. We can deal with your issues. You need to be safe, and we need to be a family."

"And this place," whispered Harper, "doesn't seem all that safe."

# CIVILIZATION TAKE TWO

Waning sunlight engulfed the saloon's windows in fiery orange.

Expecting to spend the night in Fairplay and head out first thing, Harper, Logan, and Luisa sat at one of the square tables close to the back wall. Square depressions in the beige carpet gave away where various store racks used to be. Harper kept one leg through the strap of her backpack, which sat beside her chair, in case anyone tried to grab it. The Mossberg, she kept at her left, butt on the floor, barrel pointing up, hand firmly around the barrel.

In a 'normal' setting, such as sitting at a table in a bar, having a large shotgun in her custody proved annoying. She couldn't lay it on the floor, fearing someone would grab it. Putting it on the table seemed like a hazard since no matter which way it pointed, someone would be in the line of fire. It couldn't remain on her shoulder while she sat in a chair. Balancing it across her lap also ended up putting people in danger. Hopefully, no one happened to be directly above her on the second floor.

She'd stayed at the Mushroom Cloud with Logan and Luisa while Cliff and Ken went out to scout around for an alternate place to sleep—just in case Brian and any other morons came back for revenge. Luisa had already informed Desmond of her intention to leave with her brother. The man didn't seem to mind losing a waitress, neither trying to talk her out of leaving nor acting as if her departure inconvenienced him.

For the most part, she talked with Logan, filling him in on the minor details of her survival. She described their home in Colorado Springs as 'kinda collapsed,' slumping over like a poorly made gingerbread house left out in the sun. Entry in and out of the basement required climbing a 'tunnel' of broken wood, wires, and pipes. She claimed not to have noticed any smell from their dead parents despite having been there for upward of three weeks after her father died and at least one week after her mother passed.

The group who helped her get here largely left her to her own devices once they arrived in town. She'd initially gone into the Mushroom Cloud to beg for food but ended up being hired as a waitress slash housekeeper. For the walk here, she'd been largely numb, but soon after having a place to sleep and somewhat of a sense of safety around her, she started having horrible nightmares and random panic attacks. Logan told her about Dr. Hale, and kept repeating how he'd help her get through everything.

Harper fidgeted at a frayed strand sticking out from the pocket on her jeans. She loved Logan, wanted to be with him for the rest of her life... but if anything happened to him, she doubted she'd ever care about another man. If he needed some time to be there for Luisa, so be it. Harper had no urge to rush into having babies. The world might have been pulled out from under her, but the idea of becoming a pregnant teen still carried a heavy stigma from the past world's values. With Madison and Lorelei to take care of, she felt like some girl in a Lifetime network movie whose parents died and she 'got stuck' raising her little siblings. Only, she didn't resent the obligation. It helped she didn't need to worry at all about going to school, earning money for rent and food, or really anything other than being there to protect them.

Honestly, she'd been somewhat guilty of shorting Logan on time in favor of her little sister and 'daughter', so if he did the same to help Luisa recover from her trauma, she'd understand, even encourage him to do so.

The worry spiral in her head stopped spinning when Cliff and Ken walked in. Neither man had much of a readable expression. No gunshots had gone off at any point, so she hoped Brian and his two friends would stay gone.

*Hopefully, they were drunk enough to be passed out somewhere sleeping by now.*

"Well, seems we're at a bit of a disadvantage." Cliff pulled out a chair and plopped down at their table. "This place ain't like home."

"Oh, really?" Harper fake smiled. "I hadn't noticed any differences."

Logan snickered.

Cliff pointed at her, making a 'look here, young lady' face, then chuckled. "I meant they use money still."

"Yeah." Ken took a chair from a nearby empty table, dragging it over before sitting on it. "Seems like they're using coins at face value and credit cards instead of paper bills. Probably because plastic won't disintegrate."

Luisa nodded. "Yes. I could have told you that. Amex is like a five-dollar bill. Visa, ten. Mastercard worth twenty bucks."

"No Discover?" asked Cliff.

"What's that?" Luisa bit her lip in thought. "They didn't say anything about a discovery."

Cliff shrugged in a 'what can ya do' manner. "Figures. Even after the apocalypse, no one takes Discover."

"Wow." Ken laughed.

"Prices are a bit different though." Cliff pointed a thumb back over his shoulder. "Cheapest lodging we found is twenty cents a night. Dunno about you all, but I haven't bothered carrying any cash in a while."

"Jonathan's got a whole shoebox full of cash." Harper whistled. "Maybe he had the right idea. Someday, it might be valuable again."

Logan shook his head. "I hope not. The way we're doing it is so much better."

"Yeah." Harper exhaled. "Wonder if the Express office here charges postage."

"No." Luisa brushed at a dirt smear on her sleeve. "They didn't ask me to pay to send the letter, or for the paper. I think they get food for free, so they basically trade their services for it."

Ken opened his backpack, pulling out a water bottle. "This town's probably unique in the use of money again, or it's not common. Otherwise, the Express would be trying to spread the idea around to the 'uncivilized' settlements."

"Or they're stretched thinner here for resources," said Harper. "Maybe no one wanted to be quartermaster, so they came up with the laziest possible way to manage distribution—money."

"I have some money if you want to get food." Luisa looked down. "It's the least I can do for all of you walking out here to find me."

Cliff snagged his backpack off the floor. "Thanks, but we didn't come here to take your money."

"Am I going to need it in Evergreen?"

"No, but that's beside the point." Cliff winked, opening the backpack zipper.

Luisa glanced at Logan, seemingly content until he started munching on a raw potato. At that, she huffed, stood, and went over to the bar.

"Guess I'm going to have real food tonight." Logan shrugged.

Harper kept her eye on the front door and windows, not convinced their problems in Fairplay had come to an end. This place *did* feel more 'civilized' than Evergreen in a weird sort of way, barring the semipsychotic people who seemed eager for a chance to shoot someone without consequences. She imagined the mayor, or whoever ran the place, taking the city's name and running away with the idea of 'fair play.' As in, shoot someone, die instantly to a gunshot. The more she thought about it, the less she wanted to stay here for any length of time.

*Who knows what kinds of weird punishments they'll come up with? Was the actual Wild West like this? Everyone walking around outside like we're in a movie. All that's missing are wanted posters and a dude playing that piano in the back.* She smirked. *Already had the shootout over the poker game back home. At least* here *it would make somewhat more sense as money has meaning. Freakin' idiot.*

A boy between fourteen and sixteen carried a plate of meat strips over and set them by Luisa. "Is it true you're leaving?"

"Yes." She gestured at Logan. "Tom, this is my brother."

"Oh, yeah." Tom offered a handshake. "She told me about you. Guess being in Denver worked out. We heard it got hit pretty hard."

"It did get hammered… just not *too* bad where I happened to be that morning." Logan exhaled.

"Relax, dude. We're not like dating or anything." Tom grinned. "Just both working here. Hope whoever Desmond hires to replace her isn't a pain in the butt."

Luisa blushed. "Whoever takes my place probably won't be too scared to go into the basement."

"Well, good luck." Tom squeezed her shoulder. "You deserve to be with your family."

"Thanks." She patted his hand, then looked at Logan. "Go on. Eat. Half of these are yours."

"What is it?" asked Logan.

Harper sniffed at the pile of meat strips, about the size of those chicken-on-a-stick things Mom used to always order from the Chinese place. "Smells like goat."

Logan shrugged and divided the pile in uneven halves, giving Luisa the extra odd piece. Harper munched on vegetables from her backpack, as did Cliff and Ken. At least Desmond didn't charge anything for water. Since no one spoke about rooms for the night beyond pointing out they cost money none of them had, it seemed likely the plan became 'finish eating, then we go camp somewhere.' Question being, did they hunt down a random abandoned building and hope the town wouldn't care?

About the time Harper had a third of a potato left in her hand, she spotted a scrawny man walk by the door outside carrying a pair of bolt cutters.

"Aww, crap." She hopped up and ran for the door, the Mossberg dangling from her left hand, still munching on potato she couldn't bring herself to waste.

Sure enough, the guy with the bolt cutters attacked the chain securing Cliff's bike to the railing outside the Mushroom Cloud Saloon.

"Hey!" yelled Harper, pointing the shotgun at him. "Get away from those bikes. They don't belong to you."

About a dozen people in the vicinity stopped walking, all turning to watch. Most gripped their revolvers but didn't pull them out. The thief glanced at her momentarily, disregarded her, and cut the chain. Curiously, he left the padlock intact.

*Dammit. They're all going to kill me if I shoot this guy for stealing. Wouldn't bother me so much if these creeps didn't look so eager about it.*

She stuffed the quarter-potato in her mouth, grabbed the shotgun in both hands, and rushed the guy as Cliff, Ken, and Logan raced out onto the porch. The thief—who also had a revolver on his hip—spun to meet her charge, swinging the bolt cutters at her. Harper ducked the swipe, then pretended to go for a kick to the nuts, figuring he'd expect such an attack from a girl. When the guy shoved the bolt cutters down to block her fake kick, she walloped the butt of the Mossberg across his face, knocking him sideways into a twirling fall.

The thief hit the street on his back, seemingly out cold.

Spectators, up to about fifteen now, kept watching her.

She glanced around at them. The potato still clutched in her teeth kept her from saying anything stupid like 'what are you looking at?' *Wow, is this how it feels to be a cockroach when the lights come on? They're all looking at me like 'give me a reason.'*

"The hell happened out here?" Cliff jogged up behind her.

"Mrmm," muttered Harper past the potato in her teeth while pointing at the bolt cutters.

Ken approached the bike, picked up the severed chain, then dropped it.

"Why is everyone staring at us?" asked Logan from the porch.

Harper slung the shotgun over her shoulder, then plucked the potato from her mouth. "Because… they're waiting to see if I shoot this guy so they can light me up."

Cliff leaned close, putting an arm around her. "Those two boys across the way by the street sign are trying to figure out if they should 'arrest' you for hitting him with a weapon."

She tried to inconspicuously look. Two twentysomethings dressed like post-nuclear cowboys stood beside a street sign reading Main and 6<sup>th</sup>. Both men tensed when she glanced in their direction, like gunslingers expecting to throw down at any second.

"Wow. No wonder there's no coffee left. This town drank it all," whispered Harper. "Everyone's got the dial up to eleven."

Cliff patted her on the back, then went to collect his mountain bike. "We should get outta here now or the bicycles will be gone by morning."

"Yeah."

"Getting Luisa," said Logan before darting back into the saloon.

Harper stepped toward her bicycle, but paused at a collective gasp from several spectators. Motion caught her eye—the thief lunged at her, thrusting a knife. She reacted on reflex, spinning to her right, grabbing the arm and flipping the guy to the ground using a jiu-jitsu takedown. He crashed cheek-first into the pavement, screaming as she wrenched back on his arm, applying pressure above the elbow while hyperextending his wrist. Involuntarily, his grip on the knife released, letting it fall to the road.

Cliff taught her it didn't take a whole lot of strength to break an arm when holding it in such a delicate position. Leverage worked entirely for her. Perhaps due to performing the maneuver so often while training with Cliff—and only twice for real—she'd become accustomed to not completing the maneuver fully to break the arm. She hadn't done so here, either. At least, not in one smooth motion. Cliff would've faceplanted the guy and destroyed the guy's elbow joint automatically. She could snap it if she wanted to, but hesitated.

*A broken arm could be a death sentence now.*

"Gah! My fuckin' arm," yelled the man.

She leaned her weight into the middle of his back to keep him pinned. "You came at me with a knife. You're so freakin' lucky I didn't break it already."

Cliff stomped over, picked the knife up from the road, and threw it onto the roof of the saloon. When he moved to grab the thief, Harper let go and scooted back, unnerved at the level of anger in her adoptive dad's eyes. Cliff dragged the guy upright, giving him a little shove to put fighting distance between them.

"My knife...." The man pointed at the saloon.

"You're a damn lucky son of a bitch she managed to duck, or you'd need a surgeon instead of a ladder to get it back." He glared. "Wanna take a swing at someone? Try me on for size. Or are kids more your challenge level?"

The thief twitched, his shifty stare wandering among the locals—now up to about twenty—watching them.

"Thought you were safe to steal right in front of me?" Harper folded her arms. "Figured I'd stand there since I couldn't shoot you with all these people itching to mow me down?"

Logan and Luisa emerged from the saloon, carrying everyone's backpacks.

Cliff slapped the guy. "What'cha lookin' at them for. I'm right here, pal. You got two choices right now. Find somewhere else to be but in my face, or you'll be needing the attention of a doctor real soon like. This town's got one, don't it?"

After a moment of standing there fidgeting, making faces, and twitching, the thief huffed and staggered off, rubbing his shoulder. A few spectators decided to resume going about their night, but most remained, watching them.

"Real soon like?" asked Harper. "Seriously?"

Logan handed out backpacks.

"Sorry. Place is rubbing off on me." Cliff chuckled, taking his pack and putting it on.

"She okay?" asked Harper when Logan held out her backpack.

"Yeah."

"Time to go." Cliff backed his bike away from the railing. "Besides. We can't get a room here, anyway. All I've got is Discover."

Harper almost laughed, still eyeing about twenty people who looked ready to shoot her if someone farted too loud. No one had pulled a gun out yet, and they *did* seem to have calmed a bit once she'd shouldered the Mossberg. She threw a leg over her bike, stood on the higher pedal, and let gravity start her off.

*Yeah... not coming back here if I can help it.*

# 28

# HAUNTED

A good while after leaving Fairplay, Cliff veered left off the side of Route 285.

He stopped on a small patch of dirt beside the road, an elevated spot overlooking a creek crossing via culvert below the highway up ahead. Though Harper would've liked to put more distance between them and the weird town, a ready supply of—hopefully safe—water made for an enticing camping spot. Also, it had to be past midnight by now and they'd been riding all damn day. If anyone, especially the bike thief, from Fairplay had any intention of seeking revenge or acting on their bizarre bloodlust, it didn't seem likely they'd walk this far.

A horse they'd hear coming on the road. But, someone taking a horse and chasing them out of town implied a level of commitment she dismissed as excessive for simple bloodlust or a bike thief nursing a bruised ego.

"This should be far enough to sleep in peace." Cliff stopped at the edge of the dirt, dismounted, and walked his bike down the hill to the grass below. "C'mon down here off the road. Harder to be seen."

Some moonlight made it past the hazy sky, but not enough for Harper to notice a baseball sized rock in the grass while walking her bike down the hill. She tripped over it, pitching her forward off her feet. Clinging desperately to the handlebars, she slide-surfed the rest of the way down the hill to flat ground. As soon as she stopped, the bike fell onto her.

Terrified she'd sprained or even broken her ankle, Harper didn't even try to breathe for a moment. The irrational fear she'd end up stranded out in the middle of nowhere, forty or fifty miles from home unable to walk faded in a few seconds once the adrenaline spike from the fall wore off and her brain switched back on.

*I can ride a bike with a sprain… and I'm not alone.*

"Harp?" asked Logan from somewhere above and behind her. "You okay?"

"Uhh…" She tentatively moved her right foot. It hurt a little, mostly on the sole. "Yeah. Whew. Lucky. Thought I sprained it."

"Gah!" yelled Ken. He tumbled to the ground behind her, his bike landing on top of him. "Frickin' rock."

Harper rested her chin on her hand, elbow in the ground. "Guess I'll sleep right here."

"Heh." Cliff grasped her by the backpack and pulled her to her feet. "Mind where you step in the dark. If it ain't a rock, it's dog shit. If it ain't a rock or dog shit, could be an IED."

A distant *moo* came from farther off the road.

"More likely it's cow shit than dog," said Ken. "Ouch."

Harper dusted herself off. "You really think people are setting bombs randomly around here?"

"Let's just say I'm not confident they *aren't*." He patted her on the shoulder.

She turned to keep facing him as he walked back to his 'spot.' "Where would they even get bombs?"

"Grenades. Flash bangs, that sort of thing. National Guard armories, former soldiers, police stations. Who knows?" Cliff shrugged off his backpack and dropped it on the bike. "Take nothing for granted unless you've triple checked it."

"Right…"

She exhaled… and decided she may as well sleep where she ate grass. Harper slipped out of her backpack, then lay down, using it for a pillow. Logan, to her surprise, stretched out right next to her with Luisa on his other side. She smiled, not that he could see, and snuggled up against him. Cliff and Ken wandered off to the north.

"Crap," said Harper a moment later.

"What?" asked Logan.

"We didn't talk about watch rotation."

"Haven't gotten there yet. Dealing with biological needs first," said Cliff from a fair distance off. He walked back over to the 'campsite' soon after. "Now, we can work out the watch rotation. Figure there's four of us. Hour and fifteen each. Won't get a great deal of sleep, but we ain't all that far from home and no one likes sleeping on bare ground."

"Dammit." Harper emitted a playful growl while sitting up. "You *had* to talk about peeing, didn't you? Now I have to go."

Logan groaned, as did Luisa.

*My luck, I'm going to trip and fall face first into that creek if I go too far.* Fortunately, the water reflected the moonlight enough to differentiate it from meadow. She walked a bit off from the 'campsite,' and assumed the position. Luisa and Logan also made their way out into the field in search of privacy. Harper couldn't see much of her surroundings in the weak moonlight beyond the wavering hint of grass blowing in a faint breeze. Everything appeared in shades of blue or black. Numerous dark masses appeared to be moving pretty much everywhere in the distance. Given the intermittent mooing, she figured cows from one or more farms had broken out of their enclosures and become wild.

*I don't remember it ever being so dark at night. There used to at least some moonlight. But... I'd always been in the city. We had streetlights, houses, shops, car headlights... and the sky didn't have a permanent haze of dust.*

"All right. Unless anyone else wants it real bad, I'll take first watch," said Cliff. "Ken, second?"

"Sure."

Harper yanked her pants back up. "Third?"

"Works for me. Okay, Logan. You got last watch."

"Not me?" asked Luisa, sounding timid.

"Nah." Cliff chuckled. "Math ain't my strong suit and I'm not going to recalculate the sleep time dividing by five now. Go on and get some rest."

Harper crept back to where she thought her bike was. Her shin confirmed its actual location, a little closer than she expected. "Grr. Son of a..." Scowling, she hopped around the bike and lay down again in the same spot, rubbing her shin.

"I'm going to be waking up a few times anyway," muttered Luisa. "Sorry if I scream and bother people. It's not something I *want* to do."

"It's okay." Harper looked toward the general area of void where the girl's voice came from. "I have nightmares sometimes, too. Kinda getting over them for the most part now, but they used to be bad."

"What are yours about?" asked Luisa in a hushed voice.

"My parents being killed... and a while back, I saw this guy who'd suffered serious radiation poisoning. He'd turned purple, all swollen up. Didn't really even look human anymore. Couldn't talk. Just moaned like a straight up zombie. Gave me nightmares about like radiation zombies chasing me around the ruins of a city."

Cliff groaned as if stretching. "You know, anyone who got a serious dose of rads is *long* dead by now."

"Yeah," said Logan, "but if someone spends too much time at a ground zero location, they could still get radiation poisoning over time."

"You aren't helping," deadpanned Cliff. "Trying to make your sister feel better here."

"What are your nightmares about?" asked Logan while leading his sister back over to the spot where they'd laid down earlier.

Luisa grabbed at Harper, feeling her way around to sit. Logan lowered himself to the ground between them.

"It's okay if you can't talk about it." Harper went to pat her on the shoulder but mistakenly smacked Logan in the face.

"Oof." He laughed. "Can't see a darn thing."

"Usually, I dream of Ma and Papa's rotting bodies sitting up and talking to me," said Luisa in a toneless voice. "They're not like trying to hurt me. Just saying I need to eat, and find water, and be careful. But their skin's falling off."

Harper shuddered.

Luisa sniffled. "Guess I shouldn't have stayed there with them for so long."

*Holy crap, this poor girl. At least she's crying, not emotionless. Hopefully, it means she's not gone psychotic.*

Logan broke down in tears as well.

Unable to think of anything to say worthy of the moment, Harper wrapped her arms around him and offered comfort as best she could.

Luisa hugged him from the other side. "Sorry."

"Not your fault," rasped Logan.

"I'm making you cry."

"No. You aren't." Logan fought back tears, coughed, then groaned. "I expected they died... but you know, like instantly vaporized when the bombs went off. I had no idea what happened. It's—I dunno. Thinking about them dying slowly like that, I can't..."

Harper squeezed him.

"They never said anything about being in pain," whispered Luisa. "Hours before he died, Papa made a joke about how difficult it would be to get the insurance company to fix the house."

*Joke? Or delirium?* Harper kept her mouth shut. *He couldn't have been serious.*

"You know damn well Ma and Papa wouldn't have complained about any pain," said Logan. "Not when they had you to look after. They didn't want you to be scared."

"Ma would have complained when she thought I was sleeping. I don't think they suffered any more than knowing they were definitely going to die for a couple days before it happened."

Logan sobbed once, caught himself, and rubbed his face... at least it felt as if he rubbed his face.

*It's so damn dark I can't see him and I'm close enough to hold him.*

"Maybe you won't have a bad dream tonight," said Logan, his voice cracked. "You're not alone anymore."

Luisa grabbed Harper's arm while trying to cling to Logan. "Sorry..."

"No worries. I'll get this side, you hold the other."

"Okay."

Logan gave a sad chuckle.

"Make a wish before you pull him apart," said Cliff from a few feet away.

"What?" asked Harper.

"Never heard of a wishbone?" replied Cliff.

"Nope."

He whistled. "Wow."

Harper rummaged the small blanket she'd brought out of her backpack, grateful Cliff insisted they bring them in case of unexpected circumstances. Not being able to sleep in Fairplay due to needing money hadn't been on the list of potential problems, but... at least they had blankets. She thought about the brief lecture he'd given about the loss of body heat in the night months ago for help going to sleep.

KEN NUDGED HARPER AWAKE AND PRESSED A SMALL METAL object into her hand.

She opened her eyes to void. Waking up early had *never* been cool. She had no idea what time it was, other than 'really freakin' dark.'

"Your, uhh 'watch,' Harp," whispered Ken. "Going to crash again if I don't kill myself on a rock trying to find my pack."

She almost chuckled. *If I don't get up now, I'm going to pass back out.* She sat up and glanced at the object he'd given her. Three glow-in-the-dark spots moved at different speeds in a small circle. It didn't take her sleep-addled brain *too* long to figure out he'd given her a wind-up wristwatch.

*Cliff is taking 'night watch' a bit too literally.*

The glow elements had mostly lost their charge, but considering the heavy darkness, it didn't take much energy for them to be visible. It couldn't possibly be quarter after nine as the watch indicated. Cliff had wound it up purely to measure the passage of minutes for shift rotation, not tell the time. She drank some water, found a spot to pee again so she could try to go back to sleep as fast as possible as soon as her hour-and-fifteen ended, then returned to her 'bed'. Feeling relatively safe due to being below the level of the highway, she sat in place holding the Mossberg, relying completely on her ears to warn of approaching threats.

*No one is going to be coming down the road at this hour without a light. They'll be obvious for miles.*

Ken occasionally emitted a faint snore. Logan only breathed, but it seemed loud. His sister alternated between total silence, rapid breathing, and whimpering. Occasional odd noises coming from Logan suggested his sister squeezed him in response to whatever she dreamed about.

*I've never had a nightmare about my parents as zombies coming after me. And shit. Now that I thought about it, I'm definitely going to dream it.* Luisa's story about staying in the basement next to her dead parents for weeks made her skin crawl. Honestly, the girl looked too scrawny to be able to lift and carry a dead adult on flat ground, much less drag a body out of a basement through the rubble of a collapsed house.

*What choice did she have? Go out into radiation or stay there.*

Harper's brain went off on an infuriatingly depressing tangent, trying to figure out what would have happened if she hadn't hesitated. If she shot the Lawless coming for her so Dad didn't need to turn away... could they have repelled the attack? Mom would've died anyway. Nothing Harper did or failed to do could have changed the guy stabbing her through the window. Mom shouldn't have been so close to the sink. She had a handgun.

If Harper *had* shot the guy, would she have had a breakdown and become helpless upon witnessing him die? Or gone psycho and freaked out, shooting every Lawless in sight? Would Dad have buried Mom in the yard and continued living with her and Madison in the basement, or would the attack have been the final push to get him to check out the rumors of safety they'd been hearing about Evergreen? Other survivors had gone past the house several times in the days before the Lawless attacked. She hadn't seen them, since only Dad went to the door when someone knocked.

*Did anyone who tried to talk Dad into leaving make it to Evergreen or did they die on the way?*

Of course, the way it happened, she and Madison had to run for their lives. Enough Lawless chased them, at least according to her foggy, traumatized memory, it didn't seem likely she and Dad could've fought them all off. The gang would have stormed the house, killed Dad anyway, then kidnapped her and Madison. She'd only grabbed Maddie and run because Dad died. The idea it would have been worse for everyone involved—especially her little sister—if Harper *had* shot the man without hesitation almost got her crying.

Almost.

*I promised Dad I was done crying over what happened.*

She let out a long, slow breath to calm her nerves.

*And I really need to stop thinking about it so much. Gotta move forward. Can't change the past.*

Except for the occasional moo in the distance and Ken's intermittent snores, Harper listened to silence for an hour and fifteen minutes according to the tiny bits of weak glow in her hand. Each hand had a little rectangle of phosphorescent material. She stared at the watch. *Logan's gotta pedal with his sister tomorrow. He needs the sleep more than I do. What if we get attacked? If I'm too out of it, I won't be able to hit anything.*

She flipped her hair forward over her face, sitting with her arms balanced across her knees, intending to let him remain asleep since he'd definitely be carrying extra weight tomorrow. Harper only needed to stay sharp *if* someone attacked them, not a guarantee.

A little while later, Luisa jolted awake but managed not to scream. Logan woke from the sudden, violent jump. Luisa's freakout didn't make much noise, which got Harper thinking the girl had spent some nights sleeping alone in ruined cities... and learned to stay quiet to avoid danger. Fortunately, she settled back down fairly quick.

"Hey, what time is it?" whispered Logan. "Want me to take over?"

"No idea. This watch isn't set. Just using it to count minutes and hours."

"How long before I'm up?" Logan yawned.

"Not long. Go back to sleep."

He reached around until he found her shoulder. "You're past your time, aren't you? I can tell by your voice."

"Yeah."

"What are you doing?" Logan kissed her above the ear. "You need sleep, too."

"You're carrying two people."

"She doesn't weigh much. Get some rest."

Harper looked down. "I miss being able to sleep all night without worrying someone might attack us."

"It's pretty much like that back home in Evergreen. You're not keeping night watch at your house, right?" Logan squeezed her shoulder. "Maybe it's not quite as safe as civilization, but home invasions still happened before the war."

"Yeah, you're right." She stretched, yawned, and relented, handing him the watch. "Guess you don't really need this thing since you're up until sunrise. Are you sure you don't want extra sleep?"

"Totally. Haven't been getting tons already and working on the farm is a lot more tiring than riding a bike with a skinny little passenger."

Luisa jabbed him in the side.

He laughed.

"'Kay." She reclined, again using her backpack for a pillow.

Water bottles and potatoes didn't offer the most comfort in the world, but for the moment, they worked fine.

HARPER AWOKE TO A COW'S NOSE INCHES FROM HER FACE.

Fortunately, the curious animal had approached from behind, so she didn't find herself completely under it. She gazed up past the cow at a hazy blue sky marked here and there with long, strands of cloud. It looked like the most epic swimming pool imaginable. Sleeping under only a thin blanket left her more than a little cold. The morning's chilly breeze didn't help. At least the sky didn't look dark enough to threaten rain—or maybe snow. She exhaled hard to test the temperature. Her breath didn't fog, a good sign.

After a minute or so of daydreaming about 'diving into the sky,' she shifted her gaze back to the big, black nose hovering over her. "Good morning."

The cow fired a sharp exhale from its nostrils, spraying her face with wetness.

*Eww.*

She scooted forward and sat up, torn between wiping her face on her sleeve and not wanting to have cow snot on her shirt, forcing her to wash it sooner. Trying not to let any get in her mouth, she scrambled to her feet and hurried over to the creek, crouching at the edge. Despite the iciness of the water, she scooped several handfuls into her face. Cow snot glided off on the creek's surface like strands of tiny jellyfish.

*Ick. Why did I look?*

She dried her face on her sleeves, then stood to check around for privacy.

Cliff and Ken sat near the bikes, munching on carrots and green beans. Luisa walked back to the campsite from the north. Harper headed off away from the creek and the camp in search of as much solitude as she could to water the grass. Once she found a good spot, she realized a shocking number of cows littered the fields around her, along with a much smaller number of bulls and about twenty calves. It felt as if they all stared at her.

*Grr. Can't go to the bathroom with all the cows watching me.*

It took her a few minutes—as well as closing her eyes—but she finally took care of business.

Upon her return to camp, Logan offered her a choice between a carrot and a potato. For a change of pace, she took the carrot.

"Morning." Harper yawned, then bit the front third off the carrot.

"That it is." Cliff put his backpack on. "You three about ready to head on out?"

"Yep." She held up the remaining portion of her 'breakfast'. "Just a sec to finish this."

"No rush. We've got plenty of daylight." Cliff took in a deep breath, eyes closed as if savoring the purity of it all.

Harper pulled a small bread loaf from her pack and took a bite of it, wanting a little more than a single carrot. "It *is* really pretty here. Can almost pretend nothing happened."

"Yeah." Cliff hooked his thumbs in his pockets. "They didn't have quite enough nukes to cover every square inch of land. Saved 'em for the juicy spots like military bases and big cities."

"That's good though, right?" Harper scarfed down the rest of the carrot. "Means we have a chance to rebuild since there's plenty of usable land."

"I suppose." Cliff gave a noncommittal nod. "Not sure *what* people will rebuild, but I suppose they'll get to rebuilding something. Hope it's not an exact replica of the dumbassery we created last time around."

Harper held the bread in her teeth while pulling her backpack on and dragging her bike up to the road. In the bright early morning sun, she had no trouble avoiding the rocks all over the hill. Once on the highway, she plucked the bread out of her teeth. "Maybe the cows are going to take over."

Ken laughed. "Looks like they're trying."

"Sure does." Cliff walked his bike up to the highway. "Hmm. Might as well do it right and say something properly dad-corny. Hmm... Let's blow this popsicle stand."

Harper rolled her eyes, but couldn't resist laughing.

# 29

# EVERY MOMENT

Somewhere around eleven or twelve hours later, Harper pedaled up Route 74 into the heart of Evergreen, not wanting to even look at a mountain bike ever again.

Exhaustion and soreness definitely beat stretching the trip out to three or four days each way. The ride home hadn't been without a few nerve-wracking moments, but the black bear didn't bother to chase them and the two guys they spotted wandering in Bailey more or less ignored them. The men had been a good distance away from Route 285, in the parking lot of a small church, tending a wood-burning grill made from scrap. They made no effort to attract attention, communicate, or attack.

Harper figured people content to live in small groups or alone would likely be lonely. However, they couldn't run all over the place rounding people up. If someone preferred the solitude, so be it. Except for unattended children or those in clear need of help, she'd leave people be.

She'd spent the last few hours of the ride wondering how many survivors remained in the ol' USA. What happened to the densely populated cities, especially on the coasts? How did massive concrete towers react to nuclear bombs? Did they shield people better than suburban houses or turn into collapsing deathtraps? How much of the country remained reasonably intact like Evergreen, Colorado and the surrounding areas? Did this place avoid the worst of it due to the shielding effect of the mountains or would any reasonably remote town have the same chances? A hostile nation would certainly have targeted farmland in the middle of the country, so perhaps remoteness or a sparse population alone didn't guarantee similar results.

Her mind tried to scare her with images of vast cities like Los Angeles reduced to wide open fields of grey dust populated by 'rad zombies.' Of course, she knew monsters like that only existed in video games and stories. If any big city *had* been nuked so hard it became a literal parking lot, it would likely still be too radioactive for anyone to survive in.

*They probably hit Washington DC the hardest. Bet there's a dead zone a hundred miles around it. That and Hollywood. The Russians would hate it as a 'symbol of America' or something like that. They probably felt the same way about all of California. Did they nuke Mount Rushmore, too? Of course, they hit our farms… to poison us with radiation, make the land useless for growing stuff.*

By the time they rolled up to the militia HQ, she'd stopped thinking about how soon—if at all—any sort of national identity would emerge again. Mostly, she wanted to spend a few uninterrupted hours with Madison, Lorelei, and Jonathan. She also had an attack of First World Problem, wanting to recover from so much sitting and pedaling by lounging in a hot bath for a while. If the electric worked, no big deal, but she wouldn't waste firewood on a comfort soak.

"Here we are," said Cliff, after stashing his bike back in the collection. "No one got their ass shot off."

"Surprisingly." Harper smiled.

"You sound disappointed." Cliff glanced at her.

"No, not at all. Happily surprised. I mean we *did* get shot at the other day looking for you and I thought for certain those weirdos in Fairplay were going to turn me into Swiss cheese."

He laughed. "C'mon, now. We're not in a *Mad Max* movie. Real world's a little saner... and kinda more depressing most of the time."

"Did you *see* them?" Logan whistled. "I can't tell if they're playing the Wild West thing for laughs or taking it seriously."

Luisa exhaled. "They're pretty serious about it. One guy said something about simpler times worked much better."

"Not by much." Ken got off his bike and stretched. "Ugh. I need an ass transplant. Gonna be walking funny for days."

"The bad guys in real life don't paint their faces, wear leather, and hang off the side of speeding giant pickup trucks while waving giant clubs around." Harper stared off into space. "They wear suits, tell lies, and kill millions with the stroke of a pen."

"Ain't that the truth." Cliff shook his head at the ground.

"C'mon." Logan took his sister's hand. "Gotta go see a doctor."

"I'm not sick," said Luisa.

Logan smiled reassuringly. "It's one of the rules here. Everyone needs to get looked at when they first arrive."

"Oh, okay." She shrugged and walked after him.

*Grr.* Harper wanted to simultaneously be home with Madison *and* go with Logan. She stood there looking back and forth from the clinic to the point where Hilltop Drive met Route 74.

Upon noticing her indecision, Logan waved. "It's cool if you need to let Maddie know you're alive."

She jogged after him. "I want to be there for you, too."

"It's okay. She's a kid. We've all been through rough shit." Logan looked down. "I can't be the reason your sister has a breakdown."

"Don't pull the macho stuff." She playfully punched him on the shoulder. "It's fine for boys to show emotion. Hey, let me go let her know I'm still alive, and I'll—probably both of us actually—go to the clinic to wait with you."

"Cool." Logan grinned.

"Wait with him?" Luisa blinked. "Doctors *still* have waiting rooms? How long is this going to take?"

"Got somewhere to be?" Logan tilted his head at her.

"No." Luisa shrugged. "Just saying. Sounds weird."

Harper hugged him. "Be there as soon as I can."

THE INSTANT HARPER WALKED INTO THE HOUSE, MADISON jumped off the sofa—but caught herself.

Trying to act calm, she casually crossed the living room. Carrie remained on the couch, reading to Lorelei, who cuddled up beside her. Jonathan and Mila lay on the rug, enjoying a moment of synchronicity with the universe—the PlayStation worked.

*Her eyes are bleary. She didn't sleep well.* "Hey, Termite. "I'm sorry for running off yet again."

"Thanks for feeling guilty." Madison hugged her. "It's okay. You know I'd rather you didn't, but I'm not gonna get all emo on you if you have a good reason."

Harper squeezed her. "It would take something pretty important to convince me to go on another trip. I have to be here for you. No, I *want* to be here for you. Don't think it's a begrudging obligation."

"I don't." Madison fussed at her hair. "You sound totally different when you're doing something under protest. If you're going to leave town again, will you at least wait for me to be old enough to go with you?"

"You want to join the militia?" Harper started to cringe at the idea, but, honestly, being on or off the militia didn't really change a person's odds of experiencing violence anymore.

Madison rolled her eyes. "Hell no, dork. I'm still scared because you did... but I understand why."

"Oh?" Harper scratched her head.

"You're a slacker with no real skills other than shooting." Madison folded her arms. "What else would you do?"

Harper laughed at the straight-faced delivery, then playfully scoffed. "I have skills."

"What job did you want before the world died?" Madison raised an eyebrow.

"I dunno. Didn't quite figure it out yet."

"See?" Madison gestured at her. "You coasted through school having no clue what you were going to do for a career."

"Guess so."

"At least we were happy before it all went to shit." Madison gave her an expectant look.

"Watch your language," deadpanned Harper.

Her sister grinned.

"I only said it because you wanted me to. Doesn't really seem like 'bad words' are an issue anymore… compared to everything else."

"Does that mean we can curse all we want?" asked Jonathan from the floor.

"No," said Carrie and Harper at the same time.

Madison and Mila snickered.

Lorelei looked up, seemingly confused.

"You're right." Madison bit her lip. "It's what Mom would've wanted. Gotta be eighteen to swear."

"Mom would *still* give me a sour look if I dropped an F-bomb, even though I *am* eighteen."

"Yeah." Madison laughed. "Totes."

"So, what happened out there?" asked Carrie. "Did you find Logan's sister?"

"Yeah, she's over at the clinic. Routine exam. She'll probably be fine, but I think the doctor is going to quarantine her dress. Holy cow, I've never seen clothing so filthy. Wait, no… I have. Randall's group."

The kids chuckled.

Harper gestured at the door. "I'm going to go sit with Logan so he's not alone with his thoughts." Harper nudged Madison. "Wanna come with?"

"Sure."

Carrie pointed at her. "Don't forget to tell that boy to come here tonight. He's not bringing a fifteen-year-old girl to live in a house with four other men."

"Five other men. Logan's the sixth guy in the house over there." Harper exhaled. "Yeah. He's gotta talk to Anne-Marie about taking the little place up the dirt driveway from yours."

"All right." Carrie turned the page and resumed reading to Lorelei.

Harper headed for the door, but stopped when Madison followed without bothering to put her shoes on.

"Hey, it's getting kinda cold. Shoes?"

"Cold doesn't really bother me, but okay." Madison rushed off, humming *that* song from *Frozen*.

… and Harper started humming it. *Damn it.* She went outside to Hilltop Drive, waiting on the road. A minute later, Madison ran out from the house, having put her sneakers on. She hurried across the front yard to the road. As soon as her sister caught up, Harper started walking toward Route 74.

*Wow, waiting for her to come outside so we can go somewhere feels so damn normal except for not having a car.*

"Umm, Harp?" asked Madison.

"Yeah?"

"Sorry for being a brat."

"You're not a brat."

Madison shrugged. "I mean before… like *before* before. I used to yell at you for being in my room or even sitting too close to me, but now it doesn't feel weird to take baths together. It feels weird *not* to. I hate that we used to fight, like at all. Now, I'm always thinking we could die at any minute."

"We need to be cautious, but there's no reason for us to be scared all the time."

"Yeah, I know." Madison stuffed her hands in her pockets, shivering slightly at an uptick in the breeze. "I'm not *scared*, just aware. Like, I never used to think about death at all, just figured I'd grow up and eventually get old like everyone else. Now… every moment is important. Maybe it's lame, but I like it when you wash my hair."

"You feel protected."

"Yeah. And loved, and all that sappy Hallmark stuff." Madison smirked at her. "I'll probably outgrow it once I stop being so scared all the time. Probably won't outgrow wanting to have you around. Even if you and Logan live next door, I'll be okay. That's still *around*. I'll eventually be okay not having to literally Velcro to you."

"Hah."

"Does it bother you not *expecting* to grow old?" Madison stuffed her hands in her pockets.

"Honestly? I never even thought about it before at all. Don't suppose there's really any point to losing your mind over stuff that's totally out of your control."

Madison nodded, then smiled. "Hey, at least I'm not in a hurry to grow up so I can drive anymore."

"And I'm not in any hurry to turn twenty-one."

"How long are we going to be at the clinic?"

*Got somewhere to be?* She smiled. "Not long. Just until they finish checking Luisa. I'm sure Logan is going to want some time to catch up with her tonight, all the stuff they didn't want to talk about in front of everyone else. We should have a few hours before bedtime to do something fun."

"Cool. I'm going to sleep *hard* tonight." Madison dramatically held a hand to her forehead.

"Up worrying last night?"

"No," said Madison with a straight face. "Bear tried to get in the house."

"Are you being sarcastic or serious?"

"Serious this time. It clawed a bit at the window. Might be the same one that tried to sniff the chickens. Lore and I screamed loud enough to wake Carrie up. She chased the bear off."

"She did not leave you in the house alone…" Harper blinked.

"No, she was in Dad's room." Madison lowered her voice to a fake whisper. "I think she was sad and worried he'd get hurt."

Harper half-smiled, simultaneously a bit guilty for contributing to Carrie's worry as well as happy she sincerely cared for him.

"Anyway…" Madison punted a small rock off the road. "After the bear left, it took me a long time to go back to sleep because I kept thinking there might be another bear out there somewhere biting you."

"Didn't get bit by a bear, but I had a cow snoz on my face."

"Eww!" Madison squirmed.

"Saw a cougar, too."

Madison's eyes went wide. "Really?"

"Yeah. He snuck up on me. Sniffed my butt."

"Eep!" Madison covered her mouth with both hands. "You didn't shoot him, did you?"

"No. He got bored with us and walked away." Harper ruffled her hair. "So, what do you want to do when we get home?"

"Don't care. Board game. Uno. Just hang and talk. Draw. Maybe you could read that book to Lorelei and I'll listen in."

"All right." Harper opened the door to the medical center. "We'll figure something out."

*It's our way of life these days… we figure it out.*

*fin*

# ACKNOWLEDGMENTS

Thank you for reading *The Nuclear Frontier!*

Harper's story will continue.

Thanks also to Lee Sheridan for editing and Alexandria Thompson for the cover design.

# ABOUT THE AUTHOR

Originally from South Amboy NJ, Matthew has been creating science fiction and fantasy worlds for most of his reasoning life. Since 1996, he has developed the "Divergent Fates" world, in which *Division Zero, Virtual Immortality, The Awakened Series, The Harmony Paradox, and the Daughter of Mars series* take place. Along with being an editor at Curiosity Quills press, he has worked in IT and technical support.

Matthew is an avid gamer, a recovered WoW addict, Gamemaster for two custom RPG systems, and a fan of anime, British humour, and intellectual science fiction that questions the nature of reality, life, and what happens after it.

He is also fond of cats.

Visit me online at:
   Facebook: https://www.facebook.com/MatthewSCoxAuthor
   Pinterest: https://www.pinterest.com/matthewcox10420/
   Goodreads:          https://www.goodreads.com/author/show/
7712730.Matthew_S_Cox
   Email: mcox2112@gmail.com

# OTHER BOOKS BY MATTHEW S. COX

Divergent Fates Universe Novels

Division Zero series

- Division Zero
- Lex De Mortuis
- Thrall
- Guardian
- Harbinger
- The Shadow Fixer

The Awakened series

- Prophet of the Badlands
- Archon's Queen
- Grey Ronin
- Daughter of Ash
- Zero Rogue
- Angel Descended

Daughter of Mars series

- The Hand of Raziel
- Araphel
- Ghost Black

Virtual Immortality series

- Virtual Immortality
- The Harmony Paradox

Prophet of the Badlands Series

- Prophet's Journey

Divergent Fates Anthology

(Fiction Novels - Adult)

The Roadhouse Chronicles Series

- One More Run
- The Redeemed
- Dead Man's Number

Faded Skies series

- Heir Ascendant
- Ascendant Unrest
- Ascendant Revolution

Temporal Armistice Series

- Nascent Shadow
- The Shadow Collector
- The Gate to Oblivion
- The Queen of Discord

Vampire Innocent series

- A Nighttime of Forever
- A Beginner's Guide to Fangs
- The Artist of Ruin
- The Last Family Road Trip
- The Phantom Oracle
- How Not to Summon Demons
- Ordinary Problems of a College Vampire
- A Vampire's Guide to Surviving Holidays

- An Introduction to Paranormal Diplomacy
- A Vampire's Guide to Adulting
- How to Stop a Vampire War in Six Easy Steps

Standalones

- Wayfarer: AV494
- Axillon99
- Chiaroscuro: The Mouse and the Candle
- The Spirits of Six Minstrel Run
- Sophie's Light
- The Far Side of Promise anthology
- Operation: Chimera  (with Tony Healey)
- The Dysfunctional Conspiracy (with Christopher Veltmann)
- Of Myth and Shadow
- The Girl Who Found the Sun

Winter Solstice series (with J.R. Rain)

- Convergence
- Containment
- Catalyst
- Catacombs

Alexis Silver series (with J.R. Rain)

- Silver Light
- Deep Silver
- Silver Quarrel
- Silver Crucible

Samantha Moon Origins series (with J.R. Rain)

- New Moon Rising
- Moon Mourning

- Haunted Moon

Vampire For Hire series (with J.R. Rain)

- Moon Master
- Dead Moon
- Lost Moon
- Vampire Destiny
- Infinite Moon
- Vampire Empress

Maddy Wimsey series (with J.R. Rain)

- The Devil's Eye
- The Drifting Gloom
- Dark Mercy

Samantha Moon Case Files series (with J.R. Rain)

- Blood Moon

Immortal Operative (with J.R. Rain)

- Broken Ice

Four Elements series (with J.R. Rain)

- The Elementalist
- The Black Rose
- The Wakefield Curse

Young Adult Novels

The Eldritch Heart Series

- The Eldritch Heart
- The Cursed Crown
- The Sapphire Soul

## Evergreen Series

- Evergreen
- The World That Remains
- The Lucky Ones
- Nuclear Summer
- The Nuclear Frontier

## Standalones

- Caller 107
- The Summer the World Ended
- Nine Candles of Deepest Black
- The Forest Beyond the Earth
- Out of Sight

## Middle Grade Novels

### The Adventures of Ubergirl series

- My Dad is a Mad Scientist
- Aliens Ate My Homework
- The End of all Halloweens

### Tales of Widowswood series

- Emma and the Banderwigh
- Emma and the Silk Thieves
- Emma and the Silverbell Faeries
- Emma and the Elixir of Madness
- Emma and the Weeping Spirit

Standalones

- Citadel: The Concordant Sequence
- The Cursed Codex
- The Menagerie of Jenkins Bailey

www.ingramcontent.com/pod-product-compliance
Lightning Source LLC
Chambersburg PA
CBHW031706170626
46808CB00005B/1626